Spicy ADVENTURES

ROBERT E. HOWARD

Introduction by Patrice Louinet
Edited by Paul Herman and Patrice Louinet

THE
Robert E. Howard
FOUNDATION PRESS

For Glenn Lord (1931-2011), preserver of Howard's typescripts and manuscripts, godfather of Howard studies, and the greatest fan that ever lived.

Copyright © 2011, 2024, 2026 Robert E. Howard Properties Inc. Robert E. Howard™ and related logos, names, characters and distinctive likenesses thereof are trademarks or registered trademarks of Robert E. Howard Properties Inc. unless otherwise noted. All rights reserved.

ISBN: 978-1-955446-17-4 (Paperback)
ISBN: 978-1-955446-16-7 (Hardcover)
ISBN: 978-1-955446-29-7 (eBook)

Published by the REH Foundation Press, LLC by arrangement with Robert E. Howard Properties Inc.

https://rehfoundation.org
https://rehfpress.com

Cover illustration copyright © 2024, Mark Wheatley.

https://markwheatleygallery.com

Book prepared for publication by Ståle Gismervik, Savage Studios.

Version 2.1 - Ultimate Edition.

Acknowledgments

All of the Howard stories and portions thereof contained in *Spicy Adventures* come from Howard's original typescripts, manuscripts, and carbons. Virtually all of them were scanned from the Glenn Lord collection, now at the University of Texas, Austin; the Robert E. Howard collection at Texas A&M University; or the typescript collection at Cross Plains Library.

CHANGES FROM THE 1ST EDITION: In this Ultimate Edition, previously edited versions of "The Girl on the Hell Ship," "Ship in Mutiny," and "Daughters of Feud" have been restored to typescript. Five "new" earliest known drafts have been added: "Desert Blood," "Dragon of Kao Tsu," "Murderer's Grog," "Guns of Khartoum," and "Daughters of Feud." We have also replaced the previous "early" drafts of "The Girl on the Hell Ship" and "Ship in Mutiny" with their earliest known drafts.

CHANGES FROM v2.0: Corrected errors in transcriptions.

Contents

Introduction

by Patrice Louinet

We can only imagine Howard Phillips Lovecraft's reaction upon receiving Robert E. Howard's letter of December 5, 1935, in which the Texan stated:

> "In my efforts to make new markets I've been 'splashing the field' as Price calls it. One market I tried was *Spicy Adventure*, a sex magazine to which Ed is the star contributor. I sold the first yarn I tried, but doubt if I could make that market regularly, as it requires a deft, jaunty style foreign to my natural style. However, I'll probably try it again. Why don't you give it a whirl? You can use a pen name if you like; I did, and I think most of its contributors do. The maximum length is about 5000 words. That sort of yarn is easy to write, if not to sell. If they reject it, you've only wasted a day or so. If they accept it, you're fifty bucks to the good, and they pay promptly. They like good strong plots, but the sex element is a cinch; any man can write that part of it. Just write up one of your own sex adventures, altered to fit the plot. That's the way I did with the yarn I sold them."

At the time Howard was writing those words, the "Spicies"—as they were soon to be called—were relative newcomers in the pulp publishing world. The rather notorious and infamous Harry Donenfeld had earned his money (or laundered that of others) by publishing a line of sleaze magazines. After various run-ins with the censors, he had the idea to blend the "sex" element of his earlier publications with the flourishing outlet that was pulp fiction. He had but to take an established (i.e. profitable) pulp genre and add the "spicy" element to the recipe. Thus were born *Spicy Detective*, *Spicy Western*, *Spicy Mystery*, and of course *Spicy-Adventure Stories*, the magazine where it was logical Robert E. Howard should submit his stories. Editor Frank Armer had to walk a very thin line indeed, titillating the readers with tantalizing promises that would not really be delivered while trying not to provoke the ire of the censors.

If traditional pulps were more often than not lurid at best, the Spicies catered to the lowest common denominator. The formula was simple enough, but followed strict rules. The stories should be quite short, the hero had to be American but should never be nude at any moment. The heroine should also never be stark naked, but was allowed to "strip to her underwear or transparent negligee or nightgown, or the torn shred of her garments," according to a 1934 "Writers' Guideline" issued by the Spicy magazines' editor. Howard was later to remark: "Though extremely fond of almost-nude ladies, they prefer her to retain some garment ordinarily—like a coyly revealing chemise. However this taboo isn't ironclad, for I've violated it in nearly every story I've sold them. I've found a good formula is to strip the heroine gradually—she loses part of her clothes in one episode, some more in the next, and so on until the climax finds her in a state of tantalizing innocence."

Quite tame by today's standards, there was an odor of brimstone about them when they began appearing, and most of the writers contributing to the line did so under by-lines. For his own contributions, Bob Howard adopted the name of a man he thought (wrongly, it turns out), to have been an ancestor of his, Sam Walser, supposedly a Dane from the Skaggerack.

As was his wont, and probably in the hope of landing a new series, and thus a regular market, Howard followed Kline's advice and set out to write the first tale of "Wild Bill" Clanton, a rugged Sailor Steve Costigan lookalike, but with a vicious streak. The first tale in the series—"The Girl on the Hell-Ship"—was written in late September or early October 1935, and promptly submitted. Kline commented: "Your story 'The Girl on the Hell-Ship' seems to be pretty close to what Frank Armer wants for *Spicy-Adventures*, although it may not be quite hot enough for that book." The story was apparently "hot" enough and was bought outright. It would appear in the April 1936 issue of *Spicy-Adventure Stories*, under the title of "She-Devil," the first of five published tales in the pages of that magazine.

"Ship in Mutiny"—a sequel to "The Girl on the Hell-Ship"—failed to meet approval. Howard briefly toyed with the idea of rewriting the story for *Thrilling Adventures*, but this was not to come to pass. "Desert Blood," probably written in November 1935, dumped heroine Raquel O'Shane, the *Saucy Wench* (or *Lazy Lass*, or *Saucy Lass,* the name of the ship varying depending on the versions and drafts), and the South Seas locale, and found some of its inspiration in Edgar Rice Burroughs, Howard borrowing a few names from *The Return ofTarzan*. Decidedly spicier than anything Burroughs wrote, "Desert Blood" was somewhat better than the first tale, benefiting from a small dose of humor. Hot on the heels of the scantily-clad Zouza of "Desert Blood" came the equally scantily-clad Arline of "The Purple Heart of Erlik," written in December. Both stories were quickly grabbed by the editors.

If the Clantons proved, for the most part, easy sells, Howard was not so successful with his non-Clanton offerings. Two tales—"Daughters of Feud" (probably submitted in December) and "Guns of Khartoum" (sent in early January 1936)—were rejected. "Guns of Khartoum" was probably more ambitious than necessary for a Spicy, drawing on the Mahdi revolt in Sudan. Howard had just read Achmet Abdullah's *Dreamers of Empire*, which included a chapter on "Chinese Gordon" and the events of Khartoum, and this is probably where he found his inspiration. While not a gem by any standard, the story is competent enough and could have made for a very interesting tale, if rewritten and aimed at another market. "Daughters of Feud" was another interesting offering. Howard later reflected that this tale was "too hot for them to handle," and it was probably the strong sado-masochistic strain that runs throughout the story that proved too much for Armer. Quite different in tone from the other spicies, "Daughters" resonates strangely when seen under the light of Howard's ailing relationship with Novalyne Price, a teacher at the Cross Plains high school.

After these consecutive failures, Howard ceased experimenting and was soon back to Clanton. He would only write two more, "The Dragon of Kao-Tsu" in January 1936, and after a long interruption caused by his mother's hospitalization, "Murderer's Grog" in April, a tale which would only appear in the January 1937 issue of *Spicy-Adventure*, several months after Howard's death.

Those who are familiar with the previously-published versions of these stories (either in the pulps or in the 1983 collection *She-Devil*) are in for a surprise with the texts presented in this volume. For if Kline—and us—thought that Howard's stories were perhaps too tame for Armer, it turned out, upon examination of the surviving carbons and drafts, that it was in fact exactly the opposite: all of the stories had been heavily censored when first published in *Spicy-Adventures* (and thus in the 1983 edition.) In typical fashion, Howard had gone further than the guidelines imposed, stretching the boundaries as much as possible, probably because he felt he understood what his readers wanted. This was nothing new. As early as 1932 he had commented upon selling the Conan story "Black Colossus" that: "My heroes grow more bastardly as the years pass. One of my latest sales concluded with a sexual intercourse instead of the usual slaughter. My swordwielder grabbed the princess—already considerably stripped by the villing—and smacked her down on the altar of the forgotten gods, while battle and massacre roared outside, and through the dusk the remains of the villing, nailed to the wall by the hero, regarded the pastime sardonically. I don't know how the readers will like it. I'll bet some of them will. The average man has a secret desire to be a swaggering, drunken, fighting, raping swashbuckler." For the Spicies, he was simply pushing that logic a bit further, and the less than chivalrous behavior of Clanton in some of those stories will probably make some readers cringe. There is none of the playfulness one can find in his erotic playlets written in 1929 for his friend Tevis Clyde Smith. Howard was simply going through the motions, writing these stories while his mother was literally dying under his eyes, at a time when cash was urgently needed in the Howard household to take care of the expenses. What few comments he had to offer about them (aside from the Lovecraft letter, which was obviously more tongue-in-cheek than anything else), were desultory at best, calling them "bawdies" or "bubby-twisters." He wrote to Novalyne Price in February 1936 that he hoped to "get a reaction from the readers, who, I feel, are cultured and scholarly gentlemen, who wax enthusiastic over meritous artistic efforts. . . . Wild Bill Clanton . . . carefully avoids all moral scruples in his dealings with the ladies . . . Indeed, in most of my yarns, the heroine's virtue is in more danger from the hero than from anybody else." Price would later declare that Howard considered those tales as nothing but "pot-boilers."

The tales contained in this volume were conceived as "pot-boilers", simple stories whose risqué element has become more quaint than anything else with their inventive use of metaphors and suggestive ellipses. One might be tempted to conclude by stating that one should not look for hidden philosophical meanings or intellectual puzzles in these yarns—they aren't there. But we all know how wrong such an assertion can prove, don't we?

—Patrice Louinet
Paris, France
March 2011

Spicy Adventures

The Girl on the Hell Ship

Outside, where dawn was just dispelling the fog wisps from the South Pacific waters, the sea was calm, but a typhoon was raging in the cabin of the *Saucy Wench*. Most of the thunder was supplied by Captain Harrigan—vociferous oratory, charged with brimstone and sulphur, punctuated with resounding bangs of a hairy fist on the table across which he was bellowing damnation and destruction at Raquel O'Shane, who screamed back at him. Between them they were making so much noise they did not hear the sudden shouting that burst forth on deck.

"Shut up!" bawled the captain. He was broad as a door and his undershirt revealed a chest and arms muscled and hairy as an ape's. A growth of whiskers bristled his jaws, and his eyes blazed. He was a spectacle to daunt any woman, even if she had not known him as Bully Harrigan, smuggler, blackbirder, pearl thief and pirate, when opportunity offered itself.

"Shut up!" he repeated. "One more yap out of you, you Spanish-Irish gutter-snipe, and I'll bend one on your jaw!"

Being a man of primal impulses, he demonstrated his meaning by a fervent swipe of a mallet-like fist, which Raquel dodged with the agility of much practice. She was slim and supple, with foamy black hair, dark eyes that blazed with deviltry, and an ivory-tinted skin, heritage of her mixed Celtic-Latin blood, that made men's heads swim at first sight.

"Pig!" she screamed. "Don't you dare lay a finger on me!" This was purely rhetorical; Harrigan had laid a finger on her more than once during the past weeks, to say nothing of whole fists, belaying pins, and ropes' ends. But she was untamed.

She too banged the table and cursed in three languages.

"You've treated me like a dog all the way from Brisbane!" she raged. "Getting tired of me, are you, after taking me away from a good job in San Francisco—"

"I took you—" The enormity of the accusation choked the captain. "Why, you Barbary Coast hussy, the first time I ever saw you was that night you climbed aboard as we were pullin' out and begged me on your blasted knees to take you to sea and save you from the cops, account of you knifin' a Wop in that Water Street honkytonk where you were workin', you—"

"Don't you call me that!" she shrieked, doing a war dance. "All I did in that joint was dance! And I've played square with you, and now—"

"Now I'm sick of your tantrums," quoth Harrigan, downing a horse-sized snort from a square-faced bottle. "They're too much even for a goodhearted swab like me. As soon as we raise a civilized port, I'm goin' to kick you off onto the docks. And you give me any more lip, and I'll sell you to the first Kanaka chief I meet, you blasted hellcat!"

That set her off again, like a match to the fuse of a skyrocket. She hit the roof, and for a few moments the cabin was so full of impassioned feminine profanity it even drowned out Harrigan's roars.

"And where are we heading?" she demanded, remembering another grievance. "I want to know! The crew wants to know! You've told us nothing since we left Brisbane! We've picked up no cargo, and now we've gotten into these God-forsaken seas where none of us knows where we are, except you, and all you do is guzzle booze and study this blasted chart!"

She snatched it from the table and brandished it accusingly.

"Gimme that!" he bellowed, grabbing wildly. She jumped back agilely, sensing it was precious to him, and woman-like seizing the advantage.

"I won't! Not till you promise to quit knocking me around! Get back! I'll throw it out the porthole if you come any closer!"

With a frantic roar Harrigan lunged, upsetting the table with a crash. Raquel had raised a bigger hurricane than she had expected or intended. She squeaked in alarm and leaped back, the chart waving wildly in her hand.

"Gimme that!" It was the howl of a lost soul. Harrigan's hair stood straight up and his eyes bulged. Raquel yelped with terror, too confused to make her peace by delivering the article requested. She sprang backward, tripped over a chair and fell backward, with a shriek and an involuntary abandon that tossed her bare ivory-tinted legs revealingly skyward. But Harrigan had no eye for this entrancing display. For as she fell, her arm, thrown out wildly, propelled the chart through the air; and as the Devil always controls such things, it sailed through the open porthole.

Harrigan tore his hair and rushed for the porthole. On deck an ear-splitting racket had burst suddenly forth, but the occupants of the cabin ignored it. Harrigan, glaring popeyed from the porthole, was just in time to see the chart vanish on its way to Davy Jones's Locker, and his agonized howl paled all his previous efforts—so much so that out in the passageway the bos'n, who had just reached the cabin door in breathless haste, turned tail and fled back the way he had come. Raquel had risen, in apprehensive silence, and was making some necessary adjustments in her garments. Her lovely eyes dilated at the red glare in Harrigan's eyes as he wheeled toward her.

"You threw that away on purpose!" he choked. "A million dollars right through the damn' porthole! I'll fix you—"

He lunged and she skipped back with a squeal, but not quickly enough. His huge paw closed on a shoulder strap. There was a shriek, a ripping sound, and Raquel fled toward the door minus the dress which remained in Harrigan's hand. He was after her instantly, but panic winged her small feet. She beat him to the door and slammed it in his face, and even tried to hold it against him until convinced of her folly by a big fist which, crashing through the panels, grazed her dainty nose, filling her eyes with stars and tears. She yipped pitifully, abandoned the door, and fled up the companionway, a startling figure in slippers and pink panties.

After her came Captain Harrigan, a bellowing, red-eyed, hairy monstrosity whose only passion was to sweep the deck from poop to forecastle with that supple, half-naked body.

In their different emotions of fright and fury they were not, even then, aware of the clamor going on upon deck, until they came full on a scene so unique it even checked Harrigan short in his tracks.

Not so Raquel; she scampered across the deck, unnoticed by the mob milling in the waist, and sprang into the main shrouds before she turned and stared at the spectacle which had halted Harrigan.

Hemmed in by a ring of blaspheming seamen the mate, Buck Richardson, was locked in combat with a stranger whose breeches, his only garment, dripped seawater. That Mr. Richardson should be battling a stranger was not unique; what was unique was that Mr. Richardson, the terror of a thousand ports, bucko deluxe and hazer extraordinary, was getting the prime essence of hell beaten out of him. His opponent was as big as he—a broad-shouldered, clean-waisted, heavy-armed man with wetly plastered black hair, blue eyes that blazed with the joy of mayhem, and lips that grinned savagely even when, as now, they were smeared with blood.

He fought with the gusto that horrified even his hard-boiled audience. Continually he plunged in, head down, not blindly like a bull, but with his eyes open—except the one the mate had closed—hammering the luckless bucko like a blacksmith on an anvil. Richardson was bleeding like a stuck hog, and spitting pieces of broken teeth. He was blowing like a porpoise and in his one good eye there was a desperate gleam.

"Who's that?" demanded Harrigan aghast. "Where'd he come from?"

"We sighted him just as the fog lifted," said the bos'n, spitting carefully to leeward. "He was driftin' along in a open boat, balin' and cussin' somethin' fierce. His boat sunk under him before he could get it to the ship, and he swum for it. A shark tried to scoff him on the way, but he kicked its brains out or bit it in the neck, or done somethin' atrocious to it. That's Wild Bill Clanton!"

"The hell it is!" grunted the captain, staring with new interest. Then he swore as Clanton bashed Mr. Richardson on the snout with appalling results. "They're bleedin' all over my clean deck!"

"Well," said the bos'n, "as soon as he clumb over the rail he seen the mate and went for him. From the remarks they passed before they was too winded to cuss, I gathered that Buck stole a gal from Clanton once. I went after you, but you seemed busy, so I just let 'em fight."

Bam! Mr. Clanton's left mauler met Mr. Richardson's midriff with an impact that sounded like the smack of a loose boom against a wet sail. Bam! A mallet-like right-hander to the jaw and Mr. Richardson went reeling backward and brought up against the rail with a crack that would have fractured the skull of anybody except a bucko mate on a trading schooner.

Clanton went for him with a bloodthirsty yell—then his eyes encountered Raquel, poised in the ratlines. He stopped short, batted his eyes, his mouth wide open as he glared wildly at the ivory tinted vision posed against the blue, in a sheer wisp of pink silk that tempted rather than concealing anything.

"Holy saints of Hell!" breathed Clanton in awe—and at this instant Mr. Richardson, a bloody ruin, lurched away from the rail with a belaying pin. Bam! It crashed on Clanton's head and that warrior bit the deck. Mr. Richardson croaked gratefully and bestowed himself lovingly on his victim's bosom, naively intent on beating his brains out with his trusty belaying pin. But Clanton anticipated his design by drawing up his legs, after the manner of a panther fighting on its back, and, receiving the hurtling mate on his feet and knees, he catapulted Mr. Richardson over his head.

The mate smote the deck headfirst and reverberantly, and this time the impact was too much even for his adamantine skull. But Clanton, bounding up, observed some faint signs of life still, and sought to correct this oversight by leaping ardently and with both feet on the mate's bosom.

"Grab him!" yelled Harrigan. "He's killin' the mate!"

As no spectacle could have pleased the crew better than Mr. Richardson's violent demise, they made no move to obey. Harrigan ran forward blasphemously and tugging forth an enormous revolver thrust it under the nose of Mr. Clanton who eyed it and its owner without favor.

"Are you the cap'n of this mud scow?" Clanton demanded.

"I am, by God!" gnashed Mr. Harrigan. "I'm Bully Harrigan! What are you doin' on board my ship?"

"I've been keepin' a damned sieve of a boat afloat for a day and a night," retorted the other. "I was mate aboard the *Damnation*, out of Bristol. The cap'n didn't like Americans. After I won his share of the cargo at draw poker, he welshed and put me afloat—with the aid of the crew."

Harrigan broodingly visualized the battle that must have required!

"Carry the mate to his bunk and bring him to," he ordered the men. "As for you, Clanton, you'll work for your passage! Get for'ard!"

Clanton ignored the command. He was again staring at the vision clinging to the ratlines. Raquel peeped at him approvingly, noting the clean-cut muscular symmetry that was his.

"Who's that?" he inquired, and all turned to stare. Harrigan roared like a sea lion with awakened memory.

"Drag her down!" he yelled. "Tie her to the mast! I'll—"

"Don't touch me!" shrieked Raquel. "I'll jump and drown myself."

She didn't mean that, but she sounded as though she did. Clanton reached the rail with a tigerish bound, caught her wrist, and whipped her down onto the deck before she knew what was happening.

"Oh!" she gasped, staring at him with dilated eyes. He was bronzed by the suns of the Seven Seas, and his torso was ridged with clean hard cords of muscles. In fierce admiration his gaze devoured her from her trim ankles to the foamy burnished mass of her hair.

"Good work, Clanton!" roared Harrigan, striding forward. "Hold her!" Raquel wailed despairfully, but Harrigan, reaching for her, had his hand knocked aside, and he paused and goggled stupidly at Clanton.

"Avast!" roared Clanton gustily. "That's no way to treat a lady!"

"Lady, hell!" bleated Harrigan. "Do you know what she just did? Threw away my chart! The only dash-blank chart in the world that could show me how to find the island of Aragoa!"

"Was we goin' there, cap'n?" asked the bos'n.

"Yes, we was!" yelled Harrigan. "And what for? I'll tell you! Ambergris. A barrel full! At thirty-two dollars an ounce! You bilge rats been grousin' to know where we were sailin' to—all right, I'll tell you! And then I'm goin' to tie that wench up and skin her stern with a rope's end! "A few months ago a blackbirder bound for Australia went on a reef in a storm, off a desert island, and nobody but the mate got ashore alive. They'd found a mess of whale puke floatin' on the water, and filled a big barrel with it—and it floated ashore with him. The mate stood the solitude of the island as long as he could, and then took to sea in the ship's boat he'd patched up. He'd salvaged a chart and marked the island's position. He'd been weeks at sea when I picked him up, on my last voyage from Honolulu to Brisbane. He was ravin' and let slip about the ambergris—I mean he was that grateful to me for savin' him he told me all about it, and gimme the chart for safekeepin', and right after that he got delirious and fell overboard and drownded—"

Somebody laughed sardonically and Harrigan glared murderously around.

"He called the island Aragoa," he growled. "It ain't on no other chart. And now that daughter of Jezebel has fed that chart to the sharks—"

"Why, hell!" quoth Clanton. "Is that all? Why, I can steer you to Aragoa without any blasted chart! I've been there a dozen times!"

Harrigan started and looked at him searchingly.

"Are you lyin'?"

"Belay with those insults!" said Clanton heatedly. "I won't take you anywhere unless you promise not to punish the girl."

"All right," snarled Harrigan, and Raquel sighed in relief. "But!" brandishing his gun in Clanton's face, "if you're lyin', I'll feed you to the sharks! Take the wheel and lay a course for Aragoa. You don't leave the poop till we raise land!"

"I've got to have food," growled Clanton.

"Tell it to the cook. Then get hold of that wheel." Reminded suddenly of Raquel's lightly clad condition he roared: "Get below and get some clothes on, you shameless slut!"

A heavy toe in the seat of her panties emphasized the command, and she fled squeaking for the companion.

Clanton scowled, descended into the galley, and bullied the Chinese cook into setting out a feed that would have taxed the capacity of a horse. Having disposed of this, he swaggered up the poop ladder and took the wheel. The men watched him with interest, which was shared by Raquel, peeping from the companion. She had heard of him; who in the South Seas had not? A wild adventurer roaring on a turbulent career that included everything from pearl diving to piracy, he was a man at least, not a beast like Harrigan.

Her flesh still tingled deliciously with the feel of his strong grasp on her rounded arm; she was consumed with eagerness for more intimate contact with him, but the opportunity did not come until night had fallen and the powerful figure stood in solitary grandeur at the wheel.

His shoulders bulked against the South Sea stars as he held the schooner to her course; he might have posed for the image of intrepid exploration—until a slender figure glided up the poop ladder.

"Does Harrigan know you're out here?" he demanded.

"He sleeps like a pig," she answered, her great dark eyes sad and wistful in the starlight. "He *is* a pig." She whimpered a little and leaned against him as if seeking pity and protection.

"Poor kid," he said with grand compassion, slipping a protecting arm about her waist—the paternal affect of which was somewhat marred by his patting of the swelling slope of a firm hip. A luxurious shudder ran through her supple body and she snuggled closer within the bend of his muscular arm and pressed her cheek against his shoulder.

"What did Harrigan say was the name of that island?" he asked.

"Aragoa!" She jerked her head back and stared at him, startled. "I thought you said you knew about it!"

"Never heard of it!" he declared. "I just said that to save you!"

"Oh!" She stood aghast. "What will we do when he finds out you lied?"

"I dunno," he answered. "We're in a jam that requires thought and concentration. Sneak down and steal me a few bottles of Harrigan's booze."

She cast him an uncertain glance, but moved away down the ladder, softly as an ivory-hued shadow, to return presently with an armful of darkly gleaming bottles that made Clanton's eyes glisten. He lashed the wheel, casually sighting at a star on the horizon, and sat down by the rail.

"Set 'em down here," he requested, and when she complied, he grabbed her before she could straighten and pulled her down on his lap. For convention's sake she struggled faintly for a moment, and then her arms went convulsively around his corded neck, and she gave him her full red lips in a kiss that he felt clear to the tips of his toes.

"Judas!" During the entire course of a roving life he had never encountered a human volcano like this before. He shook his head to clear his swimming brain, took a deep breath and dived. When he came up for air, she was gasping too, quivering from the dynamic impact of his kisses.

Contentedly he knocked the neck off a bottle, took a deep swig and held it to her lips. She merely sipped; the night was still young, and she needed no alcoholic stimulant to drive the hot blood racing through her veins. It was already breaking all speed records.

Clanton did not need any stimulants either; but he drank because he was thirsty; because liquor was to him what moonlight and perfume are to some men. At each swig he gulped as though he were trying to see the bottom.

By the time he had tossed an empty overboard he was saying: "To hell with Harrigan! If he gets gay with me, I'll kick his teeth out! I don't believe there's any such damn' place as Aragoa, anyway!"

"Who cares?" she breathed, leaning her supple back against his breast, and lifting her arms up and back to encircle his brawny neck. He ran an appreciative hand over her swelling firm-tipped breast, and let his other hand slip up her knee, over her round, warm thigh . . ?!!!!

Just as grey dawn stole over the sea, a terrific shock ran through the *Saucy Wench*. There was a crash in the galley, blasphemy in the forecastle, as men fell out of their bunks. The schooner lurched drunkenly—and remained motionless, with a list to starboard. Preceded by a blue-streaked haze of profanity Harrigan came hurtling from the companion and pranced up the poop ladder in his drawers.

"What the blitherin' hell?" he screamed. "My God, we're aground!"

From a litter of empty bottles Clanton rose unsteadily, stretched, yawned, spat and stared appreciatively at the jungle-fringed beach which—with only a narrow strip of shallow water between—stretched away from under the port bow.

"There's your island, Bully!" he announced with a magnificent gesture.

Harrigan tore his hair and howled like a wolf. "Did you have to run her onto the beach, you son of a slut?"

"That could have happened to anybody," asserted Clanton, and added reprovingly: "Where's your pants?"

But the captain had seen the broken bottles, and his howl had all the poignancy of a stricken soul. Then he saw something else. Raquel, awakened by the noise, rose uncertainly, rubbing her eyes childishly. She made a face, tasting again all the square face she had guzzled the night before.

Harrigan turned purple; his arm windmilled, to the fascination of the crew who watched from the deck below. He found words, lurid and frenetic.

"You stole my liquor!" he roared. "You had my girl here all night! You've run my ship aground, and by God, I'm goin' to kill you, ambergris or no ambergris!"

He reached for his gun, only to discover that he wore neither gun nor belt. Bellowing he snatched a belaying pin from the rail and made at Clanton who smote him with such effect that the captain's head fractured the binnacle as his whole body performed a parabola backward.

At this moment a frightful figure appeared at the head of the starboard ladder—Mr. Richardson, bedecked in bandages, and with one good eye gleaming eerily. Not even such a beating as he'd received yesterday could long keep a true bucko in his bunk. In his hand was a revolver, and this he fired point-blank. But Mr. Richardson's one good eye was bleared, and his aim was not good. His bullet merely burned a graze across Clanton's ribs, and before he could fire again, Clanton's foot, striking his breastbone with great violence, catapulted him headlong down the ladder at the foot of which his head again met the deck with a force that rendered him temporarily *hors-de-combat*.

But Captain Harrigan had seized the opportunity to flee down the port ladder yelling: "Gimme my gun! I'll shoot 'em both!"

"Overboard!" yelled Clanton to Raquel, and then as she hesitated, he grabbed her by the neck and crotch, tossed her over the rail, and leaped after her.

The plunge into the water snapped her out of her hangover; she screamed, gasped, and then struck out for the beach, followed by Clanton. They reached it just as Harrigan appeared on the poop with a triumphant howl and a Winchester, with which he opened up on them as they raced across the sands and dived into the trees.

Under cover Clanton paused and looked back. The antics of Harrigan on the poop moved him to hearty guffaws, smiting his dripping thigh. Raquel glared at him, wringing out her skirt, and raking back a wet strand of hair.

"What's funny about being marooned?" she demanded angrily.

He spanked her jocosely and replied: "Don't worry, kid. When the schooner sails we'll be on her. You stay here and watch 'em while I go inland and look for fruit and fresh water. She's not stuck bad; they can warp her off."

"All right." She shucked her wet dress and hung it up to dry, while she lay down on her tummy on the soft dry sand to peer through the bushes at the ship. She made an alluring picture thus, for the pink panties that had played so prominent a part yesterday were not now in evidence. Clanton admired the view for a moment, and then departed through the trees, striding lightly and softly for so big a man.

Raquel lay there, watching the men piling into boats, with hawsers, where presently they were employed in yanking the schooner loose, stern-first, by main strength and profanity. But it was slow work. The sun rose, and Raquel got impatient. She was hungry and very, very thirsty.

She donned her dress, now dry, and started out to look for Clanton. The trees were denser than she had thought, and she soon lost sight of the beach. Presently she had to climb over a big log, and when she leaped down on the other side, a brambly bush caught up her skirt, twisting it high about her ivory thighs. She twisted about in vain, unable to reach the clinging branch or to free her skirt.

As she squirmed and swore, a light step sounded behind her, and without looking around she commanded, "Bill, untangle me!"

Obligingly a firm masculine hand grasped her skirt and freed it from the branch, by the simple process of raising it several inches. But her rescuer did not then lower the garment; indeed Raquel felt him pull it up even higher—much higher!

"Quit clowning," she requested, turning her head—and then she opened her lovely mouth to its widest extent and emitted a yell that startled the birds in the trees. The man who was holding her skirt in such an indelicate position was not Clanton. He was a big Kanaka in a breech-clout. Raquel made a convulsive effort to escape, but a big brown arm encircled her supple waist. In an instant the peaceful glade was a hurricane center, punctuated by lusty shrieks that a big hand clapped over a red-lipped mouth could not altogether stifle.

Clanton heard those screams as he glided like a big bronzed tiger toward the beach. They acted on him like a jolt of electricity. The next instant he was in full careen through the jungle, leaving behind a blue streak of profanity in his wake. Crashing through the bushes, he burst full onto a scene, striking in its primitive simplicity.

Raquel was defending her virtue as vigorously as civilized nations defend mythical possessions. Her dress had been torn half-off and her white body and limbs contrasted vividly with the brown skin of her captor. He wasn't all brown, though; he was red in spots, for she had bitten him freely. So much so that irritation entered into his ardour, and, momentarily abandoning his efforts to make her assume a position on her back, he drew back an enormous fist for a clout calculated to waft her into dreamland.

It was at this moment that Clanton arrived on the scene and his bare foot, describing a terrific arc, caught the Kanaka under his haunches and somersaulted him clear over his captive, who scurried to her protector on her all-fours.

"Didn't I tell you to stay on the beach?" *Whap!* In his irritation Clanton emphasized his reproof with a resounding, open-handed slap on her upturned posterior. Raquel's shriek was drowned in a vengeful roar. The Kanaka had regained his feet and was bounding toward them, swinging a knotty-headed war club he had leaned against a tree when he stole up on Raquel.

He lunged with a yell and a swing that would have spattered Clanton's brains all over the glade if it had landed. But it flailed empty air as Clanton left his feet in a headlong dive that carried him under the swipe and crashed his shoulders against the Kanaka's legs. Bam! They hit the earth together and the club flew out of the native's hand.

The next instant they were rolling all over the glade in a desperate dogfight, gouging and slugging. Then Clanton, in the midst of their frantic revolutions, perceived that Raquel had secured the club and was dancing about, trying to get a swipe at his antagonist.

Clanton, knowing the average accuracy of a woman's aim, was horrified. The Kanaka had him by the throat, trying to drive thumbs and fingers through the thick cords of muscle that protected the white man's windpipe and jugular, but it was the risk of being accidentally brained by a wild swipe of Raquel's club that galvanized Clanton to more desperate energy.

Fighting for an instant's purchase, he drove his knee into the Kanaka's groin, and the man gasped and doubled convulsively. Clanton broke away, kicking him heavily in the belly. Surprizingly the warrior gave a maddened yell, grabbed the foot and twisted it savagely. Clanton whirled to save himself a broken leg, and fell to his all-fours. At the same moment Raquel swung the too-heavy club. She missed as the Kanaka ducked, and she sprawled on her belly in the sand. Both men gained their feet simultaneously, but the Kanaka reached for the club. As he bent over Clanton swung his right overhand like a hammer and with about the same effect. It crashed behind the Kanaka's ear with the impact of a caulking maul. The Kanaka stretched out in the sand without a quiver.

Raquel leaped up and threw herself hysterically in Clanton's arms. He shook her loose, with lurid language.

"No time for a pettin' party! There's a whole village of the illegitimates over toward the other side of the island. I saw it! Come on!" He grabbed her wrist and fled toward the beach with her, panting: "Thick brush, men cussin' on the ship. They wouldn't hear the racket we've made—I hope." She didn't ask why he hoped so.

They burst onto the beach, and saw that the *Saucy Wench* was afloat; she was anchored in clear water off the shore, and Harrigan was oiling his rifle on the poop, with the be-bandaged Richardson beside him.

"Ahoy!" yelled Clanton from behind a tree. "Harrigan! I've found the ambergris!"

Harrigan started violently and glared, head down like a surly bear.

"What's that? Where are you? Show yourself!"

"And get shot? Like hell! But I'll make a trade with you. I've hidden the stuff where you'll never find it. But I'll lead you to it if you'll promise to take us aboard and put us ashore at some civilized port!"

"You fool!" hissed Raquel, kicking his shins. "He'll promise anything, and then shoot us when he's got the loot!"

But Harrigan was bellowing back across the strip of blue water.

"All right! Let bygones be bygones! I'm comin' ashore!"

A few moments later a boat was making for the beach. Raquel danced in her nervousness.

"Are you crazy? They'll kill us! And that native you knocked out will come to and get his tribe, and—"

He grinned and stepped out on the beach, pulling her with him.

"They won't shoot us till I show them the ambergris! I'll take Harrigan inland; you wait here at the boat. And let me do the talkin'!"

She was not in the habit of meekly taking orders, but she lapsed into sulky and bewildered silence. She was badly scared.

Harrigan and Richardson piled out before the boat grounded. The captain had a Winchester, the mate a shotgun. They covered Clanton instantly.

"Stay here!" the captain told the half-dozen men who had rowed him ashore. "Now then, Clanton, lead us to that ambergris, and no tricks!"

"Follow me!" Clanton led them into the jungle while behind at the boat, Raquel watched with dilated eyes and crawling flesh.

Clanton swung wide of the glade where—he hoped—the Kanaka still lay senseless. Hardly out of sight of the beach he stumbled over a root and fell. Sitting up he groaned, cursed and tenderly felt of his ankle.

"Blast the luck! It's broken! You'll have to rig a stretcher and carry me!"

"Carry you, hell!" snorted Harrigan. "Tell us where the loot is, and we'll go on and find it ourselves."

"Go straight on about three hundred yards," groaned Clanton. "Till you come to a clump of sago palms. Then turn to the left and go on till you come to a pool of fresh water. I rolled the barrel in there."

"All right," grunted Harrigan. "And if we don't find it, we'll shoot you when we get back."

"And we're goin' to shoot you whether we find it or not!" snarled Richardson. "That's why we left the men on the beach—didn't want no witnesses! And we're goin' to leave that wench to starve here with your skeleton when we sail. How you like *that*, huh?"

Clanton registered horrified despair, and both men chortled brutally as they strode away. They vanished among the trees, and Clanton waited a minute—five—ten—then he sprang up and sprinted for the beach.

He burst onto the beach so suddenly the bos'n nearly shot him.

"Pile in and row for the ship, quick!" he yelled. "Cannibals! They've got Harrigan and the mate! Listen!"

Back in the jungle rose a sudden bedlam of shots and blood-freezing yells. It was enough. No heroic soul proposed a rescuing sortie. In another instant the boat was scudding for the schooner. Its occupants swarmed up the side, spurred by the rising clamor that was approaching through the jungle. Clanton stood on the poop and yelled orders, and they were obeyed without question. The anchor came up with a rush, and the *Saucy Wench* was standing out to sea by the time the tribesmen danced out on the beach. They swarmed to the water's edge, three or four hundred of them, yelling vengefully. One waved a blood-splashed shotgun, another a broken Winchester.

Clanton grinned; the directions he had given his enemies had led them accurately—straight into the native village! He thumbed his nose at the baffled barbarians on the beach, and turned and addressed the crew.

"As the only man aboard who can navigate, and owner of the ship, I'm assumin' the position of cap'n! Do I hear any objections?"

The bos'n demanded: "What you mean, owner of the ship?"

"Me and Harrigan matched pennies," asserted Clanton. "My share of the ambergris against his ship. I won."

"What about the ambergris?" demanded a hardy soul.

Clanton nodded back toward the receding beach. "Anybody that wants to swim back there and fight those boys for it, is welcome to try!"

In the self-conscious silence that followed, he barked suddenly: "All right, get to work! Lay onto those ropes! There's a breeze makin' and we're headin' for the Solomons for a load of niggers for Queensland!"

As the crew jumped briskly, Raquel nudged him.

"You didn't find that ambergris," she said, her eyes ablaze with admiration. "That wasn't even the right island. That was all a lie!"

"I doubt if there ever was any ambergris," quoth he. "The fellow that made that chart was probably crazy. To hell with it!" He pinched her plump hip appreciatively and added: "I reckon you go with the ship; that bein' the case I want to see you down in the cap'n's cabin, right away!"

Ship in Mutiny

The mutiny of the *Saucy Lass* began with the crash of a handspike on the mate's unsuspecting head. He never knew what hit him. The mutineers, who had crept stealthily out of the forecastle and struck murderously from behind, were just lifting the limp body over the rail when Raquel O'Shane, the captain's girl, appeared in the companion. Instantly she gave tongue piercingly: "Bill! *Bill!* Mutiny! They've killed the mate!"

"Grab that loud-mouthed wench, Lopez!" snorted Big Joe Croghan, the leader of the mutineers, and the move of the scar-faced Spaniard was a trifle quicker than Raquel's as she tried to retreat. He grabbed her by her curly blue-black hair and hauled her out on deck, shrieking and kicking.

"Lock her up in the galley!" snarled Big Joe. "Over with the mate, quick, dammit! Here comes the cap'n!"

And he was, his coming announced by a blast of lurid language. Wild Bill Clanton had heard and understood the girl's shrieks. It was a beautiful night, lovely as only a South Sea night can be. Less than a mile on the beam the narrow beach of a nameless island shone like molten silver in the moon. The *Saucy Lass* was a black, hell-reeking blot in the calm serenity of the scene. A man had just died on her deck; a shrieking girl was being dragged galley-ward by her hair to be raped, and events were rushing to a violent climax with the charge of the captain up the companion.

At the passion in his voice, the mutineers wavered, but Big Joe's bellow stiffened them. "Steady, you swabs! He's only a man like us. Jack, stand by with your belayin' pin and bash him when his head shows!"

And then Wild Bill Clanton, iron-fisted bucko of the Seven Seas, came gustily up the companionway. Jack swung his belaying pin, but Clanton had heard Croghan's order, and was ready for just such an action. He ducked and Jack, missing, fell full into a blasting uppercut that had behind it the lifting drive of Wild Bill's lunge up the stair. There sounded the snap of breaking bone, the crash of a limp body on the deck, and then, before the startled mutineers could gather their wits, the maddened captain was among them, smiting with silent ferocity. Three of them were down, knocked senseless, before they could guard themselves, and Big Joe, missing a swipe with a handspike, was driven staggering against the rail by a thunderbolt left hook under the heart, and Clanton pinned him there, driving smash after smash to his rocking head, before his dazed mates could flounder to his rescue. In desperation they swarmed over the captain, clawing, kicking and striking.

Meanwhile Lopez was having difficulty in escorting Raquel to the galley. Throwing herself on all fours, she clung to every object and projection she could reach, and some of the things she called him, in three different languages, got under even his tough skin. In his resentment he took advantage of her position to kick her savagely. He might more safely have kicked a wildcat, for she grabbed his leg and bit his bare ankle savagely. He yelled with pain and fury and sprang back, releasing her hair as he did so. She sprang up, raked back a strand of black hair, and stared like a wild thing at the knot of battling figures which surged back and forth from rail to rail, with the impact of hard fists, stamp of bare feet, and panting gasps of effort.

She glanced about for some weapon with which to go to her sweetheart's aid—then shrieked and fled toward the bows as the Spaniard, in a killing rage, came for her with his knife drawn and his bared teeth gleaming in the moonlight. She tried to double back toward the poop—saw she was trapped, shrieked and leaped desperately for the rail as his hand closed on the shoulder of her light dress. The knife went up, but with a wrench that left the torn, empty garment in his hand, she reached the rail and went over it in a long, clean dive. The Spaniard, glaring over the side, did not see her come up again after she hit water.

He spat after her and ran back to aid his mates on the port side. The helmsman had left the wheel and the ship was drifting nearer and nearer the shore. Clanton, with his back against the rail, smashed away with fists that were like iron mallets; blood spattered and when he landed solidly a man whimpered and went down. And then a blindly hurled belaying pin glanced stunningly from his skull. As he staggered, Croghan, bloody and half-blind, lowered his head and caught him in the midriff with a smashing butt that knocked him backward half over the rail. Before he could catch himself, a dozen hands grabbed his legs and heaved, and Clanton shot limply and silently down to the water that waited for him.

On the deck the mutineers still on their feet sank limply to the deck, panting gustily and wiping blood from their features as they tried to get their wind back. They did not see Clanton, revived by the shock of the plunge into cold water, rise into the moonlight fifty feet astern, shake his head and then strike out for the beach. Presently Croghan rose drunkenly, spat blood and demanded: "Where's the wench, Lopez?"

"She jumped overboard," muttered the Spaniard uneasily.

Croghan clenched his great fists and his one eye, not hidden in a mass of black and purple bruises, turned red.

"Damn you!" he bellowed. "I told you to lock her up! I led this mutiny for her as much as anything else—" With a sudden lurch he was on the Spaniard, striking hard with a belaying pin. Lopez dodged and yelped as the pin bruised his shoulder. Screaming like a wild thing he drove his knife in under Big Joe's arm. A bellow of agony burst from Croghan's lips and he struck again, with the blind fury of a dying man. And this time he did not miss. The Spaniard's skull caved in like a smashed egg, and Lopez slumped to the deck. His killer swayed drunkenly above him for an instant, then fell heavily across his body and lay still.

The battered, bloodstained crew looked on aghast.

"Now what'll we do?" moaned one. "Croghan was the only man of us that could navigate!"

"And that damn' warship lookin' for us!" whimpered another. They stared at each other in pale-faced horror. They had been mere tools of Croghan, a former captain sunk to the position of boatswain because of acts of piracy that had cost him one command after another. Wild Bill Clanton, too, was wanted by the authorities for pearl poaching. It was for this reason that a British man-of-war had been chasing the *Saucy Lass* for days, and only last night, after having run far from the regular tracks of shipping, had the schooner managed to elude her persistent pursuer. She might sight her again any time. The appearance of the warship had postponed the mutiny Croghan had planned. There were pearls hidden somewhere in the captain's cabin; Croghan had wanted Raquel; and he had wanted a ship to go pirating in on a grand scale. The men, mostly scum of the South Seas, had let themselves be led into mutiny. But now Croghan was dead, lying across the man who had killed him, and they were without a navigator, helpless victims of wind and tide, doomed to drift blindly until a storm foundered them, or starvation overtook, or the warship raised them and took them prisoners to answer for many crimes. There was one other alternative and they recognized it as they turned and stared at the island, fast falling astern.

When Raquel dived from the rail, to escape sure death at the hands of the maddened Spaniard, she hit the water with a smack that all but knocked the wind out of her. She sank deep, so deep she was suffocating for air when her head finally popped out of the waves. She was far astern of the *Saucy Lass*, on whose deck the battle was still raging, and she saw the futility of swimming after the ship or calling for help. Turning lithely, she struck out for the beach, less than a mile distant. Her scanty brassiere and brief silk panties offered no obstacle to swimming, but she knew it would be touch and go if she reached the beach before her endurance gave out. Nor would she, had it not been for a reef-like rock that jutted out of the water a few hundred yards from the beach. Straining every supple muscle, she reached it just as the last ounce of her strength ebbed out of her with a tortured sob. She clung there for a few moments, helplessly watching the ship drift on and vanish from sight beyond a point of land, and unable to tell whether or not men still fought on its deck. But she whimpered weakly as she thought of her sweetheart battling singlehanded against the odds that faced him. There were guns on the ship, but Clanton had not had time to arm himself; he was too prone to rely on the power of his naked fists. After a time she dragged her quivering body up on a ledge-like projection, and there she lay, utterly spent.

Dawn was a white streak in the east when she felt revived enough to try for the shore. She slid into the water, shivering at the thought of sharks, and presently felt the firm sand beneath her feet. A moment later she emerged, a dripping figure of pink and white loveliness—and stopped short, as a trio of astounded Polynesians, armed with spears and clad only in loincloths, sprang up from behind a clump of bushes.

They seemed dumbfounded at her appearance, and their first words told her they had no knowledge of the ship that had passed in the night.

"Who are you that you come out of the sea like a daughter of Pele?" ejaculated one in a dialect which was one of the many Raquel understood.

She had stopped short, frozen with fear at the sight of them, but now her agile brain grabbed at a chance so audacious that it would not have occurred even to her, had not the native's words suggested it.

Assuming a commanding pose, she said: "I am a goddess, daughter of Pele, the Great Goddess! I am Tarera, who left the land long ago, but am now returned to rule my people! Kneel, mortals, and do me reverence!"

They did not kneel, but they seemed impressed. They spoke together in excited whispers, and then presently clustered about her, though at a respectful distance, and indicated that she should accompany them. She didn't know whether to regard them as guards or escorts of honor, but she believed she was putting her outrageous hoax over. Otherwise the command to march would have been emphasized by the prod of a spear in the soft flesh of her round hips, molded by the wet silk of her panties.

So she marched, carrying herself with a regal hauteur, and presently, after traversing a winding path which led away from the beach, they emerged into a clearing where stood a village. The Kanakas must have been feasting the night before, for few were stirring, but the entrance of a white woman brought them pouring out of their huts.

Raquel's escort stopped in front of the biggest hut, which stood near the edge of the clearing, and from it came a tall, strongly built man, with the light skin of a half-breed, and a strong, handsome, ruthless face. His dark eyes widened at the sight of the nearly nude white girl.

"Oh, Tanoa," quoth one of the warriors, "great king of Atua, this white woman appeared to us suddenly on the south beach. There was no ship, but she rose dripping from the water! She says she is Tarera, daughter of Pele!"

An excited murmur rose from the throng of natives who formed a wide semicircle before the hut; they shrank still further back.

"Can this be?" ejaculated the king, advancing, his brown eyes beginning to burn as they swept over the slender figure posed so haughtily before him.

Raquel favored him with an arrogant stare, and announced: "I am Tarera, the daughter of Pele, returned from afar to my own land, whence I departed a thousand years ago. I demand the homage due the—*ow!*"

It was an outraged shriek of surprize and pain. Tanoa had slapped her resoundingly across the tight-fitting seat of her wet panties! A roar of mirth went up from the crowd. With one brutal, ribald gesture, Tanoa had swept away their superstitious awe. Raquel in dismay felt her pedestal of pretense crumble under her.

"There's your homage, oh daughter of Pele, and in the proper place," said Tanoa cynically and in perfect English. "You put on a good act, sister, and it might have worked on an ignorant island chief. But as it happens, I was educated in Europe!" To his people he spoke concisely and in their own tongue: "This is no goddess. It is only some silly white woman who must have come ashore from some ship that passed the island last night while we were absorbed in feasting. Pay no more heed to her. Go about your business. I will attend to her!"

And without ceremony he seized the shrinking captive by one pink ear and the seat of her step-ins and frog-marched her into the hut, ignoring her outraged protests. That the crowd had no doubt at all about his intentions was demonstrated by their shouts of jeering laughter, directed at the white woman, and the taunting, obscene gestures made by the brown girls. Raquel's ears burned with shame and anger as she was forced into the hut.

It was more elaborate than the ordinary Kanaka hut; there were chairs, and a table that must have come from a ship's cabin. And there was a couch, too, on which her attention was instantly and painfully fixed. When Tanoa let go of her to close the door, she scurried across the room, as far away from that couch as she could get.

"Why seek to flee your eventual destiny?" he asked mockingly.

"I'm a white woman!" she flared. "You don't dare!"

"I'm half-white," he told her. "When I was learning the ways of my white kin in Paris, in Vienna, and in London, I learned that white women are—merely women. The holding of white women inviolate is merely a taboo which white men force on the men of other races, so that they alone may enjoy the women of their race. In general, they are strong enough to enforce this. But here there are no white men to make me obey their creed. How you got to Atua I do not know, nor do I care. It's enough that you're here. I'm king here, and answerable to no one. When I returned here from Europe, I deposed Queen Lailu—" he smiled reminiscently, as if enjoying certain memories connected with that usurpation, then continued: "Here you are not a privileged member of a dominant race before which a man of another color must cringe; you are simply—a woman, to be used as such."

"There is an English warship in these waters," she threatened desperately. "You know what they'll do to you if you do this to me!"

"They'll never know, even if they come here. There are plenty of places on Atua to hide a woman until they've gone. What right have you to complain? I didn't ask you to come into my kingdom. You came of your own free will. Now you must dance to my tune, like any other woman!"

He advanced on her with a broad smile of anticipation on his handsome lips, and his eye sparkling with cruel humor.

"Don't!" she begged, cringing back against the wall. "Please don't—oh!"

Brutally he ripped off her brassiere, laughing tauntingly as her hands flew up to the twin globes of quivering pink loveliness thus exposed.

"That's better!" he laughed. "Beauty should never be veiled, my dear! But my curiosity is not yet entirely satisfied—"

Cheeks flaming as she realized his beastly intention, she tried to duck under his grasping arm, but he was too quick for her. He grabbed her—there was a brutal laugh, a despairing shriek, the wild, vain thrashing of white legs—and he held up the pink panties in lustful triumph, while Raquel fled sobbing to the far corner of the hut, vainly trying to conceal her nudity in the traditional feminine fashion.

"You haven't enough hands for that, my dear!" Tanoa jeered, with the cynical humor of his kind, which sees a cruel comedy in the forcible exposure of feminine charms. "But now for the real sport!"

The leering mockery on his brown face gave way to a fiercer intentness as his hot eyes devoured her cowering naked figure with a glare that seemed to burn her bare flesh. He moved toward her, towering over her like a brooding giant. His implacable advance cowed her, his utter lack of mercy or consideration left her without strength to run or fight. Her legs gave way and she sank to her knees, whimpering: "No! No! No!"

With studied cruelty he caught her chin and forced her to look up into his inexorable face, gloating over the terror in her lovely, dilated eyes. Then he caught her fiercely in his arms, and she screamed at his touch, finding action again in a convulsive struggling. It was useless. She had never before experienced the ruthlessly exerted strength of a powerful male, and the ease with which he conquered her terrified her, assuring her of inevitable defeat. The contact of his hands groping over her smooth, naked body almost drove her frantic with shame and terror. Like a man drunk and famished, he crushed her in his arms until she screamed with pain, while greedily his fingers sought out every intimate detail of her writhing figure. He had lifted her from her feet, was carrying her to the couch.

"I told you it was useless to run!" he taunted her. "You might as well have set your lovely hips on this couch when you first entered—"

A step behind him made him whirl.

Wild Bill Clanton stood before them, his eyes slits of blue balefire.

"*Bill!*" sobbed Raquel. Tanoa, realizing his deadly danger, released her and began to back away. She ran to Clanton, weeping hysterically.

"I thought they'd killed you!"

He disengaged her clinging arms and spoke quickly: "I got ashore beyond the point. Didn't know you'd made it till I heard a woman screamin' and recognized it. Go out the back way like I came in—quick!"

As he spoke he was moving after Tanoa, who backed away, eyeing Clanton as a man might eye a wild beast, and trying to edge around to the door. Raquel scurried out the back way, without stopping to retrieve her scanty garments, and Tanoa leaped suddenly for the front entrance, shouting for help. In the midst of that leap Clanton struck him.

The white man launched himself like a panther at his enemy's throat. The half-breed was bigger than Clanton, and he knew the fierce, primitive Kanaka way of fighting; also he had learned something about boxing in Oxford. But he found his tactics useless before the onslaught of the white man, driven to a murderous frenzy by the sight of his mistress writhing naked in the brown man's arms. Only to the Anglo-Saxon is allowed the gift of battling to the death with bare hands, and this Tanoa quickly learned. He was battered from side to side, from wall to wall. Only his tremendous strength kept him on his feet. Blood spattered over the couch, the table upset, chairs spun splinteringly. Tanoa's mighty swipes flailed thin air, his efforts to grapple were futile before those iron fists which sank agonizingly deep into the quivering brown torso, and smashed the brown face to a mask of blood. In a red mist Tanoa saw Clanton's wild face, a mask of murder, slitted eyes blazing, teeth bared in a snarl, sweat-glistening shoulders heaving with each thundering smash.

But for his insane fury Clanton might have wreaked his vengeance and escaped, but the American was in the grip of a berserk rage.

Intent on killing his enemy with his bare hands, he was scarcely aware when the hut was flooded with warriors until a war club, glancing from his shoulder, told him he was trapped. He wheeled, lashed out and saw a man go down with a shattered jaw, another bend double from an agony-weighted belly-smash. Then a rain of bludgeons beat him to his knees and a net fell about his shoulders, enmeshing him. Before he could tear away the clinging strands, they had hurled themselves on him, thrown him, gripped him, bound him hand and foot.

"Put a guard before the hut!" panted Tanoa, staggering up, a ghastly and bloody spectacle. "We'll find the girl and make her watch while I skin him alive! I'll make a garment of his hide and force her to wear it always about her loins to remind her how her lover died!"

A few moments later he was leading his men northward through the jungle, though he reeled a little and his head swam sickeningly. But thought of the slim white naked body he had held so briefly in his arms beat like the maddening throb of an incessant tom-tom through his bruised brain. She could not hide from him forever. Some time, somewhere on the island he would find her, and quaff the cup once dashed from his lips.

Clanton, lying on the floor of the hut, cursed and strained vainly at his bond. Through the partly open door he could see the broad back of the squatting guard, and the legs and hips of a girl who stood before him. Their soft laughter floated back to him. Then suddenly he realized he was not alone in the hut.

A native woman stood looking down at him—a woman whose magnificent figure, scantily veiled in a grass skirt, was so voluptuously formed that it drove a pulse of passion through his blood in spite of his plight. With a lithe motion she knelt to whisper in his ear. Her skin was a golden tan, and as she bent her firm, tilted breasts touched his shoulder caressingly, sending an imperative fire crawling through his veins. His fingers itched to cup those luscious breasts, even while he raged at the thought of Raquel fleeing naked through the forest before Tanoa.

"I am Lailu," whispered the woman. "Once I was queen of Atua, until Tanoa returned from across the sea, with the white man wisdom he had learned, and overthrew me and reigned in my stead. And he did to me what he means to do to your woman. Yet if he were dead, the people would again obey me, though no man of Atua now dares stand against him. If I free you, will you kill him?"

"I'll do my damndest," gritted Clanton. "But he's got his men with him now, and won't give me another chance at him. If I had a gun—"

"He hid all the guns on Atua in a spot I know!"

"Lead me to it!" he demanded bloodthirstily.

Her fingers were already busy with the cords, and in a few moments he was free, and she pressed a long knife into his hand.

"Out the back way, quietly!" she whispered. "One of my women keeps the guard occupied in front!"

A moment later they were stealing softly northward through the trees. Lailu led the way, her small soft hand grasping his; at each step the loosely woven skirt parted, baring a smooth thigh, with a hint of more generous contours further up. But for his worry about Raquel, Clanton would have felt impelled to explore the mysteries of that tempting skirt.

He spoke of his apprehensions to Lailu, who shook her head.

"If they had caught her, we could hear them yelling in triumph. Probably she has hidden in some dense thicket where it will take days for them to find her. There is no use for us to look for her now. You can help her better by arming yourself and killing Tanoa!"

Clanton felt that in any event he was going to his death. He believed that if he shot Tanoa, the Kanaka warriors would kill him before Lailu could have time to assert her former dominance. But at any rate, Tanoa should not have Raquel. He followed Lailu deeper and deeper into the jungle, hearing no sound; apparently Tanoa had swung eastward or westward and penetrated some distant part of the island.

Presently Lailu squirmed through a screen of bushes and they came into a tiny clearing in the midst of which stood a huge tree, a hollow showing some several feet from the ground.

"He hid his guns there," she said, pointing. "Lift me up!"

He bent, set her on his shoulder and rose easily, steadying her with an arm about her legs. Again fire crawled through his blood, roused by the contours of her firm hips pressing his muscular shoulder, the velvety bareness of her thighs under his grasping fingers. She cried out sharply. "He has moved them to another place! They are not here!"

She slipped to the ground, clung to him in an agony of despair. "What shall we do?"

"Find Tanoa!" he said grimly, feeling like a crippled wolf driven to bay. "I'll try to get to him and kill him with this knife."

"That would be madness," she said helplessly. "He has more than a hundred warriors. You could never reach him alive."

"Find him!" he repeated grimly, and she shrugged despairingly and turned eastward, on a venture. They had not gone far when she clutched at him. "Listen! Something there, in the bushes!"

He bent, caught a glimpse of bare white flesh through the leaves, and a low fierce cry wrenched from his throat: "*Raquel!*"

She was stretched helplessly in the tall grass. In an instant he had her in his arms, while Lailu looked on enviously. Raquel eyed the queen suspiciously.

"Who's she?"

"Queen Lailu. She's on our side. Have you seen Tanoa?"

"He turned east with his men. I hid in the bushes and they missed me." She shuddered at the memory. "Then I turned my ankle. See how swollen it is! I can't walk. But Bill!" She clutched him exitedly. "The *Saucy Lass* lies at anchor less than a mile from here!"

"What!"

"Yes! I saw it from a distance, when I was doubling to get away from Tanoa! The Kanakas didn't see it. It lies in a little bay on the north side of the island."

"They must be crazy, loiterin' here with that warship likely to show up any time!" ejaculated Clanton. "But what a break! By God! If I can kill Croghan I could make the rest eat out of my hand! I'll bring 'em ashore with rifles and we'll wipe Tanoa off the map! Lailu, I'm goin' after Croghan first! He'll be easier to get than Tanoa, with a knife."

"But Bill, the crew will have broken out the rifles!" Raquel warned him. "You'll be shot down."

He grinned. "If I wait for them to shoot me, I'll live to be a thousand. Don't stop to ask questions, let's go!"

"And quickly," added Lailu. "If Tanoa finds that ship he'll kill everyone on it, loot and sink it far out at sea to hide the crime."

"But I can't walk!" wailed Raquel.

"I'll carry you! But wait—we might run right into Tanoa, and—"

"And burdened with the girl you could neither fight nor run," said Lailu. "Then we would all be taken. I can hide her where Tanoa will not find her. Then, if you win your men back, we can come for her safely."

Raquel, staring jealously at Lailu's bare breasts and her smooth flanks peeping through the grass skirt, objected strenuously to remaining behind while Clanton went on alone with this island Juno, but Clanton, realizing the logic of the queen's suggestion, settled the matter by picking up the naked girl bodily and depositing her in a nook in the dense thicket Lailu showed him.

"Now let us run!" Lailu seized his hand and darted away. They ran until a lifting fringe of trees ahead of them betokened the nearness of the beach, and there the woman stopped, reeling and breathless. He caught her in his arms and eased her to the grass. She had reached the limit of her endurance.

"Wait!" she panted. "The beach is just beyond there—Tanoa cannot reach it without our first seeing him now. Let us rest a little—"

Impatient as he was to go on, he saw her exhaustion was not feigned. They lay there a moment, her head on his shoulder, her firm young body melting against his. As if by chance one of his hands cupped a velvety breast, the other caressed a dimpled knee, and slid up the warm, smooth length of thigh, under the scanty grass skirt. She started convulsively at his caress, then sighed gustily, and turning supplely in his arms, threw her round arms about his neck, straining herself to him fiercely. An imperative wave of passion swept over him, blotting out all other considerations. There was no fault to be attached to either. They were a man and a woman who found themselves in each others' arms. The same primal urge that is akin to the impulse that drives the seas and winds, willy-nilly, drove them. They could not have done otherwise, had the salvation of the world depended on them.

Emerging shaken and dazed from the storm of emotion, they were roused by a clamor of fierce shouts to the north.

"They have found the ship!" cried Lailu, starting up. "They have come around the beach! Oh, I never thought of that! I thought if they came, they would come through the jungle!"

Clanton swore as he leaped up and ran. That was one time when a love-bout might cost him his life. Lailu followed, contrite but not regretful. She would not be the first queen to throw away a throne for a few moments of delirious ecstasy. Even as she ran she re-lived in blissful memory the more excruciating moments of the past half hour.

A few moments later they came to the tree-fringed edge of a sloping bluff and looked down on the broad beach below. The ship was anchored in a little natural bay, and a hundred Kanakas were swarming in the water and on the beach, hurling spears and trying to climb up the sides. The sailors beat them back with rifle butts and belaying pins, but they came on again. A dozen natives had fallen, senseless, but the seamen were hard pressed, half of them bleeding from fresh wounds.

"Why don't they shoot?" wondered Lailu.

Clanton swore. "I took the firin' pins out and hid 'em! I was always afraid of a mutiny. I don't see Croghan, damn him!"

"They cannot long withstand attack," said Lailu sadly. "See? Tanoa has spoken to men who go for rifles! Now they will kill your men like sheep, and if you try to kill Tanoa, they will shoot you!"

They saw the king, standing well back out of reach of the ship, near the foot of the cliff, directing the attack. None was near him.

"I'm goin' down there," said Clanton in desperation. "Maybe I can get to him and kill him before his men see me—"

"You haven't a Chinaman's chance," bitterly spoke a voice behind them, and they wheeled, to face Raquel. The girl was leaning on a branch she had fashioned into a crude crutch. Painfully and laboriously, half-crawling, she had made her way through the forest, driven more by jealousy than fear. Now her lovely eyes dilated with anger at the sight of the dreamy expression in Lailu's eyes, an expression which Raquel understood perfectly.

"You go down there and they'll make you look like a pincushion," she told Clanton. "You watch—I'll bring Tanoa up here!"

And before they could stop her she limped out into the open and eased herself to the ground at the edge of the bluff. There she picked up a pebble and threw it so it rattled down close to Tanoa. He turned and saw her cowering there at the crest, apparently in an attitude of panic, as if she had blundered into sight by accident. She yelped and began to drag herself away, and Tanoa promptly abandoned the fray without a word to his warriors, whose attention was wholly absorbed by the ship, and came swarming up the sloping cliff, his eyes red as hell's coals.

She looked so helpless, as she crawled out of sight into the bushes, that he knew she must be hurt, and did not bother to call his warriors away from the attack to help him catch her. He swarmed over the rim, burst through the bushes—and halted short as he came face to face with Clanton. A dozen wild questions flared in Tanoa's battered face, but he never knew the answer to them. The white man did not draw his knife. With an incoherent grunt of hate, he plunged at Tanoa's throat. His plunge carried the king with him. They hit the rim and went over, head over heels down the slope, a whirling tangle of arms and legs. And when they ended that headlong, rolling tumble, one man arose, shaking his head like a bull, and one lay still. Tanoa's head was bent beneath his arm on a broken neck.

The men on the ship yelled amazedly; the Kanakas wheeled, shrieked in vengeful surprize, and started toward the victor, lifting their spears. But up on the cliff Lailu stepped into view.

"Stop!" she called imperiously. "Tanoa is dead! I am queen of Atua!"

Old habits of obedience came back to them. There was no reason why they should champion a dead Tanoa against a living Lailu. They were but tools of the stronger; and now Lailu was the stronger. They knelt humbly.

Clanton glared at the frightened faces peering over the ship's rail, and demanded: "Where's Croghan?"

"Dead, cap'n!" bawled the men eagerly. "Lopez and him killed each other. We couldn't navigate her—all we could do was put back to the island and wait till the warship come along and captured us, but it was that or drift till we starved. We nigh wrecked her gettin' her into this anchorage. It was all Croghan's fault! We won't never do it again, sir! Come aboard and let's get gone, won't you, please, cap'n?"

"All right, blast you!" Clanton climbed the cliff and, stooping, lifted Raquel with a rough tenderness.

"You could be my king if you stayed," Lailu tempted; her eyes were deep and melting, and she involuntarily swayed her luscious hips. But Raquel forgot her pique when Clanton shook his head and said: "Not for me, Lailu. Not even if I didn't have that warship to think about. You're a fine girl, but—well, this little devil is my girl, after all. Pardon my haste, but I've got to get aboard and get some liniment on her ankle, and some clothes on her. And then we've got to put some more distance between us and that damned warship."

Raquel sighed luxuriously and settled herself in his arms, dreamily revelling in the contact of his strong hands with her naked flesh; he was her man; and though often he stepped aside to follow strange women, he always came back to her.

Desert Blood

The lazy hum of ancient Tebessa's streets was only a faint echo in the little Barbary room, with its gilded ornaments and woolen rugs, where Wild Bill Clanton scowled down at the girl who stretched with feline abandon on the couch beside which he stood. Clanton was a broad-shouldered, hard-fisted, lean-waisted American whose face was browned by the suns of the Seven Seas. It was not the first time he had come to Tebessa on business not to be shouted from the housetops, but it was the first time he had been confronted by a situation like this, while mingling a little pleasure with his business.

"What the hell?" he demanded of the world at large, and particularly of the girl who smiled up at him with mocking malice. "What's the matter with you, Zouza?"

She twisted over on her supple stomach and propped herself on her elbows. There was no veil to hide her roguish features, her full, pouting lips and *kohl*-darkened lids, which now drooped amusedly over dark eyes that sparkled with hidden meaning. Her *gandourah*, the robe worn by Algerian women, was a filmy wisp through which shone the warm ivory flesh beneath. Her broad girdle, drawn close about her supple waist, outrageously emphasized the contours of her ripe hips as she lay there, one leg thrust out in a straight line, the other kicking up a trim heel in the feminine joy of tantalizing a male, so the little crimson slipper barely clung to one saucy toe.

"Women love valiant men!" she asserted.

"Nobody ever called me a coward," he growled. He was puzzled. He had been in Tebessa a week, and had fallen in with her the first day. There had been nothing elusive about her then. She had bestowed upon him the full flavor of her exuberant charms, with a youthful zest that custom had not had time to stale, rousing in him an imperative thirst for a repetition. But business had intervened then, and he had been unable to see her again until today. And now she repulsed him. Moreover it was easy to see that she was not prompted by a mere coquettish whim, rising from a desire to be deliciously mastered, after a mock resistance. He chafed, puzzled and angry.

"You fight men!" she mocked. "Have you fought beasts—the king of beasts?"

"What do you mean?" He was fascinated by the swell of her ripe young breasts under the filmy robe. His fingers itched to caress them. Impatience was playing hell with his temper.

"The man I love must be a slayer of lions!" she announced.

"And where the hell would I slay a lion?" he demanded. "I'm no hunter. Anyway, there's no lions around here. An Englishman told me—"

"*That* for your accursed Englishman!" she interrupted with an inelegant but descriptive gesture. "There are lions in the forest of Alloufa, one day's ride from Tebessa. If you were a brave man—"

"Shut up!" he yelled, stung to the quick. He had never faced a lion, it was true, but his mallet-like fists had impacted on human jaws from Frisco to Singapore, alike on ship's decks and in seaport saloons, and his was the natural vanity of a fighting man. Mingling with his hunger to crush this saucy bit of warm, scented flesh in his arms, there rose a pugnacious urge to answer this challenge to his manhood. No strong man can endure being jeered at for cowardice by the woman he desires. Circumstances had enforced a postponement of the culmination of his business in Tebessa. He felt he could safely devote the next few days to his personal affairs.

"All right! But I'll have to get a guide, and a license or permit or somethin', won't I?" A man of the sea, his ideas of landsmen's rules and regulations were extremely hazy. Zouza bent her head to hide a triumphant smile; this hard-fisted bucko was as wax in her small hands.

"The authorities will rob you," she announced. "They will make you pay so much for the permit to buy a rifle, so much for a license to hunt, and so much tax on each cartridge you buy. Besides they will make you employ a guide with a government license, and *he'll* charge you more than he is worth. Besides, you will have to buy a rifle."

"Well, what can I do about it?" he demanded. He had no reason to question the truth of her statements.

She smiled in a superior manner, and announced: "I will arrange it, and it will cost you nothing! I have a cousin who is a famous lion hunter. He is Ahmed ibn Said. You have heard of him?"

"Naw."

"*Roumis* are without knowledge," she said loftily. "Never mind. Procure a donkey and at dusk ride alone out of the city, to the Well of Mansourah, three miles to the south. If any Frenchman sees you go, he will think you go to visit some woman of the Ouled-Nayl near the Well. But Ahmed will be waiting there with horses and a rifle. He will show you how to slay a lion unbeknownst to the French, Allah curse them!"

"How do you know I want to chase off to Alloufa just to shoot a lion for you?" he grumbled. "You're not the only skirt in Tebessa!"

"But I am Zouza!" she assured him, with the naive vanity that always amused and stimulated him. "You will prove yourself a man for me!"

And with a gurgle of glee she rolled lithely on her back, kicking up her heels like a frolicsome filly, heedless of the resultant display of ivory flesh. The little red slippers flew across the room, and with a peal of silvery laughter she swung her bare legs out of Clanton's reach, snatched her robe away from his grabbing hands and sprang from the couch, taking refuge behind it.

"No, no, not yet! Not any more until you have heard *El Adrea* roar: *'Ana wa el-bin el-mera!'* Go now and do not come back until you have proved yourself a man!"

A few moments later Clanton, swearing under his breath, strode out into the streets and almost bumped into another woman, the very antithesis of Zouza. Instinctively he doffed his cap. He knew her—had met her at the consul's office in Constantine a few weeks before. She was Miss Augusta Evans, a New England school teacher on vacation, and like all her breed, of both sexes, prone to wander into all sorts of outlandish places.

The stare she returned him was frigid. Evidently she had a pretty good idea as to the nature of the place he had just left. She was handsome enough in a cold, reserved way. The riding habit she wore displayed a well-rounded figure, and there was a wealth of light hair under the British sun-helmet New Englanders feel obliged to wear anywhere east of Gibraltar. Her features were classical in their severe regularity, and easy to look at, in spite of the tight-lipped expression of disapproval she frequently wore, as at present, denoting her condemnation of anything that differed from the habits and traditions of Boston.

It was partly because of the curves betrayed by the close-fitting riding breeches, as well as an honest desire to be helpful to a fellow countrywoman, which prompted Clanton to address the girl. After all, you never could tell.

"Good afternoon, Miss Evans," quoth he, his eyes focusing somewhere south of her waistline. "I understand you're interested in archaeology. There's some Roman ruins a few miles south of town, that—"

Her voice dripped icicles as she answered.

"Thank you, Mr. Clanton, but I am quite aware of that fact. I assure you that I am in no need of your assistance. As a matter of fact, I am just now completing my plans for hiring a guide and exploring those ruins tomorrow. The consul warned me against you—he said you were suspected of being a gunrunner and worse, and the house you have just emerged from quite substantiates his opinion of you. Good day, Mr. Clanton!"

"Okay, sister!" Clanton left her instantly, smarting.

"Damn', prudified, stuck-up snip!" His tentative interest had been chilled, in spite of those tempting curves. His only emotion right now was a wish that he could pull down those enticing riding breeches and give their fair owner a good spanking.

This incident, coming right on top of his maddeningly unsatisfactory interview with Zouza, left him in a state of extreme exasperation toward women in general. He found a boy with a donkey for hire, gave him some instructions, and then, still seething with resentment and frustration, he sought a certain house of entertainment, cleverly camouflaged by an innocent-appearing silk shop. He was presently seated in a wide cellar, among a motley crew of cutthroats, watching the gyrations of half a dozen dancing girls who had just enough Sudanese blood in them to impart an untamed voluptuousness found only in mixed breeds. Tobacco smoke rose in a blue cloud, and he occasionally caught a reek that didn't need the confirmation of vacant faces and dilated eyes to tell him some of the men were smoking more than tobacco. The place was a *hashish* den also.

It was a hell of a place for a white man to be, but Wild Bill Clanton was generally to be found in places where most white men ventured only at the risk of their lives. When he yelled for liquor it was brought him by a brown-skinned Somali girl, with eloquent rolling eyes, whose short slit skirt, worn for the convenience of customers with curiosity and roving hands, gaped revealingly at each strutting step. She smiled meltingly on the white man, but Clanton, in his present mood, eyed her coldly and applied himself to the liquor. None of the Moslems objected at the presence of the forbidden liquid among them. Indeed, they eyed it wistfully, and at his invitation, laid aside their coffee cups and drank heartily at his expense.

"Good Muhammadans, yeah!" he snorted. "When the Prophet forbade wine he didn't mention brandy; so they stuff their guts with it."

And so did he. He neither knew nor cared whether these men knew why he was in Tebessa. It was a cinch the French didn't know. He had come there to arrange with the agent of certain Berber chiefs for the delivering of a cargo of rifles, from a ship of which he was captain and sole owner, and which now lay anchored safely at a certain obscure island well offshore. He had learned that it would be a week more before the agent could get in touch with him. Clanton was playing a risky game, but there was more than money involved.

He had a sincere sympathy for these mountain tribesmen, fighting for life and freedom against a ruthless European power.

The dancing girls, stimulated by the presence of a *Roumi*, outdid themselves in vigor and abandon. But Clanton, with images of Zouza and Miss Augusta Evans mingling chaotically in his brain, merely glowered. He sat and drank and drank and drank, moodily watching the brown girls as they capered and cavorted, shedding garment after garment as they frisked before him, until to his slightly glazed eyes they merged into a whirling phantasm, many armed and many legged.

He came to himself with an awareness of motion beneath him and a wind out of the desert blowing in his face. He blinked, spat, swore, and glared about him. Here were no brown girls, no drunken Arabs—not even any lights, except the crazily rocking stars overhead. He was on a donkey and the donkey was carrying him over a rocky trail.

He tried to orient himself. He had drunk more than he intended, and the close atmosphere, reeking with *hashish* fumes, had proved overpowering. Evidently the owner of the donkey had, according to previous instructions, brought the beast to the silk shop, and told the Arabs, those still sober enough to understand, that the *Roumi* had intended riding southward. They must have lifted him into the saddle and led the donkey to the southern outskirts of the city, and then left him to the mercy of Allah and the jackass, which was characteristic of the Arabic nature. Some dim instinct, not altogether submerged, had made him cling to the saddle and boozily urge his steed southward.

He pulled up and glanced at the stars. He was not exactly lost, insofar as he still knew in which direction lay the Mediterranean Ocean and the Sahara Desert. He knew he must be somewhere south of the city. But where lay the Well of Mansourah, he had no idea. The terrain was a succession of ridges, and he could not have seen the lights of Tebessa, even if it were within a few miles. And it was nearly midnight, according to the position of the stars! Either he had left the city much later than he had intended, or else he had been riding for many hours. And he was supposed to meet Zouza's cousin at dusk!

"Hell's fire!" He had no natural ambition to hear *El Adrea* roar: "I and the woman's son!" among the cork oaks of Alloufa; but it had been Zouza's ultimatum; and now doubtless Zouza's cousin had given him up in disgust, and he had lost the easiest way of accomplishing his set task.

He urged the jackass to the crest of the nearest ridge. From there he still could not see the city lights, but he did see a single, glowworm sort of a light, winking off to the northwest. He headed toward it, and presently saw that the light was in a tent which stood on a small flat with a low ridge to the north. There was only one tent; a horse nickered behind it. As he dismounted the tent flap was pulled aside and a slender figure was silhouetted against the glow. A soft voice called anxiously: "Ahmed! Ahmed ibn Said! Is it you?"

"No, it's his friend!" announced Clanton, striding out of the darkness.

The girl cried out and sprang back, but Clanton caught her wrist. The liquor fumes were still rising to his brain, just enough to make him reckless of consequences, and the sight of her supple figure outlined against the light had set hammers going in his temples.

"Don't be afraid," he soothed, following her into the tent as she backed away, trying to free her wrist. He spoke Arabic as she had done. "I'm a friend of Ahmed's cousin."

There was no one in the tent but themselves. She was prettier than Zouza, a little taller, with the sweet suppleness of limb that belongs only to Bedouin girls. With her sleeveless, low-necked vest of embroidered silk, open in front and revealing the twin ivory hemispheres that were her youthful breasts, and with her voluminous pantaloons, girdled at the waist and caught in at the ankles, she might have just stepped from a Baghdad *harim*. Her lips were full and red and passionate, her eyes dark and expressive. Her slim shoulders and naked arms had just that touch of frailty that is most appealing to a powerfully muscled man.

Fascinated by his captive, Clanton turned her about, feasting his eyes on her supple figure. She squirmed uneasily under his scrutiny, making no attempt to cover her naked breasts, but twisting her legs nervously in their filmy coverings. The fabric of her pantaloons was so sheer that the soft white flesh gleamed through it. He glimpsed hints of piquant contours that set his already hot blood a-riot.

"Are you Ahmed's wife?" he wondered aloud. "His sister?"

A mute shake of the head answered each question; he understood the situation and grinned, relieved of any scruples he might otherwise have felt.

"And he leaves you here alone?"

"He went to meet a *Roumi* at the Well of Mansourah," she answered, finding voice at last. "No man would dare touch a woman of Ahmed ibn Said!"

Clanton grinned.

"Yeah? Well, I'm touchin' you!" A broad hand slipping down luxuriantly over the right swell of a saucily prominent hip removed any doubt on that score. Beneath the filmy covering her skin was velvety to his touch. She did not shrink from his caress, nor did she seek to draw away when his arm encircled her supple waist and drew her closer to him. A warm light that was neither fear nor resentment began to glow in her dark eyes as, recovering from her first shock of surprize and fear, she began to take stock of the intruder. Arab girls admire strength, and Clanton was overflowing with that; audacity, and nobody ever accused him of timidity. She met his gaze squarely, staring at his broad shoulders, deep chest, hard waist and thickly muscled arms.

"If he should catch you in my tent he would kill you," she said. "He is a trusted man of Shaykh Ali ibn Zahir!" But she spoke without enthusiasm. Clanton sensed that her relationship with Ahmed was a one-sided affair. Without doubt he had taken her by force from some weak tribe far to the south or the east. There was still plenty of raiding and women snatching going on in the desert, and he knew Shaykh Ali was a powerful chief who dwelt somewhere south of the Atlas Range. But he did not care. The nearness of this desert beauty, the feel of her lightly veiled flesh under his fingers, was making him drunk again, and with a wilder, more reckless intoxication than that of liquor. He had forgotten Zouza; this girl had everything she had, and more; she was vibrant with that intangible quality some call glamour, which sets the natural artist apart from the willing worker, however skilled and lovely.

All his life Clanton had been following his impulses, and now there was no resisting the peremptory urge of his primitive nature. He saw in this girl's eyes the same light he knew burned more fiercely in his own, and that was enough.

"To hell with Ahmed!" In sudden savage hunger he crushed her to him, found her hot red lips, until she caught fire from his ardor and her arms locked in equal fierceness about his neck, as she gave him kiss for kiss. There was a profusion of silk pillows in one corner, to serve as a couch. She yielded meltingly in his arms as he lifted her from her feet and carried her across the tent. His fumbling fingers found what they sought, and the filmy pantaloons glided to the floor. The soft white gleam of naked flesh in the mellow light made his head swim. Then for a time, Time stood still in the little striped tent. Sometime later the girl squirmed blissfully in Clanton's arms, stretched her white arms luxuriously above her head and then threw them about his thick neck, laughing with the pure joy of living. She kissed him with a gusto their recent exercises had not satiated in the slightest.

"I love you!" she sighed. "The first man I ever loved! The first man I ever gave myself to willingly. I hate Ahmed. He is cruel. He stole me by force. I am Aicha. What is your name, beloved?"

"I'm Wild Bill Clanton," he answered, running his fingers through her silky locks. Her dark eyes flared with sudden terror and the clasp of her arms was suddenly convulsive.

"You are the man Ahmed was to meet at dusk by the Well of Mansourah! To lead to your death!"

"What are you talkin' about?" he laughed. "He's Zouza's cousin, and—"

"He is not!" She was shaking him in a very frenzy of fright. "She betrayed you! Ahmed is Shaykh Ali's spy, and for Ali he laid a trap for you! Listen, I know all about it! There are no lions in Alloufa! Zouza lied about that, as about many things, according to Ahmed's instructions. He waits at Mansourah, not to guide you to Alloufa, but to take you captive to Ali, who has ridden up from the southern desert and lies with his tents not many miles from this spot.

"Ali sent Ahmed into Tebessa to draw you from the city by trickery. So Ahmed dogged your steps until he learned you were visiting Zouza—may she sit on hot coals! Then he gave her money to trick you as she did."

"But why does Ali want to capture me?" he demanded.

"Zulaykha, his wife, who rules him even as he rules his tribe, has turned from him and refused to grant him her favor until he brings you to her. She is the sister of Muhammad Pasha."

That seemed to suggest some kind of a connection with that cargo of rifles. Muhammad Pasha was a Turkish adventurer, playing a dangerous game for high stakes in Tripoli. Doubtless he needed guns.

"The moon has risen! Let us go, quickly! There is a horse tied behind the tent which will carry us both. Ahmed may tire of waiting, and—"

Even as they stepped outside the tent door a group of riders swept over the ridge to the north and were upon them. Ahmed, weary of his long vigil at the Well, had returned. No time to run now. From a heap of firewood Clanton snatched up a heavy fagot as the Arabs sprang from their horses and rushed at him. Oaths, shouts, the impact of blows rang to the sky. Ahmed, his face convulsed at the sight of Aicha cringing beside Clanton, forgot his command to take the *Roumi* alive, and lunged in, pistol thrust out at full arm's length, firing blindly. Clanton grabbed the long barrel and twisted it aside. As the powder burned his cheek he smashed his rude bludgeon down on the frantic Arab's head, and felt the bone give way. But even as he knew he had killed his man, a rifle stock splintered on his own head, and the lights went out.

Clanton recovered consciousness bound in a saddle, riding among his captors. The first streaks of dawn were lighting the eastern sky. Profanely he demanded to know where they were taking him, and what had become of Aicha.

"We take you to Shaykh Ali ibn Zahir," they answered, without resentment. "As for the girl, she sprang on a horse tied behind the tent, and fled away when we tried to seize her."

The sun was up when they topped a low ridge and saw half a dozen tents before them.

Shaykh Ali ibn Zahir, a tall, stately man with a pointed black beard, and half a dozen wild-looking cutthroats behind him, stood before the largest tent. He eyed Clanton murderously, but restrained his obvious anger and said quietly: "Your enemy, my wife, awaits you."

"I'm no enemy of hers," grunted Clanton. "I never saw her."

"Perhaps not. But you helped the Italians catch her young brother and send him to prison, she says. She has denied herself to me, until I brought you to her." He meditated for a moment, wryly. "Never in the history of *Al-Islam*," quoth he, "has a *shaykh* led a *Roumi* in to his wife, and left them alone! Yet that is what she requires! What she means to do, I do not know. I know this: that she is safe from you, because your hands will be tied behind you, and my most faithful eunuch on guard over you. Who can fathom the whims of women? Her whim is to punish you, alone in her tent. Perhaps she will let you live, after certain alterations. But you must understand that I cannot. It is shame enough that I let her have her way in this thing. You understand that I cannot let you live after you have been in my wife's tent, whatever the reason."

"Sure," said Clanton sardonically. "I understand. A hell of a *shaykh* you are, lettin' your wife boss you around!"

But the white man knew that petticoat domination in the desert is much more common than Westerners generally realize; and if Zulaykha was anything like her brother, it was not surprizing that she should dominate Shaykh Ali, who was not noted for any particular strength of character.

He was led to the tent and thrust through the door. The flap was closed behind him. A dark-haired, dark-eyed beauty, unveiled, lounged on a great pile of velvet cushions. Near the door stood a huge impassive Soudanese, like an image cut out of black basalt, with a scimitar in his hand and the butt of a Luger jutting from his girdle.

Clanton scowled at the woman, who was an olive-skinned Turkish Juno, plumper and darker than Aicha, with generous contours only partly veiled by her sheer *gandourah* and the silk vest beneath. Clanton knew very well what sort of punishment a masculine captive might expect at the hands of a Turkish woman, but he was too mad to be apprehensive.

"What the hell you mean by tellin' your husband that lie?" he demanded. "I never helped send any brother of yours to jail, and you know it."

"I had to give him some excuse," she answered calmly. "My husband is a sluggard, caring for nothing but women. He is but a pawn in the game my brother plays. I thought he was a man when I married him. I find he is a coward. Had he known my real reason for wanting you, he would never have brought me up from the south and captured you for me. Enough. My brother has learned you have a cargo of rifles to deliver to the Berbers. I want you to write a letter to your mate, telling him to deliver the rifles to my brother, at a spot on the coast I shall designate."

"I won't do it!" he snarled.

"There are ways of persuasion!" Her heavy lids drooped over her glittering eyes, and she looked dangerous and cruel enough for any torture or bloody mutilation. But Clanton was not impressed. He was as tough as he looked.

"Go on and shoot the works," he growled. "I'm a gone goose anyway. Those guns are goin' to friends of mine, not to your fat-bellied brother. They're patriots. He's a blasted thief! You can't hurt me bad enough to make me write that letter."

Zulaykha eyed him with more respect, recognizing in him a man who might be led by a woman, but who was not to be driven.

She rose suddenly, came to him, untied his wrists and drew him toward the cushions.

"Let us be friends," she urged. "You could go far, with my brother and me. Never mind the black man. He is my servant—not Ali's. And he is faithful to me."

Clanton wondered just which one of them was mistaken about the Negro. He understood her game, but he was a man who plucked fruit when he found it, and not even the realization that only a miracle could keep his severed head from rolling in the sand within the next hour could cool the customary ardour of his reckless blood. He was not one to let a woman do all the wooing. Zulaykha, preparing to vamp him with all her arts, found the game taken out of her hands as he drew her onto his lap without hesitation. Always adaptable, she yielded supplely.

"Ally yourself with me!" she whispered, throwing her round arms about his neck, and rubbing her full, velvety cheek against his. "Let Muhammad have the guns! I will make Ali spare your life!"

He knew she lied deliberately. Whatever her dominance of the Shaykh, she could never persuade him to spare a man she had taken into her tent, even though Ali suspected nothing of this lovemaking.

"Leave Ali and ride with me to Tebessa," he suggested, fighting for his life with every trick that occurred to him, even while he explored the perfumed recesses of her *gandourah* and the filmy vest beneath. "We'll sneak out the back side of the tent, grab horses and ride!"

"I cannot," she breathed, seizing his hand and drawing it down between her warm, firm breasts. "Ali is a fool, but we need his tribe, Muhammad and I, and his money in our schemes. Write the letter for me! You shall have what I have refused Ali, and freedom and gold besides!"

He knew she lied. Once she got that letter, Ali could have his head. He pretended to be intoxicated by his passion, replying incoherently to her urgings as he sparred desperately for time and a plan of escape. And his head *was* beginning to swim a little; and Zulaykha's shudders of ecstasy were not all feigned, as his caresses grew more and more intimate. The black eunuch yawned, whether with indifference or to conceal envy, Clanton did not know. But he did know the moments of his life were fast slipping away. Zulaykha dexterously withheld the ultimate favor, increasing her importunities. He couldn't stall her off much longer. Presently she'd realize his game, and turn from seduction to torture. Well, at least his hands were free, and he'd go down fighting.

Outside, suddenly, a voice shouted: "*Sidi!* A white woman! Riding alone, within a mile from camp!" It was a lookout on the ridge.

An instant clamor answered him, Ali's voice exultantly yelling orders. Zulaykha sat up on Clanton's knees, a little irritated.

"Listen at them! Ali shows decision and determination only in the matter of women! Hear them saddling and mounting? He could never resist the opportunity to turn up a white woman's petticoats."

"You mean he'll snatch her?" demanded Clanton incredulously.

"Why not?" she demanded impatiently. "Nobody will know. We'll be deep in the desert by nightfall. Ali is terrified by the thought of revolt and intrigue—that's why I deceived him about the rifles. But he'll risk his neck for a woman—especially a white woman."

"Well, he won't get away with this!" Clanton leaped to his feet, spilling Zulaykha in a sprawl of bare, olive-tinted legs and hips. She swore at him in Turkish, French, and Arabic.

"What do you care?" She herself felt no jealousy toward a chance-caught captive. "Let the fool do as he wishes with her. You and I—"

"To hell with that!" He sprang toward the door, as the drum of hoofs diminished in the distance. Zulaykha screamed: "Stop him!" The black swung with his scimitar. Clanton ducked and swung with his right. It connected. The black kissed the carpet, with a fractured jaw. Clanton snatched the pistol from his girdle and burst out of the tent, ignoring Zulaykha's profane screams. The camp was empty, but spare horses were picketed nearby. He jammed a bridle on one and leaped up, bareback. On the ridge north of the camp he paused an instant, glaring at the broken field below him. He saw a horseman riding hard before the whooping Arabs. And he swore at the sight of the familiar riding habit and sun helmet. Miss Augusta Evans! What the hell! And riding as he'd never expected to see her ride.

She was making a wide circle, swinging back to the south again, and her horse was magnificent. She was drawing steadily away from all of them except Ali and he was barely holding his own.

Clanton cut straight across the wide semicircle, riding with a recklessness acquired by a boyhood on a Western ranch, before he went to sea. They were not far ahead of him as he rode to cut their path, when the woman's horse stumbled and threw her over its head. The girl staggered dizzily to her feet, just as Shaykh Ali swept down, yelling, sprang off and grabbed her in a way that showed plainly that he did not intend to postpone his favorite pastime.

Then Clanton heard him cry out fiercely and saw him dash his captive to the ground in a paroxysm of anger the white man could not understand. But he came sweeping in, and his yell was a challenge that brought Ali around, whipping out a pistol. They fired simultaneously. Clanton heard the whine of Ali's slug, and the Bedouin fell, with a bullet through his head. Nearly half a mile back his followers yelled with panic, pulled up and scattered to cover, not recognizing their former prisoner at that distance, and fearing an attack in force.

Clanton leaped down and grabbed the girl, who was just getting on her feet. The helmet had fallen off, revealing a profusion of *black* hair!

"Aicha!"

She clung to him.

"Oh, my lover! When they rode away with you toward Ali's camp, I rode for Tebessa, to beg the French to come and aid you, though I feared they would arrive too late. But then Allah put the means of saving you in my hand!

"I knew Ali would ride forth with all his men if he sighted a white woman riding alone. So I showed myself in these garments to his sentry on the ridge, intending to draw them all away, outride them and double back to set you free before they could come up. But the horse stumbled."

"But where'd you get these clothes?" he asked.

As I rode toward Tebessa, I met a white woman with spectacles on a donkey, and a boy guiding her whom I knew. Yussef, son of Hassan. So I gave him money, and we took her garments—"

"*What?*"

"Aye. Yussef helped me strip her. She made many lamentable cries, and wept with shame. Aye, she blushed from head to foot! She could have had *my* garments, but while I was preparing to change, Yussef put her upon her donkey and it ran away toward the city, she clinging to the saddle horn, and—"

The rest was drowned in Clanton's roar of laughter as he was overcome by the thought of Miss Augusta Evans, on a runaway donkey, approaching the crowded streets of Tebessa, clad only in horn-rimmed spectacles. Aicha watched him, naively puzzled at his mirth, but glad that her new lord and master should be pleased with her. "And then Yussef ran away," she concluded, "and I rode on to Ali's camp, and all befell as you have seen."

Still laughing he caught his horse and hers, which were grazing nearby. He spanked her playfully as he lifted her into the saddle; she filled those provocative riding breeches even more deliciously than had Miss Evans.

"I'll have to sneak you into Tebessa and get you some more clothes before you're spotted with those duds on, and arrested for highway robbery! As soon as I've delivered those rifles to my Berber friends, I'm going to take you to sea with me. Ever been to sea, Aicha?"

She shook her head. He grinned with pleasurable anticipation.

"You'll like it, kid; wait till you see the bed in my ship's cabin!"

The Purple Heart of Erlik

"You'll do what I tell you—or else!" Duke Tremayne smiled cruelly as he delivered his ultimatum. Across the table from him Arline Ellis clenched her white hands in helpless rage. Duke Tremayne, world adventurer, was tall, slim, darkly mustached, handsome in a ruthless way, and many women looked on him with favor. But Arline hated him, with as good reason as she feared him.

But she ventured a flare of rebellion.

"I won't do it! It's too risky!"

"Not half as risky as defying me!" he reminded her. "I've got you by the seat of your pretty pants, my dear. How would you like for me to tell the police why you left Canton in such a hurry? Or tell them *my* version of that night in Baron Takayami's apartment—"

"Hush!" she begged. She was trembling as she glanced fearfully about the little curtained alcove in which they sat. It was well off the main floor of the Bordeaux Cabaret; even the music from the native orchestra came only faintly to their ears. They were alone, but the words he had just spoken were dynamite, not even safe for empty walls to hear.

"You know I didn't kill him—"

"So you say. But who'd believe you if I swore I *saw* you do it?"

She bent her head in defeat. This was the price she must pay for an hour of folly. In Canton she had been indiscreet enough to visit the apartments of a certain important Japanese official. It had been only the harmless escapade of a thrill-hunting girl. She had found more thrills than she wanted, when the official had been murdered, almost before her eyes, by his servant, whom she was sure was a Russian spy. The murderer had fled, and so had she, but not before she had been seen leaving the house by Duke Tremayne, a friend of the slain official's. He had kept silent. But the murderer had taken important documents with him in his flight, and there was hell to pay in diplomatic circles. It had been an international episode, that almost set the big guns of war roaring in the East. The murder and theft remained an unsolved mystery to the world at large, a wound that still rankled in the capitals of the Orient.

Arline had fled the city in a panic, realizing she could never prove her innocence, if connected with the affair. Tremayne had followed her to Shanghai and laid his cards on the table. If she did not comply with his wishes, he'd go to the police and swear he saw her murder the Jap. And she knew his testimony would send her to a firing squad, for various governments were eager for a scapegoat with which to conciliate the wrathful Nipponese.

Terrified, Arline submitted to the blackmail. And now Tremayne had told her the price of his silence. It was not what she had expected, though, from the look in his eyes as he devoured her trim figure from blond hair to French heels, she felt it would come to that eventually. But here in the Bordeaux, a shady rendezvous in the shadowy borderland between the European and the native quarters, he had set her a task that made her flesh crawl. He had commanded her to steal the famous Heart of Erlik, the purple ruby belonging to Woon Yuen, a Chinese merchant of powerful and sinister connections.

"So many men have tried," she argued. "How can I hope to succeed? I'll be found floating in the Yangtze with my throat cut, just as they were."

"You'll succeed," he retorted. "They tried force or craft; we'll use a woman's strategy. I've learned where he keeps it—had a spy working in his employ and he learned that much. He keeps it in a wall safe that looks like a dragon's head, in the inner chamber of his antique shop, where he keeps his rarest goods, and where he never admits anybody but wealthy women collectors. He entertains them there alone, which makes it easy."

"But how am I going to steal it, with him in there with me?"

"Easy!" he snapped. "He always serves his guests tea. You watch your chance and drop this knock pill in his tea."

He pressed a tiny, faintly odorous sphere into her hand.

"He'll go out like a candle. Then you open the safe, take the ruby and skip. It's like taking candy from a baby. One reason I picked you for this job, you have a natural gift for unraveling Chinese puzzles. The safe doesn't have a dial. You press the dragon's teeth. In what combination, I don't know. That's for you to find out."

"But how am I going to get into the inner chamber?" she demanded.

"That's the cream of the scheme," he assured her. "Did you ever hear of Lady Elizabeth Willoughby? Well, every antique dealer in the Orient knows her by sight or reputation. She's never been to Shanghai, though, and I don't believe Woon Yuen ever saw her. That'll make it easy to fool him. She's a young English woman with exotic ideas and she spends her time wandering around the world and collecting rare Oriental art treasures. She's worth millions, and she's a free spender.

"Well, you look enough like her in a general way to fit in with any description Woon Yuen's likely to have heard. You're about the same height, same color of hair and eyes, same kind of figure —" his eyes lit with admiration as they dwelt on the trim curves of bosom and hips. "And you can act, too. You can put on an English accent that would fool the Prince of Wales, and act the high-born lady to a queen's taste.

"I've seen Lady Elizabeth's cards, and before I left Canton I had one made, to match. You see I had this in mind, even then." He passed her a curious slip of paper-thin jade, carved with scrawling Chinese characters.

"Her name, of course, in Chinee. She spends a small fortune on cards like that, alone. Now go back to your apartment and change into the duds I had sent up there—scarlet silk dress, jade-green hat, slippers with ivory heels, and a jade brooch. That's the way Lady Elizabeth always dresses. Eccentric? You said it! Go to Woon Yuen's shop and tell him you want to see the ivory Bon. He keeps it in the inner chamber. When you get in there, do your stuff, but be careful! They say Woon Yuen worships that ruby, and burns incense to it.

But you'll pull the wool over his eyes, all right. Be careful he doesn't fall for you! Couldn't blame him if he did."

He was leaning toward her, and his hand was under her dress. She flinched at the feel of his fingers questing under her dress. She flinched at the feel of his caresses, but she dared not repulse him. He was arrogantly possessive, and she did not doubt that when—and if—she returned with the coveted gem, he would demand the ultimate surrender. And she knew she would not dare refuse him. Tears of helpless misery welled to her eyes, but he ignored them. Grudgingly he withdrew his hand and rose.

"Go out by the back way. When you get the ruby, meet me at room Number 7, in the Alley of Rats—you know the place. Shanghai will be too hot for you, and we'll have to get you out of town in a hurry. And remember, sweetheart," his voice grew hard as his predatory eyes, and his arm about her waist was more a threat than a caress, "if you double-cross me, or if you flop on this job, I'll see you stood before a Jap firing squad if it's the last thing I do. I won't accept any excuses, either. Get me?"

His fingers cupped a handful of soft, firm breast, and as he voiced his threat, he dug them in like talons, emphasizing his command with a brutality that made Arline bite her lip to keep from crying out with pain.

"Yes, I get you."

"All right. Get going." He spanked her lightly and pushed her toward a door opposite the curtained entrance beyond which the music blared.

The door opened into a long narrow alley that eventually reached the street. As Arline went down this alley, seething with rebellion and dismay for the task ahead of her, a man stepped from a doorway and stopped her. She eyed him suspiciously, though concealing a secret throb of admiration for a fine masculine figure.

He was big, broad shouldered, heavy fisted, with smoldering blue eyes and a mop of unruly black hair under a side-tilted seaman's cap. And he was Wild Bill Clanton, sailor, gunrunner, blackbirder, pearl poacher, and fighting man de luxe.

"Will you get out of my way?" she demanded.

"Wait a minute, kid!" He barred her way with a heavy arm, and his eyes blazed as they ran over the smooth bland curves of her blond loveliness. "Why do you always give me the shoulder? I've made it a point to run into you in a dozen ports, and you always act like I had the plague."

"You have, as far as I'm concerned," she retorted.

"You seem to think Duke Tremayne's healthy," he growled resentfully.

She flinched at the name of her master, but answered spiritedly: "What I see in Duke Tremayne's none of your business. Now let me pass!"

But instead he caught her arm in a grip that hurt.

"Damn your saucy little soul!" he ripped out, anger fighting with fierce desire in his eyes. "If I didn't want you so bad, I'd smack your ears back! What the hell! I'm as good a man as Duke Tremayne. I'm tired of your superior airs. I came to Shanghai just because I heard you were here. Now are you comin' across, or do I have to take it away from you?"

"You wouldn't dare!" she exclaimed. "I'll scream—"

A big hand clapped over her mouth put a stop to that.

"Nobody interferes with anything that goes on in alleys behind dumps like the Bordeaux," he growled, imprisoning her arms and lifting her off her feet, kicking and struggling. "Any woman caught here's fair prey."

He kicked open the door through which he had reached the alley, and carried Arline into a dim hallway. Traversing this with his writhing captive, he shoved open a door that opened on it. Arline, crushed against his broad breast, felt the tumultuous pounding of his heart, and experienced a momentary thrill of vanity that she should rouse such stormy emotion in Wild Bill Clanton, whose exploits with the women of a hundred ports were as widely celebrated as his myriad bloody battles with men.

He entered a bare, cobwebby room, and put her on her feet, placing his back against the door.

"Let me out of here, you beast!" She kicked his shins vigorously. He ignored her attack.

"Why don't you be nice?" he begged. "I don't want to be rough with you. Honest, kid, I'd be good to you—better than Tremayne probably is —" For answer she bent her blond head and bit his wrist viciously, even though discretion warned her it was probably the worst thing she could do.

"You little devil!" he swore, grabbing her. "That settles it!"

Scornful of her resistance, he crushed her writhing figure against his chest, and kissed her red lips, her furious eyes, her flaming cheeks and white throat, until she lay panting and breathless, unable to repel the possessive hand that bared the white mounds of her tilted breasts. She squirmed and moaned with mingled emotions as he sank his head, eagerly as a thirsty man bending to drink, and pressed his burning lips first to the tender vale between those dainty hillocks, and then to each quivering hemisphere in turn. One hand wandered lower, under her skirt, and insatiably explored the cool, velvety flesh beneath, seeking out intimate contours that made her whimper with shamed ecstasy.

In a sort of daze she found herself on the dingy bed, with her skirt bunched about her hips. The gleam of her own white flesh, so generously exposed, brought her to her senses, out of the maze of surrender into which his strong, dominating hands were forcing her. Her agile mind worked swiftly. As he tilted her back on the bed she shrieked convulsively.

"My back! Something's stabbed me! A knife in the mattress—"

"What the hell?" He snatched her up instantly and whirled her about, but she had her hands pressed over the small of her back, and was writhing and moaning in well-simulated pain.

"I'm sorry, kid—" he began tearing the bed to pieces, trying to find what had hurt her, and as he turned his back, she snatched a heavy pitcher from the washstand and smashed it over his head.

Not even Wild Bill Clanton could stand up under a clout like that. He went down like a pole-axed ox—or bull, rather—and she darted through the door and down the hall. Behind her she heard a furious roar that lent wings to her small high heels. She sprang into the alley and ran up it, not stopping to arrange her garments. As she emerged into the street, a backward glance showed her Clanton reeling out into the alley, streaming blood, a raging and formidable figure. But she was on a semi-respectable street, with people strolling past and Sikh policemen within call. He wouldn't dare come out of the alley after her. She walked sedately away, arranging her dress as she went. A few loungers had seen her run from the alley, but they merely smiled in quiet amusement and made no comment. It was no novelty in that quarter to see a girl run from a back alley with her breasts exposed and her skirt pulled awry.

But a few deft touches smoothed out her appearance, and a moment later, looking cool, unruffled and demure as though she had just stepped out of a beauty shop, she was headed for her apartment, where waited the garments she must don for her dangerous masquerade.

An hour later she entered the famous antique shop of Woon Yuen, which rose in the midst of a squalid native quarter like a cluster of jewels in a litter of garbage. Outside it was unpretentious, but inside, even in the main chamber with its display intended to catch the fancy of tourists and casual collectors, the shop was a colorful riot of rich artistry. A treasure trove in jade, gold, and ivory was openly exhibited, apparently unguarded. But the inhabitants of the quarter were not fooled by appearances. Not one would dare try to rob Woon Yuen. Arline fought down a chill of fear.

A cat-footed Chinese bowed before her, hands concealed in his wide silken sleeves. She eyed him with the languid indifference of an aristocrat, and said, with an accent any Briton would have sworn she was born with: "Tell Woon Yuen that Lady Elizabeth Willoughby wishes to see the ivory Bon." The slant eyes of the impassive Chinaman widened just a trifle at the name. With an even lower bow he took the fragment of jade with the Chinese characters, and kowtowed her into an ebony chair with dragon-claw feet, before he disappeared through the folds of a great dark velvet tapestry which curtained the back of the shop.

She sat there, glancing indifferently about her, according to her role. Lady Elizabeth would not be expected to show any interest in the trifles displayed for the general public. She believed she was being spyed on through some peephole. Woon Yuen was a mysterious figure, suspected of strange activities, but so far untouchable, either by his many enemies or by the authorities. When he came, it was so silently that he was standing before her before she was aware of his entrance. She glanced at him, masking her curiosity with the bored air of an English noblewoman.

Woon Yuen was a big man, for a Chinaman, squattily built, yet above medium height. His square, lemon-tinted face was adorned with a thin wisp of drooping mustachioes, and his bull-like shoulders seemed ready to split the seams of the embroidered black silk robe he wore. He had come to Shanghai from the North, and there was more Mongol than Chinese in him, as emphasized by his massive forearms, impressive even beneath his wide sleeves. He bowed, politely but not obsequiously. He seemed impressed, but not awed by the presence of the noted collector in his shop.

"Lady Elizabeth Willoughby does my humble establishment much honor," said he, in perfect English, sweeping his eyes over her without any attempt to conceal his avid interest in her ripe curves. There was a natural arrogance about him, an assurance of power. He had dealt with wealthy white women before, and strange tales were whispered of his dealings with some of them. The air of mystery and power about him made him seem a romantic figure to some European women.

"The Bon is in the inner chamber," he said. "There, too, are my real treasures. These," he gestured contemptuously about him, "are only a show for tourists. If milady would honor me—"

She rose and moved across the room, with the assured bearing of a woman of quality, certain of deference at all times. He drew back a satin curtain on which gilt dragons writhed, and following her through, drew it together behind them. They went along a narrow corridor, where the walls were hung with black velvet and the floor was carpeted with thick Bokhara rugs in which her feet sank deep.

A soft golden glow emanated from bronze lanterns, suspended from the gilt-inlaid ceiling. She felt her pulse quicken. She was on her way to the famous, yet mysterious, inner chamber of Woon Yuen, inaccessible to all but wealthy and beautiful women, and in which, rumor whispered, Woon Yuen had struck strange bargains. He did not always sell his antiques for money, and there were feminine collectors who would barter their virtue for a coveted relic.

Woon Yuen opened a bronze door, worked in gold and ebon inlay, and Arline entered a broad chamber, over a silvery plate of glass set in the threshold. She saw Woon Yuen glance down as she walked over it, and knew he was getting an eyeful. That mirror placed where a woman must walk over it to enter the chamber was a typical Chinese trick to allow the master of the establishment to get a glimpse at the more intimate charms of his fair customers, as reflected in the mirror. She didn't care, but was merely amused at his ingenuity. Even Woon Yuen would hardly dare to make a pass at Lady Elizabeth Willoughby.

He closed the door and bowed her to an ornate mahogany chair.

"Please excuse me for a moment, milady. I will return instantly."

He went out by another door, and she looked about her at a display whose richness might have shamed a shah's treasure house. Here indeed were the real treasures of Woon Yuen—what looked like the plunder of a thousand sultans' palaces and heathen temples. Idols in jade, gold and ivory grinned at her, and a less sophisticated woman would have blushed at some of the figures, depicting Oriental gods and goddesses in amorous poses of an astonishing variety. She could imagine the effect these things would have on some of his feminine visitors. Even her eyes dilated a trifle at the sight of the smirking, pot-bellied monstrosity that was the ivory Bon, looted from Allah only knew what nameless monastery high in the forbidden Himalayas. Then every nerve tingled as she saw a gold-worked dragon head jutting from the wall beyond the figure. Quickly she turned her gaze back to the god, just as her host returned on silent, velvet-shod feet.

He smiled to see her staring at the idol and the female figure in its arms.

"That is only one of the conceptions of the god—the Tibetan. It is worth, to any collector—but let us delay business talk until after tea. If you will honor me—"

With his guest seated at a small ebon table, the Mongol struck a bronze gong, and tea was served by a slim, silent-footed Chinese girl, clad only in a filmy jacket which came a little below her budding hips, and which concealed none of her smooth-skinned, lemon-tinted charms. This display, Arline knew, was in accord with the peculiar Chinese belief that a woman is put in a properly receptive mood for amorous advances by the sight of another woman's exposed charms. She wondered, if, after all, Woon Yuen had designs—but he showed no signs of it.

The slave girl bowed herself humbly out with a last salaam that displayed her full breasts beneath the low-necked jacket, and Arline's nerves tightened. Now was the time. She interrupted Woon Yuen's polite trivialities.

"That little jade figure, over there on the ivory shelf," she said, pointing. "Isn't that a piece of Jum Shan's work?"

"I will get it!"

As he rose and stepped to the shelf, she dropped the knockout pellet into his teacup. It dissolved instantly, without discoloring the liquid. She was idly sipping her own tea when the Mongol returned and placed the tiny figure of a jade warrior before her.

"Genuine Jum Shan," said he. "It dates from the tenth century!" He lifted his cup and emptied it at a draught, while she watched him with a tenseness which she could not wholly conceal. He set the cup down empty, frowning slightly and twitching his lips at the taste.

"I would like to call your attention, milady—" he leaned forward, reaching toward the jade figure—then slumped down across the table, out cold. In an instant she was across the room, and her white, tapering fingers were at work on the teeth of the carved dragon's head. There was an instinct in those fingers, a super-sensitiveness such as skilled cracksmen sometimes have. In a few moments the jaws gaped suddenly, revealing a velvet-lined nest in the midst of which, like an egg of some fabled bird of paradise, burned and smoldered a great, smooth, round jewel.

She caught her breath as awedly she cupped it in her hands. It was a ruby, of such deep crimson that it looked darkly purple, the hue of old wine, and the blood that flows near the heart. It looked like the materialization of a purple nightmare. She could believe now the wild tales she had heard—that Woon Yuen worshiped it as a god, sucking madness from its sinister depths, that he performed terrible sacrifices to it—

"Lovely, is it not?"

The low voice cracked the tense stillness like the heart-stopping blast of an explosion. She whirled, gasping, then stood transfixed. Woon Yuen stood before her, smiling dangerously, his eyes slits of black fire. A frantic glance sped to the tea table. There still sprawled a limp, bulky figure, identical to Woon Yuen in every detail.

"What —?" she gasped weakly.

"My shadow," he smiled. "I must be cautious. Long ago I hit upon the expedient of having a servant made up to resemble me, to fool my enemies. When I left the chamber a little while ago, he took my place, and I watched through the peephole. I supposed you were after the Heart."

"How did you guess?" She sensed the uselessness of denial.

"Why not? Has not every thief in China tried to steal it?" He spoke softly, but his eyes shone reddishly, and the veins swelled on his neck.

"As soon as I learned you were not what you pretended, I knew you had come to steal something. Why not the ruby? I set my trap and let you walk into it. But I must congratulate you on your cleverness. Not one in a thousand could have discovered the way to open the dragon's jaws."

"How did you know I wasn't Lady Elizabeth?" she whispered, dry lipped; the great ruby seemed to burn her palms.

"I knew it when you walked across the mirror and I saw your lower extremities reflected there. I have never seen Lady Elizabeth, but all dealers in jade know her peculiarities by reputation. One of them is such a passion for jade that she always wears jade-green step-ins. Yours are lavender."

"What are you going to do?" she panted, as he moved toward her.

A light akin to madness burned in his eyes.

"You have defamed the Heart by your touch! It must drink of all who touch it, save me, its high priest! If a man, his blood! If a woman—"

No need for him to complete his abominable decree. The ruby fell to the thick carpet, rolled along it like a revolving, demoniac eyeball. She sprang back, shrieking, as Woon Yuen, no longer placid, but with his convulsed face a beast's mask, caught her by the wrist. Against his thickly muscled arms her struggles were vain. As in a nightmare she felt herself lifted and carried toward an ornate velvet couch which stood in an alcove. Her eyes sweeping the room helplessly, she saw the ivory Bon leering at her as through a mist. It seemed to mock her.

The alcove was walled with mirrors. Only Chinese cruelty could have devised such an arrangement, where, whichever way she twisted her head she was confronted by the spectacle of her own humiliation, reflected from every angle. She was at once actor and spectator in the beastly drama. She could not escape the shameful sight of her own writhings and the busy, denuding hands of Woon Yuen. As she felt the lustful yellow fingers on her naked flesh, she saw, in the mirrors, her quivering, bare white breasts, her dress bunched high about her hips, the scarlet skirt in startling contrast to the bare white thighs, with only a wisp of silk between them as they frantically flexed, twisted and writhed—then with a sucking gasp of breath between his grinding teeth, Woon Yuen tore the filmy step-ins from her body.

At the tea table the senseless Chinaman still sprawled, deaf to the frantic, agonized shrieks that rang again and again through the inner chamber of Woon Yuen.

An hour later a door opened into a narrow alley in the rear of Woon Yuen's antique shop, and Arline was thrust roughly out, her breasts bare, her dress tucked above her waist. She fell sprawling from the force of the shove, and the door was slammed, with a brutal laugh. Dazedly she rose, shook down her skirt, drew her dress together over her bosom, and tottered down the alley, sobbing hysterically.

Inside the room from which she had just been ejected, Woon Yuen turned to a lean, saturnine individual, whose pigtail was wound tightly about his head, and from whose wide silk girdle jutted the handle of a light hatchet.

"Yao Chin, take Yun Kang and follow her. There is always some man behind the scenes, when a woman steals. I let her go because I wished her to lead us to that man. Follow her, and when she joins him, send Yun Kang back to me. On no account kill him yourself. I, and only I, must feed the Heart with their vile blood—hers and his."

The hatchetman bowed and left the room, his face showing nothing of his secret belief that Woon Yuen was crazy, not because he believed the Heart drank human blood, but because he, a rich merchant, insisted on doing murder which others of his class always left to hired slayers.

In the mouth of a little twisting alley that ran out upon a rotting abandoned wharf, Arline paused. Her face was haggard and desperate. She had reached the end of her trail. She had failed, and Tremayne would not accept any excuse. Ahead of her she saw only the black muzzles of a firing squad to which his lie would deliver her—but first there would be torture, inhuman torture, to wring from her secrets her captors would think she possessed. The world at large never knows the full story of the treatment of suspected spies. With a low moan she covered her eyes with her arm and stumbled blindly toward the edge of the wharf—then a strong arm caught her waist and she looked up into the startled face of Wild Bill Clanton.

"What the hell are you fixin' to do?"

"Let go!" she whimpered. "It's my life! I can end it if I want to!"

"Not with me around," he grunted, picking her up and carrying her back away from the wharf lip. He sat down on a pile and took her on his lap, like a child. "Good thing I found you," he grunted. "I had a hell of a time tracin' you after you slugged me and ran up that alley, but I finally saw you duckin' down this one. You pick the damndest places to stroll in. Now you tell me what the trouble is. A classy dame like you don't need to go jumpin' off of docks."

He seemed to hold no grudge for that clout with the pitcher. There was possessiveness in the clasp of his arms about her supple body, but she found a comforting solidity in the breast muscles against which her flaxen head rested. There was a promise of security in his masculine strength. Suddenly she no longer resented his persistent pursuit of her. She needed his strength—needed a man who would fight for her.

In a few words she told him everything—the hold Tremayne had on her, the task he had set her, and what had happened in Woon Yuen's inner room.

He swore at the narrative.

"I'll get that yellow-belly for that! But first we'll go to the Alley of Rats. Try to stall Tremayne along to give you another chance. In the meantime I'll work on a Eurasian wench I know who will tell me plenty about him—and she will, too, or I'll skin her stern. He's been mixed up in plenty of crooked rackets. If we get somethin' hot on him, we can shut his mouth, all right. And we'll get somethin', you can bet."

When they entered the Alley of Rats, in a half-abandoned warehouse district in the native quarter, they did not see two furtive figures slinking after them, nor hear the taller whisper: "Yun Kang, go back and tell our master she has led us to a man! I will watch the alley till he comes."

Clanton and Arline turned into a dingy doorway, and went down a corridor that seemed wholly deserted. Groping along it, in the dusk, she found the room she sought and led Clanton into it. She lit a candle stub stuck on a shelf, and turned to Clanton: "He'll be here soon."

"I'll wait in the next room," he said, reluctantly taking his arm from about her waist. "If he gets rough, I'll come in."

Alone in the candle-lighted room she tried to compose herself; her heart was beating a wild tattoo, loud in the stillness. Somewhere rats scampered noisily. Time dragged insufferably. Then quick, light steps sounded in the hall, and Duke Tremayne burst through the door, his eyes blazing with greed. They turned red as he read defeat in her eyes; his face contorted.

"Damn you!" His fingers were like talons as he gripped her shoulders. "You failed!"

"I couldn't help it!" she pleaded. "He knew I was a fake. Please don't hurt me, Duke. I'll try again—"

"Try again? You little fool! Do you think that Chinese devil will give you another chance?" Tremayne's suavity was gone; he was like a madman. "You failed, after all my planning! All right! I'll have a little profit out of you! Take off that dress—" The garment ripped in his grasp, baring a white breast which he seized greedily, wrenching a scream of pain from her lips. The inner door swung open. Tremayne wheeled, drawing a pistol, but before he could fire, Clanton's fist crashed against his jaw and stretched him senseless. Clanton bent and picked up the gun, then whirled as the hall door opened behind him. He stiffened as a tranquil voice spoke: "Do not move, my friend!"

He looked into the muzzle of a gun in Woon Yuen's hand.

"So you are the man?" muttered the Mongol. "Good! The Heart drinks—"

He could fire before Clanton could lift the pistol he held. But behind the American Arline laughed suddenly, unexpectedly.

"It worked, Bill!" she exclaimed. "Our man will get the ruby while we hold Woon Yuen here! The fool! He hasn't yet guessed that we tricked him to draw him away from his shop after I'd found where he hid the gem!"

Woon Yuen's face went ashen. With a choking cry he fired, not at Clanton but at the girl. But his hand was shaking like a leaf. He missed, and like an echo of his shot came the crack of Clanton's pistol. Woon Yuen dropped, drilled through the head.

"Good work, kid!" Clanton hissed exultantly. "He fell for it—hard!"

"But they'll hang us for this!" whimpered Arline. "Listen! Somebody's running up the hall! They've heard the shots!"

Stooping swiftly Clanton folded Duke Tremayne's fingers about the butt of the smoking pistol, and then kicked the man heavily in the shins. Tremayne grunted and showed signs of returning consciousness. Clanton drew Arline into the other room and they watched through the crack of the door.

The hall door opened and Yao Chin came in like a panther, hatchet in hand. His eyes blazed at the sight of Woon Yuen on the floor, Tremayne staggering to his feet, a pistol in his hand. With one stride the hatchet man reached the reeling blackmailer. There was a flash of steel, an ugly, butcher-shop *crunch*, and Tremayne slumped, his skull split. Yao Chin tossed the reeking hatchet to the floor beside his victim and turned away.

"Out of here, quick!" muttered Clanton, shaking Arline who seemed threatened with hysteria. "Up the alley—in the other direction."

She regained her poise in their groping flight up the darkened alley, as Clanton muttered: "We're in the clear now. Tremayne can't talk, with his head split, and that hatchetman'll tell his pals Tremayne shot their boss."

"We'd better get out of town!" They had emerged into a narrow, lamp-lit street.

"Why? We're safe from suspicion. Besides, I can't wait any longer!" She knew what he meant, but she did not resent the suggestion now. A little tingle of pleasure ran through her as Clanton turned into a doorway and spoke to a grinning old Chinaman who bowed them into a small neat room, with curtained windows and a couch.

"This is what I've been waiting for, kid!" As the door closed behind the old Chinaman Clanton caught her hungrily to him, finding her red lips, now unresisting. Her arms went about his thick neck as he lifted her and carried her to the couch. Supply she yielded to his swift, disrobing fingers. She had only exchanged masters, it was true, but this was different. There was a delicious sense of comfort and security in surrendering to a strong man who could fight for her and protect her. There was pleasure in the dominance of his strong hands on her naked body. With a blissful sigh she settled herself luxuriously in his powerful arms.

The Dragon of Kao Tsu

The girl who stormed into the back room of the Purple Dragon Bar where Wild Bill Clanton sat sipping a whiskey-and-soda, looked out of place in that dive. She advertised her place in the social register from her insolently tilted beret to her high French heels. She was tall and slender, but all her lines were supple and rounded, with melting curves that would make any man's mouth water. Just now her purplish eyes flashed and her pertly-tilted breasts swelled stormily.

"You," she accused Clanton, "are a thief, a liar, and a rat!"

"So what?" he retorted unimpressed, as he poured another drink.

"Why, you low-lifed—!" Her refinement skidded a trifle in her resentment, and she began sketching his genealogy with language she never learned in the Junior League, when he interrupted her peremptorily.

"Now you hold on! Some things nobody can call me, not even a lady! Sit down and cool off before somethin' unpleasant happens to you!"

She wilted at the threat and drooped into the chair opposite him.

"This," she said bitterly, "is what I get for associating with a gorilla like you. Why I do it I don't know."

"I know," he retorted. "Because you wanted Shareef Ahmed's ivory dragon and I was the only man who could get it for you."

"Yes, you were!" There was rancor in her tone, and her basilisk glare made him uneasy. You never could tell about these society dames! If she yanked a knife out of her garter, he meant to smack her down.

But she had no knife in her garter, as he could tell when she crossed her silk-clad legs with the regal indifference of a true aristocrat. She twitched down her skirt an inch or so, but not before he had a glimpse of white flesh that made the blood boil to his head. Her indifference to his emotions was maddening. Probably it had never occurred to Old Man Allison's pampered daughter Marianne that a man on Clanton's social plane would even think of making a pass at her, but he had to clench his hands to keep them off of her.

"What's eatin' you?" he demanded.

For answer she produced something from her handbag and smacked it down accusingly before him. It was a small but potbellied ivory dragon, exquisitely carved and yellowed with age.

"It's a fake!" she declared.

"It's the one Ram Lal stole from Shareef Ahmed," he asserted.

"It's a fake," she contended moodily. "Either you've gypped me, or that babu you hired to do the job has, or Ahmed's fooled us all."

"Well, what of it?" he asked. "All you want it for is to show to your society friends back in the United States and brag about it bein' a rare antique. They won't know the difference."

"Some of them will," she answered, lighting a cigaret with an injured air. "The collection of Oriental antiques is a great hobby in my set. It's been a game to see who could get the rarest relic by fair means or foul. Betty Elston got hold of a priceless Ming vase in Canton, and she's gloated over the rest of us until I've wanted to kick her little—well, anyway, I heard about the Kao Tsu dragon in San Francisco, and I came all the way to Singapore to get it. It dates from the Early Han Dynasty, and it's the only one of its kind in the world. I knew Ahmed wouldn't sell it, so I hired you to have it stolen for me."

Clanton picked up the yellowed figure and turned it about.

"I dunno," he mused. "Ram Lal got into Ahmed's house and swiped this. He's the slickest thief on the Peninsula. But if it's the wrong one, he might be afraid to risk another try. Ahmed's bad business."

"But he's been paid, and it isn't the right dragon!" she snapped. "What kind of a man would he be to take money under false pretenses?"

"Hire a thief and then squawk if he gyps *you!*" he mocked her. "But keep your pants on. I'm a man of my word, anyway. I've taken your dough, and I aim to deliver the goods. Ram Lal's so scared of Ahmed he's hidin' in an old warehouse down on the waterfront. Maybe he just got the wrong dragon by mistake. Or he may be holdin' out on us for more dough. You leave this thing with me, and tonight I'll go down there and talk to him. If he's on the level, maybe he'll try again. If he's tryin' to put somethin' over, well, we'll see."

"I'm going with you," she decided. "I don't trust either of you."

"It's no place for a white woman," he warned her.

She tilted a scornful nose.

"I can take care of myself, *Mister* Clanton—otherwise I'd never have dared to have any dealings with you! I'll pick you up near the mosque on Muscat Street. And I don't want to have to drag you out from under some table, or off of some brown-skinned wench, either."

"I'll be there, sober and respectable," he assured her. "But how about a few drinks before you go?"

"No, thanks!" she declined. "I prefer to keep our relationship on a strictly business basis; and whiskey has too elevating an effect on men's minds—and women's petticoats! I'll see you at dusk."

And she swung out of the room with a long-legged, hip-swaying gait that made Clanton moan with despair and grab the whiskey bottle. She had him buffaloed. If she'd been anybody else, he'd have grabbed her and headed for the nearest bedroom, regardless. But there was a limit even to his audacity, and he didn't dare try any rough stuff on the daughter of Old Man Allison, millionaire and woolly wolf of finance that the old devil was.

He turned the ivory dragon about in his hands and frowned.

"Antique collectin', eh? Hokum!"

Rising he bellowed to a half-caste waiter, plunked a coin on the table and barged out of a side door. A few moments later he was seated in a silk shop kept by one Yakub, an old Jew who had a finger in many enterprises besides the one advertised by the sign over his door, and whose ear was always close to the mysterious pulse of the East. Clanton set the ivory dragon before him and demanded: "What's that?"

Yakub donned square, steel-rimmed spectacles, and regarded it.

"That's the Kao Tsu dragon," he said. "But I wouldn't handle it for you. You must have stolen it from Shareef Ahmed. I love life too much to handle anything stolen from that devil."

"It's a fake," asserted Clanton.

"If it's a fake, I'm a Gentile," answered old Yakub, lovingly fondling its smooth surface. "Tchk, tchk! Such a pity! I'd buy it myself if I wasn't afraid of Ahmed. He'll slit your throat for this, sure."

"You'll swear it's genuine?" Clanton demanded.

"My head on it!" The old man's sincerity was convincing.

"Hmmm!" Clanton's scowl deepened. "I wonder what that hussy's tryin' to put over?"

Then he asked Yakub a strange question, and received a stranger answer.

If Marianne Allison had known of that conversation her poise might have been a trifle less confident when her big coupe purred up to the curb where Clanton stood, just as the streetlights were coming on. He climbed in beside her and she turned off down a side street according to his directions.

"Did you bring any money, in case Ram Lal wants more?" he asked.

"I should say not!" she retorted. "He's been paid enough. He owes me any future service it takes to get the right dragon."

"You're an arrogant wench," he observed, his eyes glued on a rounded knee. Through accident or design her dress had worked up again, baring an inch of white flesh above the stocking top.

"When you get through studying my legs," she suggested, "you might tell me which way to turn at this next intersection."

She smiled cruelly as he reluctantly turned his attention to the street. Feeling perfectly safe from him, she took a feminine delight in tantalizing him. She was aware of her effect on him, and she enjoyed seeing the veins in his forehead swell with frustrated emotion.

"Pull up here," he directed presently, and they rolled to a halt in a shabby side street in the native quarter. "Have to leave the boat here. They may steal the wheels off of it before we get back, but it won't navigate the alley we've got to follow. Here, this is it."

It was dark in the alley. They groped their way along and presently came out into an open space, lined on one side by rotten, deserted wharves.

"That's the warehouse." Clanton indicated a building looming darkly before them. "He's got a camp cot and some canned grub in one of the lower rooms, and he aims to hide there till I let him know what move Ahmed's makin' about that theft."

No light showed behind the shutters of the barred windows. Clanton knocked and softly called: "Ram Lal!" No answer. He tried the door and found it to be unlocked. He pushed it open and Marianne pressed close to his heels as he entered. She jumped and grabbed his arm as they stood in the darkness.

"The door! Somebody pushed it to behind us!"

"Wind must have blown it shut," he grunted. "But where the hell's Ram Lal?"

"Listen!" She clutched him convulsively. Somewhere in the darkness sounded a steady *drip-drip* as if somebody had left a faucet partly open. But Clanton's hair began to rise, because he knew there wasn't any faucet in that room. He struck a match in a hurry and held it up. Marianne clapped a hand over her mouth to stifle a shriek. Clanton swore. In the wavering light they saw Ram Lal. The fat, swarthy babu slumped drunkenly in a chair near a table. His head lolled on his breast and his eyes were glassy. And from a throat slashed from ear-to-ear blood still oozed sluggishly to fall drop by drop in a widening crimson puddle on the floor.

"Godlemighty!" muttered Clanton. "We've got to get out of here—*ow!*"

Something that glinted swished at him out of the shadows. Marianne had a brief glimpse of an arc of gleaming steel and a dark contorted face behind it. Then the match went out, clipped from Clanton's hand by that slashing blade, and the dark filled with hair-raising sounds. Marianne dropped to the floor and scurried on all-fours in the direction she hoped the door was. She'd lost touch with Clanton, but he couldn't be dead, because no corpse could put up the fight he was putting up. Lurid Anglo-Saxon oaths mingled with Asiatic yowls, and she almost pitied his adversaries as she heard what sounded like beeves being knocked in the head with a maul, but which she knew to be the impact of his massive fists on human skulls. Howls of pain and rage filled the room, the table overturned crashingly, and then somebody stumbled over her in the dark.

It was a Malay. She could tell by the smell, even in the dark. She heard him floundering on the floor near her, and her blood froze at the *wheep-wheep* of a keen blade being whirled at random. It was close behind her, and the flesh of her hips contracted as she scuttled away on her all-fours. Her groping hands found a door and pulled it open, but no light came in, and she felt steps leading upward. But any avenue of escape from that blind blade flailing the blackness was welcome.

She shut the door behind her and went up the stair as fast as she could and eventually emerged into an equally dark space that felt big and empty and smelt musty. There she crouched, shivering, while the noise of battle went on below, and presently culminated in an amazing crash that sounded as though somebody had been knocked bodily through a closed door. Then the sounds died away and silence reigned. She believed that Clanton had broken away from his attackers and fled, pursued by them.

She was right. At that moment Clanton was racing down a winding alley, hearing the pad of swift feet close behind him, and momentarily expecting a knife thrust in the back. They were too many for even him to fight with his bare hands, and they were gaining on him. With a straining burst of effort he reached an empty, dim-lit side street ahead of them, and before he vanished into an entrance on the other side, he cast something on the paving in the light of the dim streetlamp. Startled yelps escaped his pursuers, and abandoning the chase, they pounced on the yellowed ivory dragon Clanton had discarded.

Back in the loft of the deserted warehouse Marianne crept down the stair. For some time she had heard no sound below. Then just as she reached the stairs door, she checked, her heart in her throat. Somebody had entered the room beyond. But this man wore the boots of a white man; she could tell by his footfalls. Then she heard a smothered, English oath.

Clanton must have eluded his pursuers and returned. She heard a match struck, and light stole through the crack under the door. She pushed the door ajar. A brawny figure, wearing a seaman's cap, with his back to the door, was bending over the corpse slumped in the chair.

"Clanton!" she exclaimed, stepping into the room—then checked in her tracks as a perfect stranger whirled around with an oath. He was as big as Clanton and much uglier. His bloodshot eyes glared, his black beard bristled, and he levelled a snub-nosed revolver at her quivering tummy.

"Don't shoot!" she gasped. "I—I won't hurt you!"

The stranger's reply was unprintable. Evidently her sudden appearance had given him a bad shock.

"Who the blinkin' hell are you and what're you doin' here?" he concluded. "Well, talk before I start sweepin' the floor with you!" He flourished a fist the size of a breakfast ham under her shrinking nose.

She shuddered and spoke hastily: "I lost my way and wandered in here by mistake—I've got to go now—glad to have met you—"

"Stow it!" bellowed the irate intruder. "You can't pull the wool over Bull Davies' eyes like that!" The aforesaid eyes narrowed wickedly in the light of the candle on a wall shelf. "Oh, I get it!" he muttered. "Of course! You're after the dragon yourself! You killed Ram Lal to get it! Well, hand it over and you won't get hurt—maybe!"

"I haven't got it," she answered. "And I didn't kill Ram Lal. Shareef Ahmed's men did that. They were waiting in the dark when I and my companion came in here. I don't know where they went, or what happened to the man with me."

"Likely yarn," grumbled Mr. Davies. "Ram Lal knew my boss wanted the dragon. He sent me word to come here tonight and make him an offer. He'd stole it from Shareef Ahmed. I just now got here, and found him dead and the dragon gone. It ain't on him—it must be on you!" He pointed a hairy and accusing finger at Marianne.

"I tell you I haven't got it!" she exclaimed, paling. "I want it, yes! If you'll help me find it I'll pay you—"

"I've already been paid," he growled. "And my boss would cut my throat if I sold him out. You've got that dragon on you somewheres! You dames are smart about hidin' things on you! Off with them clothes!"

"No!" She jumped back, but he grabbed her wrist and twisted it until she fell to her knees with a yelp of pain.

"Are you goin' to shed 'em yourself, or do I have to tear 'em off?" he rumbled. "If l have to, it'll be the worst for you, blast you!"

"Let me up," she begged. "I know when I'm licked. I'll do it."

And under his piglike eyes she shed garment after garment until she stood before him clad only in a scanty brassiere and ridiculously brief pink panties. As she discarded each garment he snatched it and ransacked it, snarling his anger at finding his quest fruitless. Now he glared at her, silent and wrathful, and she squirmed and made protecting motions with her hands. Red fires that were not of rage began to glimmer murkily in his bloodshot eyes.

"Isn't this enough?" she begged. "You could see if I had anything on me the size of that dragon."

"Well, maybe," he admitted grudgingly, laying a heavy hand on her naked shoulder and turning her about to inspect her from every angle.

"Baby, you've got what it takes!" he muttered thickly, clapping a hot, sweaty hand down on each curving hip. "No, you ain't got that dragon hid in your pants—nor in your bust band!" He grinned wickedly as he slipped his hand inside her bandeau. The feel of his fingers on her naked breasts was too much. She shrieked and slapped him resoundingly, and instantly regretted her indiscretion. He grabbed her in a bearlike embrace and his ardour wasn't lessened a bit by the glassy stare of the dead man in the chair.

He was carrying her, squirming and fighting, toward the camp cot in the corner when he stiffened. Outside the door sounded a faint babble of approaching voices. He blew out the candle and turned through an inner door, clapping a big paw over Marianne's mouth when she tried to scream, and hissing: "Shut up, you little fool! Do you want your throat cut? That's Ahmed's men!"

He seemed to know his way about the warehouse, even in the dark. He stooped, fumbled at the floor, raised a trapdoor, hissed: "If I hear one peep out of you I'll come down there and twist your head off! I'll get you out later—if you're a good girl!"—and dropped her.

She was too scared to yell, even if she'd had breath for it. She did not fall far till she hit on her feet on a slimy floor. She heard the trapdoor settle back in place, and then the creak of the stairs. Evidently Davies was taking refuge in the loft. She thought she heard an outer door open, and a mumble of voices, but forgot it the next instant at the sight of small red eyes winking fiercely at her from the gloom. Rats! She had all a woman's natural fear of rodents, and she had heard horrifying tales about the ghoulish wharf-rats. But they made no move to attack her and she began to explore her prison, shivering in her nudity. The stone floor stood in several inches of water, and she found no opening in the slimy walls. She had been dumped into a cellar and the only way out was up through that trapdoor above her head.

She squealed as a rat ran across her foot, and jumped back against the wall, bruising her hip and tearing her panties on a broken plank.

"This is what I get for associating with people like Bill Clanton," she told herself bitterly, and then the rats started fighting in a corner. Their hideous racket snapped her taut nerves. She screamed. She yelled. She was too panicky to care for Davies' threat. Having her head twisted off seemed preferable to being devoured by rats in that black well. She didn't care who heard her, just so somebody did, and got her out of that damnable cellar. She didn't care much what they did to her afterward.

And almost instantly her shrieks were answered by sounds overhead. The trap was lifted and she blinked in the glare of a lantern. But it was not Davies' bearded face which was framed in the opening. It was a dark, saturnine, handsome face—the face of Shareef Ahmed!

"Well, our little guest didn't run away, after all!" he commented satirically. "Help her up, Jum Chin."

A tall, gaunt Chinaman reached his long arms down, caught her lifted wrists and swung her up lightly and easily. The trapdoor fell again and she found herself standing before Ahmed, whose dark eyes devoured her from head to foot. Four Malays with *krises* in their belts and the Chinaman feasted their hot eyes on her nudity. They were marked generously from Clanton's fists, from that fight in the dark room.

"A curious interlude!" smiled Ahmed dangerously. "You enter the building fully clothed, with that dog Clanton. Apparently you escape in the melee. But less than an hour later we find you imprisoned in the cellar, light clad—and with torn panties!" He lightly slapped the white hip exposed by the accident. She flinched, but did not reply nor resent the indignity. She was scared as only a girl can be who knows herself to be in the power of men absolutely merciless and cynical in their attitude toward women.

"Where is the Kao Tsu dragon?" Ahmed demanded peremptorily.

"I haven't it!" Her wits were working like lightning on a scheme.

Ahmed's eyes were poisonous.

"You must have it! Ram Lal stole two dragons out of my house. Clanton dropped one in his flight." He displayed it. "But it is not the right one. You must have it. Ram Lal must have stolen them for you, otherwise Clanton, who came here with you, would not have had this one. You have the other, or know where it is. Must you be *persuaded* to talk?"

"I had it," she said hurriedly, as the Malays moved toward her, grinning evilly. "But Bull Davies came while you were chasing Clanton—"

"Davies?" It was a snarl from Ahmed. "Has that dog of General Kai's been here?"

"He *is* here—hiding upstairs. He took the dragon from me."

"Search the upper floor," snapped Ahmed, and his men made for the stair, soft footed as weasels, with naked blades glimmering in their hands. Marianne breathed in momentary relief. At least she'd saved herself from torture for the moment. Ahmed was watching the stair, and she essayed a sneaking step toward the other door. But he wheeled and caught her wrist.

"Where are *you* going?"

"Nowhere, apparently." She flinched at his sarcasm. "Please, you're hurting my wrist. Why, the body's gone!"

"We threw it in the river after we returned from pursuing Clanton," said Ahmed absently, gazing at her half-exposed breasts. "I meant to take Ram Lal alive and make him talk. But he attacked my faithful servant, Jum Chin, who traced him here, and Jum Chin was forced to kill him. I arrived with the rest of my men just after he had killed Ram Lal. We had just completed a fruitless search of the body when we heard you and Clanton approaching. Why did you come here when you already had the dragon?"

"I came to pay Ram Lal," she lied, afraid to admit the truth, now that she had already professed to have had possession of the dragon.

"Forget the dragon for a space," he muttered, his eyes burning on her naked limbs. "My men will capture Davies and get it for me. Meanwhile—there's a cot in the other room—"

Realizing his intentions she sprang for the nearest door, but he was too quick for her. He was slender but his thews were like steel. She yelped as he tore off her brassiere—squealed despairingly as she felt her remaining garments torn from her hips. His greedy fingers exploring the intimacies of her sleek body filled her with shame and fury. She clenched a small fist and struck him in the face, and in return got a slap that filled her eyes with stars and tears. He picked her up, fighting and kicking, and started toward the other room with her, when upstairs a shot banged, blows thudded, men yelled and heavy boots stampeded down the stair.

Ahmed dropped Marianne sprawling on the floor and turned to the stair door, drawing a pistol. An instant later Bull Davies, plunging through the stair door, brought up short at the threat of that black muzzle. In an instant the five Orientals who were tumbling down the stair after him had fallen on him from behind, borne him to the floor, and had him bound hand and foot. Swift hands ransacked his garments, and then Jum Chin looked at Ahmed and shook his head. Ahmed turned on Marianne, who rose from the floor, rubbing her hip.

"You slut! You said he had it!" Ahmed grabbed a pink breast and pinched it viciously.

"Wait!" she begged, assuming a Venus de Medici pose as he started to go even further in his third-degree methods. "He must have hidden it!"

This was going to be just too bad for Davies, she knew, but it was his hide or hers. Maybe she'd get a chance to slip away while they were giving him the works.

At a word from Ahmed, Jum Chin ripped Davies' shirt off. A Malay applied a lighted match to his hairy breast. A faint smell of singed hair arose and Davies bellowed like a bull.

"I tell you I ain't got it! She's lyin'! I dunno where it is!"

"If he's lying we'll soon know," rasped Ahmed. "We'll try a test that will unlock the jaws of the stubbornest. If he still persists, we must conclude that he's telling the truth, and the girl's lying."

Jum Chin stripped off the prisoner's socks, and Davies broke into a sweat of fear. Intent on the coming torture, Ahmed relaxed his grip on Marianne's wrist—or maybe it was a trick to trap her into a false move.

As his fingers relaxed she jerked loose and darted into the outer room. He was after her in an instant, and just as she reached the door that opened into the alley, his fingers locked in her hair. But that door burst suddenly inward.

A big form loomed in the door and an arm shot out. There was a crack that sounded as if Ahmed had run his face into a brick wall. But it was a massive fist he had run into, and the impact stretched him groaning on the floor. His conqueror swooped on the pistol that flew from his victim's hand, and Ahmed's henchmen, rushing from the inner room, checked at the menace of the leveled Luger, their hands shooting ceilingward.

"Clanton!" panted Marianne. He refused to look at her. With six desperate men before him, he couldn't risk being demoralized by the spectacle of loveliness her unclad figure presented.

"Put on some clothes!" he snapped. "And you, Ahmed, get up!"

Ahmed staggered up, a ghastly sight, minus three teeth and with his nose a gory ruin. Clanton grinned pridefully at the sight of his handiwork; few men could have done so much damage with only one clout. He profanely silenced Ahmed's impassioned ravings, and backed all his prisoners into the inner room, whither Marianne followed, having salvaged the tablecloth which she wrapped rather sketchily, sarong-fashion, about her.

Briefly she explained the situation to Clanton, and he ordered the men to lie on their bellies and put their hands behind them, while she tied their wrists and ankles with their belts and turbans. He watched her in ecstatic silence while she was thus employed. The improvised sarong was something more than revealing, as she moved about, allowing glimpses of curvy contours that sent the blood to his head.

When she had finished the job he inspected each man, grunting his approval of her technique, and searching them for weapons. He lingered longer over Jum Chin, and when he rose, she was amazed to see a grey pallor tinging the Chinaman's face. Yet Clanton had done nothing to hurt him.

Clanton then untied Davies, and growled: "I ought to bust your snoot for pullin' off Miss Allison's clothes and throwin' her in that cellar, but I'm lettin' you off, considerin' what Ahmed did to you. Get out!"

"I'll get even with somebody, I bet!" sniveled Mr. Davies, and departed hastily, aided in his exit by the toe of the Clanton boot. When his lamentations had faded in the night, Clanton addressed his glowering prisoners.

"We're leavin'. I'll send back a coolie to untie you. Ahmed, you better forget what's happened tonight. The dragon's gone. Only Ram

Lal knew what became of it, and he's dead. And if the British find out you killed him, they'll hang you, sure as hell! You let us alone, and keep your mouth shut, and we'll keep ours shut."

Fear gleamed in Ahmed's one good eye at the mention of hanging. He was sullenly silent as Clanton followed the girl into the outer room and closed the door behind them.

"Do you think he'll drop the matter?" she asked nervously. "I can't afford to have this story get in the papers."

"No, you can't," he agreed. "Theft, murder, torture, bribin' a thief like Ram Lal and a pirate like me—it would ruin any debutante. Best thing you can do is to get out of Singapore as quick as you can. Ahmed won't forget this. He'll work under cover to get us, if he can. I ain't afraid of him, but you better take the first ship back to the U.S.A."

"But I've *got* to have that dragon!" She was almost frantic.

Then her eyes dilated as he took something from his pocket—an ivory dragon, not so yellow nor so exquisite as the other she had seen.

"The Kao Tsu dragon!" She snatched at it, but he withheld it.

"You wait a minute!" He fumbled with the potbelly for a moment, and then a section of it swung open. He drew out a strip of parchment, which had been rolled in the interior. One end remained fastened in the belly. The parchment was covered with tiny Chinese characters.

"Then you knew!" She was considerably agitated.

"I knew you wasn't any art collector, and I found out that the dragon Ram Lal gave me for you was the genuine Kao Tsu. So I did some sleuthin' and found out plenty. You wanted this for your old man, and he sent you after it because you're smarter than anybody workin' for him.

"That writin' is an agreement signed by the Chinese warlord they call General Kai, givin' your old man an option on an important oil concession. He gave it to your old man a few years ago, in a moment of generosity, and like a Chinaman, rigged the agreement up in the belly of this dragon, which is a clever copy of the original

Kao Tsu. Your old man thought all the time it *was* the Kao Tsu, and that's what you come after.

"Because a few months ago your old man decided to develop that concession so's to recoup his stock market losses, but General Kai had changed his mind. He wanted to give that concession to another firm. But if he refused, in the teeth of his own signed agreement, he'd lose face. So he had it stolen from your old man, meanin' to destroy the agreement and then claim he never made it, but Shareef Ahmed, who don't overlook many bets, had it stolen from Kai's agent. He already had the original Kao Tsu.

"Then Ahmed offered it to the highest bidder. Your old man had lost so much money in the stock market crash he was afraid General Kai would outbid him, so he sent you to steal it. General Kai also had his agents after it, Bull Davies bein' one of 'em. Ram Lal stole both dragons. He gave you the real Kao Tsu, but he kept the one with the contract in it, and was goin' to sell it to General Kai's agent. You know the rest."

"But the dragon—" she exclaimed bewilderedly. "That one, I mean!"

"Easy!" he grinned. "Jum Chin had it all the time. He killed Ram Lal and must have found the dragon on him before Ahmed got there. Ahmed trusts Jum Chin so it didn't occur to him to suspect him. An Arab's no match for a Chinaman in wits. I found it on Jum Chin when I searched him. He won't dare tell Ahmed we've got it because that'd betray his own treachery. I sneaked back when they quit chasin' me and was waitin' outside for a break. Well, I got it."

"Give the dragon to me!" she exclaimed. "It's mine! I paid you!"

"You paid me for the genuine Kao Tsu," he said, his eyes devouring a sleek thigh the sarong left bare. "You got it. This comes extra."

"How much?" she demanded sulkily.

"Money ain't everything," he suggested.

Suddenly she smiled meltingly and came up to him, laying a slender hand on his arm. Her nearness made him dizzy, and she did not resist as he passed an arm about her waist.

"I understand," she breathed. "You win. Give me the dragon first, though."

Trustingly he placed it in her hand—and quick as a cat she plucked the pistol from his belt and smashed him over the head with the butt. The next instant she was streaking for the door. But she underestimated the strength of his skull. To her dismay he did not fall. He staggered with a gasping curse, then righted himself and leaped after her. He caught her as she grasped the knob, slapped the pistol out of her hand and spun her back into the room, crushing her wrists in one hand as she tried to claw his eyes out.

"You little cheat!" he snarled. "You've never kept a bargain yet! Well, you're goin' to keep this one! You've got what you want, and I'm goin' to get what I want! And you can't squawk, because you can't have the world knowin' about this night's work!"

Knowledge that this was true pepped up her struggles, but to her dismay she found them useless against the strength of her irate captor. All her kicking and squirming accomplished was to disarrange the sarong—but that didn't matter for he yanked it off anyway, and caught his breath at the sight of pink breasts, sleek thighs, rounded hips—

"You don't dare!" she gasped, as he forced her down on the cot. "You don't dare—"

Even as she spoke she realized the fallacy of her assertion.

When at last he rose and grinned down at her, he almost pitied her helpless and humiliated wrath.

"Well," he said philosophically, caressing a pouting breast, "that's what you get for associatin' with people like me!" Marianne's reply was not printable.

Murderer's Grog

When Wild Bill Clanton climbed the stair that led up from the mud-walled courtyard to the rooms of Sonya Ormanoff, he was already fighting mad. Who wouldn't be, when faced with the prospect of losing all his present investments and future profits, and acquiring a possible prison sentence as well? The incessant clamorings and babblings that were the noises of the streets of Peshawur whetted the edge of his irascibility. Here, in the richest trading city south of Bukhara, there were fortunes to be made, both legal and illegal, and one of those golden troves had been almost within his fingers; but now he feared it was going to elude his eager grasp. His brow was dark as he climbed the stair, but his expression lightened somewhat, and the apprehensive anger in his eyes gave place to another expression as he heard a silvery feminine laugh gurgle tantalizingly above him. That was Sonya, and his blood pressure started rising, just to hear her.

He made the last three steps at a bound, and rapped urgently on an ornately carved door, rich with gilt work. It opened a crack and a pretty, dark-eyed Punjabi girl looked out at him. Her lovely eyes widened a bit, as if she had expected to see someone else, and was not too pleased to see Clanton. She made no move to open the door wider, but Wild Bill attended to that himself. Over the girl's shoulder he had glimpsed Sonya, lounging in voluptuous ease on a silken divan, and the maid had as much chance of keeping him out of the room as she would have had of keeping a wild Afridi out of the wine bazaar. Clanton swept the door open and brushed her aside, scarcely hearing her indignant protests, and strode across the threshold, his eyes glowing.

Sonya glanced idly over her ivory shoulder, then came to life and sat up with a startled suddenness which, had Clanton been in any mood to analyze, was scarcely flattering. Nor was there much encouragement in the way she drew her light *harim* robe together over her luscious thighs, scarcely veiled by the gauzy ankle-length trousers that adorned rather than concealed them.

Sonya was one of the mysteries of that city of mysteries. She was the one white woman who habitually lived in the native city, and as such was hardly welcome in that other world on the other side of the railroad, where the white residents of Peshawur made a little western world of their own amidst their bungalows and rose gardens. But Sonya was indifferent to what the people in the British cantonment thought of her. If she could not go to them, they could come to her—and the loiterers in the *bazaars* whispered strange tales of *sahibs*, both in khaki and in mufti, who climbed her stair by night. Yet no man could truthfully boast that he had had his way with her, whatever he may have had in the way of information and secret tales that drift up and down the long caravan trails between Samarkand and Karachi. The winds blew these tales through Sonya's house and her slim, white fingers sifted out what she desired. So many men sought her, some with the lust of gain—and others like Clanton, with just plain lust. And still she remained a mystery. She claimed to be simply a wealthy young woman who, tired of the conventional monotony of western high society, had come East to study Oriental psychology at first hand. At which claim the British population snickered in its well-tailored sleeve. But could prove nothing.

She made a ravishing image as she sat on the couch, even after she had pulled her light silk robe about her lower limbs. She was blond, with a glorious wealth of light gold hair, and her flesh was as purely white as unstained Northern snow. Her eyes were deep, grey and enigmatic, with that mysterious allure characteristic of the Slav, and Clanton knew they could burn and smolder with passion. On the one former occasion when he had seen her he had glimpsed a lighted spark, and he had come back expecting to fan it to a full-grown flame.

But there was no inviting blaze there now. They were frigid as the surface of grey ice.

"Oh, it's you!" The greeting was not ardent. But Clanton was used to the ways and moods of women, real and assumed, and he was not abashed.

"Sure! Didn't I tell you I'd come? Tell the girl to scram."

The maid salaamed and exited at an impatient wave of her mistress's hand, and Clanton sat down on the couch, devouring his reticent hostess with eager eyes. Her manner had distinctly changed since he had met her in the *bazaar* the day before and received her invitation to call on her, but he gave no heed. A woman like Sonya had always to be on the defensive—at first. Manlike, he believed he could break down that barrier of reserve which so many men had failed to overcome—and which fact made her all the more desirable. After all, he was there at her own invitation, and the look he had read in her eyes when she gave it had been one not easily to be misunderstood.

His gaze dwelt hotly on her bare, superb neck, the arrogant swell of her breasts only half-confined by a low-neck, armless velvet vest fastened with a single gold clasp. She had not bothered to draw her open robe across her bosom, and he glimpsed generous contours of white flesh which seemed ready to burst its confines. From beneath the robe peeped slender red slippers, sewn with pearls, and the trimmest ankles he had seen north of Lahore.

"Do you want wine?" she asked, but he shook his head and put an arm about her waist. He was a man of impulse and action. The uncertainty of life—as he led it—had taught him to take what he wanted when it was offered—and frequently when it wasn't. She did not exactly resist him, yet she did not yield to him. The contact of her smooth flesh went to his head quicker than any wine she could have offered him. His other hand defeated her efforts to keep the robe pulled together over her knees. The touch of her delicious contours, even beneath her filmy trousers, intoxicated him.

"Don't!" She squirmed, crossed her legs and pushed his hand away by main force. It instantly ascended and began fumbling at the brooch which held her vest together, and which, for the moment, defied his persistence. A glint of amusement showed maliciously in her marvelous eyes.

"I hear you had a run-in with the deputy commissioner," she said. "You'd better be careful. Your reputation with the British isn't any too good, as it is. And after all, they run India."

"That's what he told me," grunted Clanton, scowling again at the memory. "In fact, he gave me just twenty-four hours to get out of Peshawur."

"You'd better go," she advised.

"Where? Into Afghanistan? I came down through that way, and believe me, I outstayed my welcome. I was lucky to get down the Khyber with a whole skin. Hell, I couldn't get a pass back there for all the gold in India. Anyway, I'm broke."

"Then you'll have to go south," said she. "Or into the Independent Territory."

He shot her a quick, suspicious glance. There was a hint of mocking malice in that last remark. Could it be that she knew it was into the Territory that he passionately desired to go—must go, if he was not to be beggared?

"If I go south without any money, the British will find some excuse to pick me up and heave me into the brig," he muttered. "I *want* to go into the Territory—oh, hell, I know the British wouldn't give anybody permission to go in there now, not even me, though they'd feel grateful if some bandit shot my head off. But to Hell with them. I don't need their blasted permits. I can slip over the border and be out of their reach any time I want to—but—"

"But what?" Was she interested, or merely encouraging conversation to divert his attention from her lightly-clad charms? His hands were quiet when he talked.

"You know what," he growled. "If I stepped over the border without protection they'd hang my hide on a rock before I could turn around. Those tribes in the Territory don't recognize either British or Afghan authority. But if I went into their country under the protection of some big chief like Baber Ali Khan of the Adam

Khel Afridis, I'd be safe from his tribe, and the men of the other clans would hesitate to offend him by harmin' me. If they shot me, it'd be an insult to him and he'd feel obliged to declare blood feud. Well, I got word in to Baber Ali Khan, and I've been waitin' for an answer, but it hasn't come. I don't understand it. It's to his advantage as well as mine, confound him!"

"You want to put over some kind of a deal in the Territory, and are willing to split the profits with him, for protection?" she asserted, rather than asked.

"Yeah. And I've got plenty of money tied up innit. If I don't get a safe-conduct from him within twenty-four hours, I'll have to pull out, flat broke. And the British will get me in jail, on charge of vagrancy or somethin', and deport me as an objectionable character, as sure as hell."

"I'll lend you enough money to get to Bombay," she suggested.

He shook his head, with stubborn pride.

"I ain't borrowin' money from any woman, much less you. And if I go, what then? I lose every penny I sunk in the deal, and all I expected to make. But what the hell! I didn't come up here to talk business. Not that kind. I came up here to forget my troubles, and—"

His expression was eloquent as his arm tightened about her waist, drawing her to him unwillingly. His fingers got busy again, and in spite of her reluctance, the silk robe slid off, leaving her arms and shoulders bare. The brooch gave way to his efforts, and his gaze was dazzled by the magnificent arrogance of her ripe breasts. He was endeavoring to unfasten the drawstring of her baggy silk trousers when her resistance became determined. She jerked free and sprang up, a vibrant, resentful figure.

"What's the matter?" He too rose, startled, sensing at last that her resistance was not feigned.

"Don't you know when you're not wanted?" she lashed out at him, her eyes growing tawny in her anger. There was something feline about her now, something elemental and ready to rend and tear, and the primitive anger always close to the surface, rose in him in response.

"What the hell?" he ripped out. "What's the matter with you? You gave me plenty of encouragement in the *suk* yesterday. You said plenty with your eyes when you asked me to come up here. Blast it, you did everything but turn up your dress right there!"

"I can't afford to have anything to do with a man who's out of favor with the British," she answered coldly, turning away with a gesture as if dismissing an underling. But Wild Bill Clanton wasn't so easily dismissed.

With an oath he grabbed her shoulder and jerked her around.

"That's a lie! You never showed the door to a man before on account of the British! It's your boast that you don't give a damn what they think! It's something else—some other man—"

"Yes, another man!" she spat, trying to strike his hands aside. "When I saw you yesterday, I *was* attracted to you, because of your size, your strength and animal vitality. I did contemplate an affair with you. I admired you as I might admire a stallion, or a tiger. But right after I saw you, I met a real man! The first man I've ever wanted to possess me! The sight of him swept you out of my mind! And now get out of here before I have you thrown out!"

"Why, you little—!" Smoldering rage at the world in general, smarting vanity, and thwarted desire combined to make Bill Clanton a raging demon. He grabbed her, ignoring her biting teeth and clawing nails, swept her off her feet and carried her to the couch where he deposited her, shrieking and kicking. She fought his hands away from the waistband of her pantaloons for an instant, and then the triumphant gleam of her eyes, as she looked over his shoulder, gave him unintended warning. He wheeled sidewise and the bludgeon swung by a huge Shinwari man-servant crashed numbingly on his right shoulder instead of braining him. A groan burst involuntarily from his lips and his knees buckled, but with a supreme effort he drove a left hook deep in the Pathan's belly as the man was lifting the club again.

The Shinwari gasped and collapsed, and Clanton was stooping for the club when another servant landed squarely on his neck, bearing him to the floor. Other servants rushed through the doors and fell on the American with a hearty good will. Clanton fought as only he could fight, but his right arm was useless and the odds were too heavy. These men were Tajiks, sturdy northern tribesmen, muscular and pugnacious. Three or four were gasping on the floor, green faced from kicks in the belly or groin, or left-handed clouts delivered in spite of the close grapple, but the others heaved the white man up, rushed him tumultuously across the room, urged on by Sonya's cruel laughter, and tumbled him down the stair into the courtyard where he lay half-stunned.

Indeed he looked so much hors-de-combat that the spiteful Lahore maid ventured down, carrying his cap, to indulge in the age-old feminine sport of taunting the fallen. But she underestimated his recuperative power. She carelessly came within his reach, when she tossed his cap down at him with an indelicate jeer, and was caught off-guard when he sat up suddenly and grabbed her. There was a brief struggle, feminine shrieks, and then the girl fled up the stair, minus her trousers, and Clanton rose and cast the tattered remnants of the garment after her. The sight of bare feminine hips twinkling up the stair in humiliated haste gave him an angry satisfaction which, however, was but a drop in the raging maelstrom which was his present state of mind.

He glared balefully at the door at the head of the stair, now closed and doubtless bolted, and then he turned and strode blaspheming into the street.

He didn't know which made him madder—the treatment he had received at Sonya's hands, or the delay in hearing from Baber Ali Khan. Why was the old devil holding up on him, now of all times, when the demand for guns in the Territory, always urgent, was more extravagant than ever, with two rival clans on the verge of a war of extermination? Clanton had brought a batch of rifles down from Russia—fine, breech-bolt guns of the kind the Soviets manufacture especially for the tribes subject to their rivals. These guns were far superior to the weapons made in the native hand-factories, and cheaper than the German rifles smuggled up by the Arab traders from the Persian Gulf.

But the Russians didn't give them away. Any man who handled their guns had to pay for them in advance, though they'd help him in getting past certain borders. Clanton had sunk his whole wad in this cargo, sure of about three hundred percent profit if he could get them into the Independent Territory, that turbulent strip of feud-haunted hell that lies between Afghanistan and British India. He couldn't work the Afghan tribes, because Russian agents were there ahead of him, and jealous of their trading privileges. He winced as he thought of the work he'd had in getting the guns down through Afghanistan, bribing officials at every turn.

There was no bribing of British officials, but there were ways of getting even smuggled guns across the Afghan frontier. Even British soldiers couldn't watch every mile of it all the time. The rifles were now hidden snuggly near the border of the Territory, guarded by the three loyal, taciturn Turkomen who had accompanied him on that long journey from the North. But he didn't dare to try to sell them on this side of the line, and he didn't dare cross the border without Baber Ali Khan's protection. Clanton rubbed his sore shoulder and cursed.

"*Sahib!*"

He whirled to see just the man he had been waiting for—Mirza Pasha, a Persian who said he was the son of a prince, and who acted as Baber Ali Khan's Peshawur agent. He was a tall, slender man, no darker than Clanton, with the finely chiseled Caucasian features frequently seen in high caste Iranians. He was a strikingly handsome man, Oxford bred, the black sheep of a fine Teheran family which traced its genealogy back to kings who ruled in purple palaces when Clanton's ancestors were loping over the heather clad in wolfskins and bashing each other's skulls with flint-headed clubs.

Clanton grabbed him, brushing aside amazed inquiries as to his appearance.

"Never mind what's happened to me! Have you got the safe-conduct from Baber Ali Khan?"

Mirza Pasha spread his hands helplessly.

"I have news, but not what you wished, alas. Baber Ali Khan will have nothing to do with it. He says the British will not like it if he buys Russian guns, or protects one who sells them, and the money he'd get isn't worth risking the loss of their friendship."

"The British!" raged Clanton, clenching his huge fists. "Always the damned British—"

Abruptly he turned away, ignoring Mirza who anxiously called after him, asking him what he meant to do. Natives scrambled out of the American's way as he went down the street with the lurching roll of a seaman. Even the tall hillmen, truculent and with knives in their shawl girdles, stepped aside after a glance at his dark, convulsed face. Mirza watched him go, smiled enigmatically, then turned away, in the direction from which Clanton had come. Neither of them noticed the lean one-eyed Waziri who slouched out of an alley and followed the American. Nor did they have any way of knowing that he had been skulking after Clanton all day, and had been watching Sonya's house while Wild Bill was within.

Mirza entered a certain courtyard, climbed the stair down which Clanton had recently tumbled, and was admitted through the ornate door by a Punjabi maid who wore a brand-new pair of baggy pants.

Sonya rose and came toward him, arms outstretched, tawny eyes glowing with the flame Clanton had hoped to kindle. He bowed with the polished elegance he had acquired at European schools, but she brushed his formality aside, slipped lithely into his arms and lifted her lips for his kiss. He abandoned his Western airs instantly and caressed her with an ardor possible only to an Oriental and a knowledge of feminine anatomy and psychology acquired by a long and exhaustive study of the subject under many conditions.

"You have done as I told you?" she asked at last, panting from the fire of his kisses.

"I did it, all right." A slight uneasiness tinged his expression. "When I look at that fellow's fists, I have misgivings—but he won't dare stay here now, after what the deputy commissioner told him. He'll leave Peshawur before midnight."

But Clanton wasn't preparing for flight just then. Even as Mirza was speaking, the smoldering American was shouldering his way into a certain dive crowded with hairy, dangerous-eyed figures, and demanding something liquid with a kick. Frustration turns some men to drink, and Clanton had had his bellyful of frustration that day. He knew he was licked, and the knowledge maddened him. There was nothing he could do but pull out for Bombay as best he could, leaving his fine rifles to rot in their hiding place, a total loss, and his followers to make their way back to Turkistan if they could. The few coins in his pocket represented his entire roll.

He kicked a place for himself among the men squatting along the wall, answering the glares of the dispossessed with a snarl that chilled their blood, sat himself down. The resentful hillmen, feudists and murderers with knives hidden in their *kaftans*, glanced dubiously at his brawny shoulders and massive corded forearms, and edged away from him. They could scent the berserk mood from afar, these war-bred hill-hawks, and they knew a fighting man when they saw one.

Clanton glared belligerently about him at the men squatting along the walls, smoking opium, drinking the Prophet-forbidden wine, and watching the dancing girls frisking in the open space in the middle of the big room, and he snorted as they studiously avoided his glare, and repeated his demand for liquid dynamite.

"Opium?" queried the dive-keeper hopefully. "Brandy? *Charas?*"

"Anything," growled Clanton. "Just so it's got power. And hustle, will you?" he yelled in a voice which wafted the startled dive-keeper to an inner door as if blown by a typhoon. Clanton did not notice that another man followed the fellow into the back room—a one-eyed Waziri who had come in right after the American. Clanton leaned back and grumpily watched the caperings of half a dozen Baluchi dancing girls, lithe ivory-skinned hussies with roller-bearing hips and eyes that flashed with naughty significance. The presence of a *sahib*, however scowly, flattered them and if their friskings had left anything to even a dull imagination before, they now corrected this error to the ecstatic appreciation of the tribesmen ranged along the walls, an appreciation Clanton would have shared had his smoldering wrath left him any room for any other emotion.

Meanwhile, in the backroom, the one-eyed Waziri was muttering to the dive-keeper, as he jingled a handful of coins seductively.

"Give the *ferengi bhang*, Musa."

"It is the drink of murder," expostulated Musa. "It will drive him mad. He will belabor the men about him, and one of them will stab him, and the police will come and close my house and throw *me* in jail."

"Nay, *bhang* makes a man remember old grudges! He will go forth in his madness and seek the deputy commissioner. I have been following him all day, and I know he has a quarrel with that *sahib*. Almost he smote him then. With the madness of *bhang* on him, he will fall upon the deputy commissioner and push him with his fists very hard in the face and make his foot go behind, as is the custom of the *sahibs*. So the British will take him and fine him and deport him."

"And how will this be to your advantage?" asked Musa.

"He brings guns from the North," answered the Waziri. "I have a friend in Kabul who has sent me word—he is an official whose palm the *ferengi* had to oil with gold. They are Muscovite guns, and if they are sold in the Territory, it will hurt the business of honest men—my brother and I, to be exact. We make good lever-action rifles in our hand factory over the border, and in ten days we make a gun for which we ask eighty rupees. The Russian guns are better than ours, bolt action, with a heathenish range, but until recently they demanded four hundred rupees, and only rich men could buy them. But this *Melakani* means to sell his guns for a hundred and seventy rupees, and all men will buy them, especially the men of Yussef Jehungir, chief of Khor, and Yar Abdullah of Secunderam, who are about to go to war. If the sahib Clanton is imprisoned and cannot sell his guns, Yussef and Abdullah will buy their guns from us. Their agents are even now in Peshawur, borrowing money for the war from the Hindu usurers."

Musa nodded, took the small, weighted pouch, and proceeded to mix *charas*, made from crushed hemp-plant leaves, with water, mare's milk and sugar, while the Waziri watched approvingly.

Roars from the outer room, rising above the shrilling of the dancing girls, speeded Musa's movements, and he hurried forth with the concoction barely in time to placate Clanton, grown furious at the delay. The American gulped the stuff, made a wry face—possibly because of the unfamiliar taste of the water in it—and called for more. He didn't like the flavor, but he could tell it packed dynamite. A few drinks and his brain began to do cartwheels. Men sitting near him moved hastily away, seeing his eyes turn red as coals of fire. The murderer's grog began churning in his brain, filling it with crimson visions. A saucy wench, swaying seductively and revealingly before him, was rewarded with a resounding smack of his open hand that sent her scampering, squealing as she tenderly caressed smarting hip. Dashing the cup on the floor, Clanton heaved up, brandished his huge fists and profanely demanded if there was any eternally condemned son of a female canine in the joint who wanted a fight. A discreet silence greeted him, whereat he snorted loudly in contempt, hurled his scanty bankroll on the floor, and rolled out of the door.

"He has gone to cut the throat of the deputy commissioner," said the one-eyed gunmaker piously. "Wonderful are the ways of Allah!"

"*Allaho akbar!*" agreed Musa, dexterously thieving the money pouch of a drunken Orakzai.

But again speculations regarding Clanton's conduct were erroneous. He was heading for Sonya's house under full sail, and there was in his addled brain no room for thought of the deputy commissioner. He did not reel in his gait. No man could have told that he was drunk, unless one looked at his eyes, which blazed in the lights of the streetlamps like those of a mad dog. Without knowing, he had drunk the most hellish mixture in the world—the stuff Oriental despots have fed to their bravoes since the days of the *Shaykh-al-Jebal* to enflame them to bloody deeds, the stuff professional murderers swing to nerve themselves up to a frenzy that ignores all possible consequences.

The Waziri had told the truth when he said *bhang* made men remember their enemies; but it was Sonya, and not the deputy commissioner whom Clanton remembered with an insane fury. And naturally so, for the Sonya episode was the more recent. The Waziri did not know what had happened in Sonya's chambers, though he had seen Clanton emerge from her courtyard bruised and disheveled. But it was not uncommon for a man to come out of a woman's house looking like that.

But craft accompanies the madness of *bhang*. With the cunning of a jungle beast Clanton left the streets and stole along narrow twisting alleys until he reached a certain back door, over which a dim light burned. Night had fallen while he sat in the dive of Musa. He rapped on the door and waited, grimly massaging the muscles of his right arm. The shoulder was still sore, but the numbness was gone. A gruff voice within demanded his pleasure and Clanton, summoning his stock of *Pashtu*, answered in what he hoped was a disguised voice: "I come from Sulayman of Kabul. Open the door!"

"Art thou mad?" snarled the voice within. "I know no Sulayman of Kabul, and thou speakest like a man with his head in a bag! Stand, until I see thy face, or—"

The upper half of the door was jerked open and the Shinwari's turbaned head was thrust out. Recognition flared in the wicked black eyes, and the Pathan snatched at his girdle.

"Dog—"

Bam! He crumpled at the impact of Clanton's thundering right-hander to the jaw, and lay like a sack over the lower half of the door. Clanton hauled the limp body over the barrier, let it slump to the earth, and reaching an arm over, found the lock and slid the bolt. An instant later he was in the dim-lit hall beyond.

He poised an instant, tense as a jungle killer, intent only on one thing—to wrest revenge from Sonya's mocking white body. Fear of consequences, which would have checked him if sober, had been swept away by the crimson tide of the *bhang*. That the path he was traveling was leading him straight to a British gallows he knew and did not care.

Somewhere nearby came a low murmur of voices, lascivious feminine laughter and the heavier, insistent mutter of men's voices. He bent to a heavy door and listened. He recognized the voice of the Punjab maid he had unbreeched that day, and other voices mingled with hers—those of men and other girls. He grinned wolfishly as he braced a massive chair against the door, effectively imprisoning all those in the room. Sonya's servants were enjoying a revel of their own. That meant their mistress had dismissed them for the night, and *that* meant—

With eyes like those of a demented tiger he slid noiselessly up the back stair. Another, low murmur of voices reached him as he came into an upper hall. Crouching at a door which he knew opened into the room from which he had been ejected that evening, he listened. One voice was Sonya's, liquid with passion; the other—he stiffened, recognizing the voice of Mirza Pasha.

"How could he know that my spies had discovered where he hid his rifles?" the Persian was saying. "But I wish we had laid our plot before I got that pass from Baber. He'll wonder why Clanton doesn't show up."

"Tell the chief Clanton double-crossed him," came Sonya's voice. "We have nothing to fear. Clanton's left town by this time. Anyway, he wouldn't dare—"

Clanton's brain was a whirling ball of fire as he drew back and crashed his brawny shoulder against the door. It splintered inward and he burst into the room, raging and terrible. Mirza and Sonya sprang up from the couch. The woman wore only a light silk robe which she caught about her as she rose. Mirza was pale in the lamp light as he drew a pistol. Before he could fire Clanton was on him, and the gun spun through the air, tinkled through a window. Mirza went reeling across the room from a savage smash to the ear. Sonya was screaming for her servants.

"Yell your gizzard out!" mouthed Clanton, turning on her. "I've got 'em all locked up downstairs—"

But not all the Tajiks had been taking part in that debauch downstairs, for three of them rushed suddenly into the room. Clean berserk with *bhang* madness, Clanton whirled to meet them. Before they could check he was among them like a blood-mad tiger among hounds, mallet-like fists flailing with blinding speed and devastating fury. A whirl of terrible blows, thunderous impact of iron-hard knuckles against flesh and bone, and the three Tajiks were down and out before they had a chance to fight back.

Clanton turned on Mirza, just staggering up, dazed and bleeding.

"Don't hit me again!" begged the Persian. "It's all *her* fault! I had no intention of double-crossing you, at first. I got the pass from Baber, just as you wished, and came here yesterday, looking for you. She became infatuated with me, and persuaded me to double-cross you, and Baber. She persuaded the deputy commissioner you ought to be run out of town, and I lied to you about Baber Ali Khan. He's waiting for you beyond the border, right now! I'd found where you hid your guns, and we planned to get you out of the way, so we could get hold of them ourselves. She planned to sell them all to Yussef Jehungir, so he could wipe out Yar Abdullah—so we'd make an ally out of Yussef. She's a Russian spy!"

At that damning accusation, Sonya shrank back with a low, bitter cry.

"Where's Baber's pass?" snarled Clanton.

"Here!" Fumbling in his pocket Mirza produced an ornately scrawled parchment. Clanton grabbed it, scanned it briefly, stuck it in his pocket, and then seized Mirza by the collar, and frog-marched him to the head of the stair which led down into the courtyard. A reverberant kick in the pants sent the descendant of Persian shahs headlong down the steps, and Clanton turned back to Sonya, who cowered pale and speechless in a corner of the room. The madness of the *bhang* had passed in the frenzy of battle. His eyes were sane now, but at the light in them she gasped, and darted into an inner bedroom. He sprang after her and caught her before she could slam the door. The robe slipped from her in the struggle and the sight of her white, writhing body went to his head like wine.

"I suppose you'll tell the British I'm a spy if I don't come across!" she raged, deliriously beautiful in her rage; her breasts heaved stormily.

"To hell with them!" He laughed at her struggles as his fingers invaded each intimated charm. "I'm no telltale, nor blackmailer! I'm not threatenin' you—I'm *makin'* you! I'm man enough to *take* what I want!"

"You can't do it!" she stormed defiantly, as he forced her down on the bed. "You're *not* man enough. You can't—you can't—" Her defiance broke in a despairing shriek as she realized the futility of her resistance.

Presently he rose, and fumbled in his pocket as he looked down at her where she lay weeping in rage, shame and humiliation. He started to speak, then changed his mind, shrugged his shoulders and headed for the door. There was no mercy in the game she played, and she had no reason to expect any. With the safe-conduct in his hand he descended the stair; revenge was behind him, promise of golden gain ahead, where Baber Ali Khan waited for him beyond the border.

Guns of Khartum

Emmett Corcoran shook the perspiration out of his eyes and cursed the glare that beat up from the dusty, deserted street. A pulse in his temple throbbed sickeningly, but above that he heard the deep rumble of the cannon, as he had heard them for longer than he could, in his present daze of fatigue, remember. He knew they spelled the doom of Khartum. For ten months the wild hordes of the Mahdi had ringed the city; for ten months they had beaten in vain at its crumbling walls. But the defenders could not hold out much longer.

The street along which Corcoran walked wearily was empty. Whites and blacks kept indoors these days as much as possible, the whites in despairing fear, the blacks in sinister anticipation. There were traitors in the city. Corcoran wiped his brow shakily. His face was blackened with gunpowder smoke, and his shirt gaped, revealing his hairy, muscular chest. A Dervish sword had slit that shirt, and the Dervish had died, quickly. Grimly Corcoran touched the bone hilt of the saber at his side.

A sudden shriek, startling in the stillness of the street, brought him about. He was passing a flat-roofed house with barred windows, and the sound came from within. A woman had screamed, and she had not screamed as a black wench howls under the lash—a fairly common sound in Khartum. He reached the door with a single stride, and it swung inward at his touch. He stepped inside, blinking in the comparative darkness. Sounds of a struggle came from beyond a curtained doorway, and he sprang across the room, tore the curtains aside.

He was looking into a room which opened onto an enclosed courtyard. The last radiance of the setting sun came through an open doorway. Two women were struggling before him, and one was white—a slender girl whose hair caught the dying sun in glints of burnished bronze. It was she who had screamed, and now she screamed again as her assailant, a pantherish Somali half-caste, forced her down across a couch. The brown girl's handsome face was convulsed with rage, and as she pressed the white girl down on her back, she lifted an Egyptian dagger. Her victim's dress had been torn open at the bosom, exposing her white breasts. Between those quivering ivory mounds the Somali meant to plunge her blade.

Corcoran had never struck a woman, white or brown. But his blood was still hot from the fury of fighting and killing; months of bitter strife had roused all the racial feeling in his soul, making him hate the sight of all skins not white. Before the knife could fall he gripped the brown girl's arm, wrenched her about with a violence that brought a scream from her lips, and smashed his fist against her jaw. She stretched her length on the floor, blood trickling from her mouth. Stooping, he grasped her by her long hair and dragged her through the front room, thrust her out into the street. She tumbled into the dust and lay whimpering.

He slammed the door and turned back into the inner room. The white girl had risen and stood clutching at a hanging for support, while she fumbled her torn dress together. He stood unspeaking, devouring her with his eyes. White women were scarce enough in Khartum; women of her blond beauty were scarce anywhere. Even the distant hammering of the guns was forgotten as he stood there, silent. Desire, numbed by the constant stress of long fighting, was waking in him. Her white flesh, against a remembered background of black and brown and yellow skins, was like a cool Northern dawn.

"Who—who are you?" she gasped, frightened by his silence, by his haggard and formidable appearance.

He shook himself out of his trance.

"Corcoran," he said. "Emmett Corcoran. I was passing when I heard you cry out. I should have killed that slut."

She shook her head, then shuddered.

"She is—was—my servant, Zelda. She's been growing insolent lately. A little while ago she became so insulting I threatened to whip her. It's the custom to whip servants here, you know. But she flew into a fury, and swore she'd kill me. Said the Mahdi would soon cut all white throats in Khartum, and she'd begin with mine—oh, you're wounded!"

He involuntarily rubbed his hand on his pants' leg.

"It's not my blood. We made a sortie outside the fortifications—"

"Oh, please forgive my stupidity!" she exclaimed contritely. "Sit down and let me get a basin of water, and food—there's still a little in the house."

He sank down on the couch, grateful for its softness and suddenly realizing the full extent of his fatigue.

"You're not a soldier?" she asked, as he plunged his hands and face into the bowl she brought.

"No. I'm an American. I was hunting ivory deep in the Sudan when the Mahdi rose. I was lucky to get into Khartum. I've been doing my part to defend the town, of course."

"I've heard of you!" Her fine eyes lighted with interest. He watched them in fascination, so different from the hot brown eyes he had been used to for so long. "Men speak of you as a fighting man! Was the sortie successful?"

He shrugged his shoulders.

"They ran before us. We lopped a few heads and chased them for a few hundred yards—then rode back with a thousand devils yapping at our heels. These sorties are mainly to keep them occupied—to keep them from attacking in full force. There are breaches in the walls we can't mend—if the Dervishes ever find them—"

"We can't hold out much longer unless reinforcements come from Egypt," murmured the girl, seating herself beside him. Her eyes were shadowed with fear. "My name is Ruth Brenton. I came here a year ago to visit my uncle, a merchant. He was killed in the early days of the siege. I couldn't get away, of course. I'm afraid—terribly afraid! This country and all about it is so terrifyingly different from England. And there's a French renegade in the Mahdi's army—Gerard

Latour. I met him at Cairo and he followed me here—annoyed me until my uncle drove him from the house. Later we learned he was even then a spy for the Mahdi. He's out there, with them—" Her white hand swept vaguely in the direction of the Nile, and the color ebbed from her face. "He sent me a message that he would have me, if he had to tear the city to pieces with his bare hands."

Suddenly she turned and threw her arms about Corcoran's corded neck, as if seeking security in the contact of a strong man.

"Oh, I'm afraid! I'm afraid!"

Corcoran gathered her in his arms. Their faces were close together, his fierce blue eyes blazing into hers. The feel of that supple white body in his arms, the first white woman he had touched for three years, drove a pulse of fire through his veins. He forgot the encircling menace drawing closer and closer about the walls of the doomed Khartum—forgot the fatigue that, after thirty-six sleepless hours, had driven him from the ramparts. As she read the flame in his eyes she tried to draw away from him. But his arm was about her supple waist, pinning her to him. His other hand fumbled her torn dress apart, and a deep sigh escaped his lips as his fingers cupped a firm warm globe of white and pink flesh. He felt her resistance melting; the supple arms straining against him glided once more about his neck. With a gasp he thrust his fingers deep into her red-gold curls, crushing her crimson lips against his. The tip of her tongue was sweet as burning honey between his lips, and as she took fire from his flaming kisses, her embrace became convulsive, a low whimper of ecstasy ebbed from her panting mouth. His hand glided lower, caressed the velvet of a bare thigh, drew her dress upward.

The sun had set; the swift African dusk was deepening into night. Outside the street was silent. Over the flat roofs of the houses came the mutter of the guns of Khartum.

On the couch in the room that opened on the courtyard where palm trees hung their fronds in the windless air, Emmett Corcoran awoke suddenly and sat up, a sense of impending peril clutching at his throat. There was no moon, but the white limbs of the girl who slept beside him were a soft glimmer in the starlight that filtered through door and barred windows. He rose swiftly, reaching for pistol belt and saber which hung on a chair near the couch. The guns were ominously silent. A tense, shuddering silence lay over Khartum.

Ruth awakened and sleepily reached her arms for him.

"Is it dawn?"

He kissed her, gently caressed her firm young breasts.

"No. But get up and dress. Something's brewing. I don't like this stillness. It may presage a night attack—*God!*"

Ruth shrieked as she sprang from the couch and clutched him, but her cry was drowned in the devil's clamor that had burst outside. All hell had broken loose in Khartum. The silent town came to frenzied life in a hideous discord of screams, yells, curses and shots. A red glare of burning houses rose over the flat roofs.

"The Dervishes!" gasped Corcoran, electrified. "They're inside the walls!"

And they were. Fifty thousand of them. In the darkness they had crept through a breach in the wall cut by the river. They were in the city before the defenders knew their peril. After that it was butchery.

In Ruth's house Corcoran snatched on his boots and spoke quickly to the terrified girl.

"We've got to find a boat, somehow, and try to sneak down the Nile. This house isn't so far from the river wall, and—"

A rush of feet in the street, a bestial, exultant howling drowned his words. The outer door began to splinter under the assault of hammering musket-butts, and above the savage yells a European voice shouted commands.

"Latour!" cried Ruth, going white.

"Out into the courtyard!" snapped Corcoran. "No time for you to dress now. Maybe we can get out the back way—"

They ran into the court just as a small door in the wall opened to admit a flood of wild black faces and tossing torches. Sabers gleamed, eyes rolled white in the smoky glare. At the sight of the girl, clad only in a thin low-necked chemise, a roar went up. The soft gleam of white limbs and naked breasts maddened these brutes from the southern grasslands. Beyond them Corcoran glimpsed the triumphant face of Zelda, the Somali. She had led the ravishers upon them.

Corcoran backed into an angle of the wall, thrusting Ruth behind him. A black threw up an ancient musket and when it flashed and bellowed the ball hummed by Corcoran's ear. Corcoran shot the warrior through the head, and his bullets raked the court, spilling writhing figures on the flowerbeds, sending the charge reeling back in red ruin. But they came on again, frenzied with the sight of the half-nude woman cowering behind him, and his Colt was empty.

Corcoran's saber cut the torchlight like a flicker of blue lightning and a Negro dropped with his skull split. Again and again the tall American struck and a man dropped at each stroke. He loomed like an image of death among the Dervishes, and his mighty blows beat down their blades, the swiftness of his onslaught blinded them. For an instant the impossible happened, and one man held a horde at bay.

Then another band came pouring into the court from the house—the group which had broken in through the street door. A tall figure in Arab garb fired with a pistol over the heads of the milling mob. Corcoran swayed and his saber clanged on the flags. He fell as a tree falls and lay still, blood oozing from his head. A dozen spears went up, but before they could fall Ruth flung herself, screaming, on his body, sheltering his flesh with her own. The spears checked, hovered. Then the crowd was split by the rush of the man in Arab dress. He bent, grasped Ruth's arm and hauled her to her feet. In the torchlight a lean, mocking, saturnine face regarded her from beneath the flowing *kafieh.*

"Latour!" she sobbed.

"Your faithful admirer, mademoiselle!" he answered ironically. "Come to claim you—as I swore I would!"

"You beast!" she moaned. "You've killed him!"

"I seldom miss," he agreed calmly. "Enough! I have what I came for. Why struggle, you little fool? Would you not rather be my slave than the slave of one of these black brutes? Khartum has fallen; the Mahdi is master of the Sudan—and I am high in his favor! Come! In my tent we shall celebrate the victory of this night!"

Laughing at the revealing whirl of white limbs as she struggled vainly, the renegade lifted her in his arms and strode toward the open gate. Though she fought him like a wild thing, she hardly felt his lustful hands on her naked thighs, her bare breasts. She scarcely heard the brutal laughter of the warriors, mocking her nudity. Staring over her captor's shoulder, her dilated eyes were fixed in frenzied despair on the figure that lay limply in the angle of the wall, amidst a litter of mangled black figures.

The gate closed behind the renegade and his straggling horde. A slim, brown-skinned figure, vague in the glow of a fallen torch, stole from the shadows and bent over the senseless American. He was heavy, but her slender arms were strong. Still it was all she could do to drag him across the court and into a room. There she drew the blinds carefully before she lighted a candle.

Perhaps it was the gleam in his eyes that roused Corcoran. He blinked about and sat up, fumbling at his empty belt. He stared stupidly at Zelda, posing insolently before him, her hands on her hips.

"Where's Ruth?" he demanded. Now that his head was clearing he could hear the sounds that accompanied the sack of Khartum—distant screams, howls of triumph, shots. Blood was dried on his scalp.

"Latour took her," answered Zelda. "He shot you, but the ball only cut your skin and grazed your skull. They all thought you were dead."

Corcoran cursed and reeled to his feet, swaying with weakness.

"I'll kill him! He shan't have her!"

"He *has* her!" Zelda moved before him, swaying her insolent hips, molded by her short skirt. Through its slit her sleek brown flanks gleamed in the candlelight and her eyes reflected less an invitation than a demand. "Don't be a fool! He's taken her to the Mahdi's camp near the river shore. How can you hope to reach her, much less rescue her?"

Despair settled over him like a cloud.

"What's your game?" he muttered.

She came close to him with a swaying, provocative gait that revealed to him the full length of a sleek thigh and the contour of a full ripe hip through the gaping skirt. She pressed her hands below her already tilted breasts and forced them even more prominently upward.

"Am I not beautiful?" she demanded. "I love strong men. You are strong. I did not hate you for the blow you struck me, as a weak white woman would hate you! I could love you, *caphar!* When you slew the warriors in the garden I was hot with desire for you!"

He knew that women of her sort had a barbaric admiration for brute strength and courage, and only contempt for gentleness. But he scowled at her. With the feel of Ruth's white body still tingling his nerves, Zelda was almost repugnant to him, that is, as much as a handsome woman can ever be to a normal man. Zelda was not negroid. She was Somali-Arab. And she was beautiful in a wild, bold, sensual way.

"I hold you in my power," she said scornfully. "Khartum has fallen. Gordon is dead. I have seen his head stuck on a spear. The Mahdi is the master of all the Sudan. I saved your life because I love your strength, but I can cry out and men will come and take your head. Choose!"

It was not fear of death that decided him. But dead he could never follow and take Ruth from Latour as he determined to do; living there was still hope for rescuing the girl. He choked down the urge to seize the sneering brown girl and break her neck.

"Choice?" he growled. "This is my answer!"

Catching her roughly in his arms he tore the skirt from her body and threw her on the couch. And as his hands explored her breasts and all the intimate mysteries of her bold, brown body, he did not have to feign the fire that kindled in his veins.

Ruth Brenton looked wearily through the gilded bars of the small window which formed almost her only contact with the outer world. The sun was setting over the straggling mud houses of Omdurman, the barbaric capital of the Mahdi. Five months had passed since the fall of Khartum—five months of shame and terror for Ruth Brenton. From beyond the curtained doorway of the room in which she stood sounded the voices of other women—Turkish, Arab, Egyptian women who shared her slavery. She was Latour's favorite—not his only woman. The Frenchman had sunk as low as any wild tousle-headed Sudanese who followed the Mahdi's banner. The Dervishes were growing rich with plunder; they were building them houses of stone and mud to replace the grass-thatched *tokuls* they were born in, and the slave markets were thronged with captive women.

Ruth was dressed like any seraglio slave, in little red sandals and a light silk *gandourah*, which, belted at the waist by a broad velvet pearl-sewn girdle, displayed the contours, while barely veiling the intimate details of her dainty figure.

She shivered as she looked out on the barbaric scene. The alley into which the window opened ran into a market square in which she could see black men and women moving about, jesting, quarreling, making love. One solitary figure was idling in the alley near the window—a tall man in the robes and headdress of an Arab. Something about his bearing sent a strange, nameless throb through her, a sense of familiarity, though she knew she had never seen him before. He moved idly toward the window and she was about to withdraw from it, when he lifted a fold of his *kafieh* and looked full at her. The last rays of the sun fell on his lifted face and she almost cried out. She caught the bars of the window to keep from falling as a deadly weakness surged over her. It was the face of a man she had long mourned as dead—the face of Emmett Corcoran!

In an instant he had drawn the fold of the *kafieh* across his face, and paused below the window, leaning on a staff. Idly he scribbled in the sand with the tip, as Arabs often do. But there was method in the scratching. Plainly traced in the sand, she read: "Be ready; I'm coming for you soon after dark."

Then he drew his sandal across the sand, erasing what he had written, and moved away down the alley, to mingle with the crowd in the market. Ruth sank down on a couch, feeling stifled by the drum of her heart. Hope for her own rescue was submerged by a wild joy that he was alive, a sick terror that he would fall into the hands of their enemies. He must know the awful risk he ran, moving among them in disguise, when a false word or gesture might unmask him to a hideous death. She had seen the enemies of the Mahdi burned and flayed alive in the marketplace.

Then followed a fear that she would betray her excitement. She must hide it, especially from Zelda. The girl had come into camp and joined Latour's household shortly after the sack of Khartum. She had been sullen and savage, as if harboring a bitter disappointment or frustration. And though she feared Latour's anger too much to venture far in her revenge, she did not fail to vent her spite on Ruth as much as she dared. Ruth hated and feared her, and of late there had been a new and vicious meaning in Zelda's leering smile, promising some cruelty of which only the Somali was aware.

Ruth sprang up as Latour entered. The Frenchman had degenerated. Continual debauches had made his features coarser and flabbier. Physically and mentally he was crumbling, just as men whispered the Mahdi too was crumbling. Latour had no love for his master. He lived in constant fear that Muhammad would learn of Ruth and take the white girl away from him. For that reason he kept her more closely confined than he would have otherwise, for there was no chance for her to escape the city alone. Ruth too, lived in horror of the Mahdi. She loathed and hated Latour, but her fear of the Mahdi was a nightmare. She had seen him, riding through the market, huge, black and bearded, and he haunted her dreams with terror.

But of late Latour had treated her cruelly enough. He had taught her many things, including the sting of a rhino-hide *kourbash* on her naked body. Now he kissed her roughly, pulled her down on his knee and began playing with her bare breasts. She yielded submissively, but with greater reluctance than ever. The sight of Corcoran had made her slavery seem more abominable than ever. Latour sensed her reluctance and it angered him.

"So you cringe at my caresses!" he snarled. "You need a taste of the whip! You grow arrogant again!"

"No!" she begged, terrified by the threat. She forced herself to clasp her arms about his neck. "Please don't whip me! I always obey you!"

"Yes," he snarled, "but with reluctance. With obvious loathing. You hate me, damn your British soul! Don't try to deny it! I—"

A sudden tramp of feet sounded in an outer corridor. There was a squealing of women fleeing from the adjoining room, and then the curtains of the door were torn away and a band of warriors stood before them, led by an ostrich-plumed chief with a naked sword in his hand.

Latour sprang up angrily.

"What do you mean by entering my house in this manner?"

"I need give no explanation for obeying the command of our lord, the Mahdi," replied the *emir* arrogantly. "I have come at his order to convey that English girl there to his palace."

Latour trembled and for an instant it seemed that he would draw his sword and leap at the speaker who waited, smiling grimly. There was no love between the renegade and the native chiefs. But fear mastered the Frenchman's rage. A grey pallor overspread his swarthy cheeks and he said sullenly: "Take her, then. I obey the Mahdi's command."

"Well for you, white man," said the *emir* haughtily. "You know the law—all captives must be brought to the *Beit-el-Maal*, the treasure house of our master, there to be apportioned or appropriated by himself as he deems fit. This law you disobeyed when you took the white woman for yourself. The Mahdi generously spares your life, because of your past services. But beware!"

Seizing Ruth roughly by her shoulder he thrust her toward the door.

"Latour!" she cried frantically, writhing in her captor's brutal hands. "Don't—for God's sake, don't let them take me to that beast!"

Sullenly the Frenchman lowered his eyes, refusing to meet her frantic gaze. The *emir* slapped her soft hips contemptuously and pushed her ahead of him. Helplessly she was marched out of the room and down the corridor. Presently the outer door banged with a brazen clangor.

Latour staggered toward a wine jug on a table in the adjoining room, cursing vilely. As he lifted the jug he caught a movement of the tapestry on the wall. Dashing down the jug he sprang, jerked the hanging aside and dragged Zelda, the Somali girl, from her hiding place.

"Why were you hiding there?" he demanded.

"I was afraid of the soldiers," she replied.

"When did you ever hide from men?" he snarled. "You lie! You—" Suddenly light burst on him at the malicious smile lurking on her lips. He burst into a torrent of curses, shaking her savagely. "Damn you, you are the cause of this! *You brought the soldiers here!* You told the Mahdi I had a white girl in my *harim!* You hated her—and me!—you slut!"

She screamed as he ripped out his saber—her scream choked as his blind thrust tore through her breast. She caught at the blade with her bare hands and sank down, writhing. Latour, cursing like a madman, tore the steel from her dying body, kicked her savagely and again staggered toward the wine jug. And again he checked. The curtains over an outer door billowed and a tall figure stood there before him. A man in Arab garb, a big pistol in his hand. He rasped, in English: "Where is she, Latour?"

"Who?" gasped the astounded renegade.

"Ruth Brenton!"

"The Mahdi took her! But—" Latour's eyes narrowed. "By God, you are Corcoran! I thought I killed you!"

"So did others. That wench on the floor there saved me for her own purposes. I finally got away from her and was trying to slip into Omdurman when some slave traders grabbed me, and took me far into Darfur. It's taken me this long to get away from them and get back here. And now—"

"And now the Mahdi is enjoying your sweetheart!" The Frenchman was lashing himself into a frenzy of jealous hate. "He took her from me—but I'd rather he had her than you! She loved you. That's why she hated me! And for that I'll have your head! Oh, you dare not shoot! It was easy to sneak in here in that disguise, but a shot will bring a hundred men about your ears! I'll send your head to the Mahdi, dog!"

And whipping out his saber he rushed at Corcoran, laughing wildly.

Corcoran dared not fire. He stepped aside, drawing his own saber. Latour laughed like a wolf as he came on. He had learned swordsmanship in the fencing schools of Paris; but Corcoran had learned his on the desert, where no one lived to repeat a mistake.

Latour feinted and lunged. Corcoran swayed his body at the waist, and took the point in the slack of the loose *abba*, under his arm. Too late Latour saw his mistake. The scream that rose in his throat was severed as Corcoran's down-lashing saber split his skull to the teeth. He fell across Zelda's body and lay twitching, his shattered head in a puddle of blood and brains. Corcoran spat at the corpse and turned away. There had been no clang of steel to rouse the household, and the thick carpets had muffled the stamp of sandaled feet. None heard or saw the figure that glided out of a side door and melted into the dark alley.

Corcoran hurried toward a certain point of the town, near a market square. There he was to meet a Copt who had escaped from his Dervish master and yearned for Egypt. The Copt knew where a boat could be stolen for the perilous journey down the Nile. Corcoran had expected to meet him at the appointed rendezvous with the girl. Now he must tell the Copt that they must postpone their flight until he, Corcoran, could attempt the desperate venture of stealing her out of the Mahdi's palace. Already he was working out a plan. In the few days he had spent in Omdurman, searching for Ruth, he had obtained a good idea of the plan of Muhammad's palace, though he had not expected to have to invade it.

Fires blazed in the market and men reeled and shouted drunkenly. A few steps more and he would reach the alley where the Copt would be waiting to tell him where he had hidden the boat. Corcoran glanced absently at the severed heads adorning stakes in the square.

In that hell-town fresh heads decorated the points almost every day. And an icy hand clutched his heart. In the firelight he recognized one of those vacantly grinning, glassy-eyed trophies. It was the head of the Copt who had intended escaping with him. The man must have been recognized as a runaway slave, while on his way to the rendezvous. Punishment had been instant.

Corcoran stood paralyzed with the disaster. Then he turned toward the Mahdi's palace in a red mist of fury, in which black figures reeled against a hellfire background. Fate had dealt against him, but at least the author of his misfortunes should not survive him. He would kill the Mahdi, kill the girl, mercifully, and then wreak havoc on the black hordes until a sword thrust quieted his seething soul.

Ten minutes later he was gliding into the mouth of an alley that ran along the side of Muhammad's palace. It was dark there but not too dark for him to see a man squatting on his haunches, a naked scimitar beside him, his chin resting on his knees. Ostrich plumes nodded over his head. Corcoran knew the man was an *emir* and that he must be in temporary disfavor with the Mahdi. This menial task, of guarding a back alley, had been set as punishment. The posting of guards was more a formality than anything, since the Mahdi did not believe any enemy could reach him, in the midst of the hordes which worshipped him as the successor of the Prophet.

Like a shadow Corcoran loomed over the sleeping *emir*. The alley was a blind one; this was the only entrance. To enter he must step over the man, and that would surely waken him. Thrice he lifted his saber, and thrice he lowered his arm, cursing his squeamishness. But he could not bring himself to kill a sleeping man, not even a Dervish. Lifting the saber again he struck with the hilt, stretching the *emir* senseless.

Only one door opened into the alley. It was barred, but a thin knife blade slipped between door and jamb lifted the bar. The next instant he was in a short, carpeted and tapestried hall, lit with brass lamps. Within a few feet it ended at a curtained doorway, and beyond that curtain came sounds that brought the red mist again before his eyes—hysterical sobbing of a woman, and the brutal, throaty laughter of a man.

He tore aside the curtains, and a huge black man whirled to meet him. The Dervishes, accustomed to the tattered *djibbeh* the Mahdi affected in public, would scarcely have recognized the resplendent figure in silk and gold that faced the maddened American. Beyond him Ruth dropped the golden vase with which she had fought off the brute, and sank to the floor, crying out with relief.

The Mahdi had been a notable fighting man once. He was still quick enough to elude Corcoran's first, vengeful thrust. It slit the skin of his fat neck and brought blood, and before Corcoran could strike again, the Mahdi had closed with him. For an instant Corcoran felt the play of giant muscles. But he had gripped the fat throat, strangling the Mahdi's yell, and suddenly the giant figure crumpled in his grip. Evil living had made a shell of a once mighty frame. Too close to use the blade, Corcoran smashed hilt to jaw, and the Mahdi fell and lay sprawling, blood oozing from the scratch on his neck. Corcoran lifted the sword to strike off his head, when a sound behind him brought him around.

The *emir* he had struck down in the alley stood in the curtained door, grey faced, eyes wide with horror.

"The Mahdi!" he gasped. "You've killed him! His throat is cut—"

"Yes, I killed him!" snapped Corcoran, his mind working like lightning. "And you helped us!"

"You—you are mad!" The man's eyes were starting from his head.

"Yes? Who'll believe you if you deny it? You were in disfavor or you wouldn't have been on guard duty in that blind alley. That's a slave's job. How could I get in without your assistance?"

"You can't prove it! The people will tear you to pieces!"

"Sure! But they'll tear you, too. I won't have to prove anything. I'll just tell them you helped us. They'll be eager for victims. They won't give you a chance to prove your innocence."

The *emir* fell to his knees, completely demoralized, and begged: "Mercy, in the name of Allah! Let us go our ways and keep silent about this!"

"That's not enough," said Corcoran. "You've got to help us get away. It'll be several hours before anyone discovers the Mahdi's dead. They know he had taken a new woman, and won't dare interrupt his pleasures until dawn, at least. As an *emir* you can take what you want in the square—we'll take camels, food, water, a few soldiers for an escort. Your authority will get us out of town. Within an hour we can be well on our way to safety."

"It is far to Egypt," shivered the *emir*.

"Who mentioned Egypt? I have friends in Abyssinia. We'll cross the river south of the town and strike for the border. We'll ride fast and keep ahead of the news. I'll vouch for you to my Ethiopian friends, and among them you'll be safe from the vengeance of the Dervishes."

"Let us go!" The *emir* sprang up, tense with eagerness to be gone.

Corcoran muffled Ruth in a cloak caught from a couch and cautioned him: "Don't try any tricks! If you try to betray me I'll shout to the people that you helped me kill the Mahdi. Let's go!"

A moment later they were stealing down the alley. Five minutes later in a nearby square the *emir's* muttered orders were sending slaves darting about saddling camels and filling food pouches and waterbags, while two muffled figures stood in the shadows behind him, but always close enough to touch him. A short time later a dozen racing camels were swinging southward at a swift pace.

Only when the lights of Omdurman were dwindling behind them did Ruth venture to whisper to Corcoran: "Was the Mahdi really dead?"

He placed his lips to her ear. "No. Just knocked out, and I was afraid I'd give it away to the *emir* if I tried to finish him. But the *emir* won't know, because we'll travel so fast we'll keep ahead of all news from Omdurman. He's our passport to the border, but I'm his passport beyond that, so he won't dare kill us himself. We're safe, girl! And the Mahdi's doomed. I heard his rotten heart pumping like a war-drum. He can't live long."

Corcoran spoke prophetically, though he could not know it, for the Mahdi had less than a week of life left to him. But just now the American was more interested in the girl in his arms than anything else. He drew her close to him, feeling her slender arms about his neck, seeing her eyes lifted to his a-gleam in the starlight. Behind them lay terror and peril; ahead lay safety and happiness, happiness promised in the soft resilience of the firm young breast he fondled with caressing fingers.

Daughters of Feud

Braxton Brent, new schoolmaster in the little mountain school of Whiskey Run, sprang to his feet as smoldering hate burst into flame between Joan Kirby and Ann Pritchard, daughters of feuding families. They came together in the aisle between the rude, hand-hewn desks, in a whirl of skirts and thrashing limbs. Garments disarranged by their violence displayed generous expanses of white flesh. Mountain girls fought like wildcats. The other pupils, used to such scenes, sprang up and moved back, giving them room. They did not shout excitedly, like city-bred children; they maintained a tense silence, but blazing eyes and pale, hard-set lips told of fierce emotions within. Whiskey Run School, where old hates simmered, was a powder keg that might explode at any instant with devastating results.

Ann screamed like a wild thing, clawing, tearing, trying to gouge the other girl's eyes out, but Joan fought in silence, striking and kneeing like a man. Before much damage could be done on either side, Brent reached them and tore them apart by main strength. The new master was young, well-built and athletic; it was his first experience as a schoolteacher, and he was getting plenty.

Ann screeched, fighting to get at her enemy, but Joan was scornfully quiet. Her splendid bosom, heaving, told of her angry passion within. Her dress had been ripped open, and the sight of those full, white globes as they rose and fell stormily quickened Brent's pulse. A sleek white thigh peeping through a rent in her skirt that ran from hip to hem did not tend to make him any more tranquil. Ann was not so disheveled as to clothes; Joan had fought to damage flesh, not garments. A trickle of blood seeped from the corner of Ann's sullen mouth.

"Let go me, damn you!" raged the Pritchard girl. "Let me git my hands onto her! I'll tear off every stitch she's got on!"

"Why didn't you do it when you had the chance?" retorted Joan disdainfully. "If he hadn't pulled me off, I'd a-beat yo' haid into mush. You better let us alone, mister; we'll have it out in spite of you!"

"Shut up, both of you!" he snapped, interposing his trim, athletic frame between them. "Didn't I forbid fighting in school?"

Behind him a boy laughed jeeringly. Ann spat at him, and Joan laughed insolently. She was a magnificent figure as she stood there, scornful and angry, yet smiling defiantly, heedless of the display of her splendid bosom. She was fair, Ann was dark; both were handsome as only mountain girls can be. And both were wild, untamed young barbarians, eager to make life miserable for the "foreign" schoolteacher. Brent realized he faced a crisis and in spite of himself he turned cold inside. There was insolence in the faces all about him, the pupils realizing he faced a test of his authority, and doubting his ability to master it. Ann sneered openly, wiped the blood from her lips and tossed back her black hair insolently; the quiet, dimpling smile on Joan's lips was just as arrogant. Anger began to stir in Brent's bosom.

He had been warned of what he might expect by Judge Harrison, the one educated man in the community, and head of the board of trustees, who had hired Brent. Harrison was wise, with the hard, cynical wisdom of the backwoods. Concisely he had told Brent how he must meet his problems. Brent stood aghast.

"Why, good God, man, that's barbarous! A custom that went out of fashion a hundred years ago, even in Europe! It's medieval!"

"Whiskey Run's medieval," answered the Judge. "Actually, these mountain people are all living in the eighteenth century."

"And you mean to tell me that I'm expected to punish pupils—including grown girls—in this barbarous and indecent manner?"

"That or let them kick you all over the place. It's the only way to make these hillbilly youngsters respect you. Let them get the idea that you're afraid to handle them roughly, and they'll make life hell for you, and eventually run you off, just as they did the last three or four men who tried to teach them."

"But won't their parents object?"

"Some will and some won't. In the former case you'll just have to fight the parents! You look capable—but remember, mountain men don't fight according to civilized rules!"

"A nice position!" quoth Brent bitterly. But when a man is flat broke, he can't be fastidious. He had taken the job; and now he was face to face with a situation which would determine his status in Whiskey Run. If he let these saucy hussies get away with this, his pupils would run him off the place. If he mastered these nineteen-year-old culprits the way Harrison had advised, he'd probably have their relatives gunning for him. He was in for it, whichever way he turned. Resentment at the position into which he was forced, rebounded on the culprits. At the insolent smiles on their faces he saw red. All right! They'd put him on the spot, and they'd take the consequences. Whatever happened to him afterward, he'd take it out of their skins now.

"School's dismissed," he said crisply. "All pass out except Ann and Joan. You young ladies have a date with me in the woodshed!"

Ann snarled, and the smile was wiped off Joan's face. In the faces of the other pupils grew a grudging respect. The new teacher was not a softy, after all. Silently they gathered their dog-eared books and trudged out, boys and girls of all ages, from tiny tots to gawky youths nearly grown. Brent locked the door after them. The windows had heavy wooden bars, and the only other door led into the woodshed. Pocketing the key, he turned grimly to the culprits who faced him still scornful, but with apprehension beginning to manifest itself.

"You don't dast lick me!" Ann spat. "My folks'd skin you alive!"

He thought it quite probable. Might made right in the mountains, and customs, like laws, were obeyed only when somebody had the power to enforce them. But he was too mad to answer her taunt. He grabbed her by her shoulder and propelled her through the door, into the small lean-to shed where the wood was piled. There was a bench there, too, and on a peg near the door hung a leather strap, worn smooth by frequent use. It was because of reluctance or inability to use that strap that Brent's Northern predecessor had been beaten up and run out of the school by the young barbarians he was trying to control. The most successful teacher the school had ever known had been a local giant who licked boys and girls mercilessly and impartially, fought enraged parents with knives and shotguns, and eventually retired full of years and honor. Since then one teacher after another had been routed in ignominious defeat.

"Damn you, let go a-me!" gritted Ann, twisting in his grasp, as Brent took the strap from its peg. "You don't dast lick me, you bastard! You don't dast—"

She was quickly disillusioned. She was strong and supple as only a mountain girl can be, and she fought like a wildcat, but Brent was an athletic young man, and he was mad clear through. There was a brief whirl of struggle, and then his superior strength made itself evident. Crushing her resistance, he sat down on the bench and imprisoned her, cursing and kicking, across his knee, and pulled up her skirt. He had already learned that the girls of Whiskey Run wore no underwear. Ann was no exception.

"Now, you little devil," he said grimly, "I'm going to show you who's the boss here!" And firmly grasping his raging captive, he employed the strap on her bare, squirming, upturned hips with a vigor inspired by his determination to assert his authority once and for all. He didn't want to have to repeat this scene. At each resounding smack a broad crimson weal appeared on her olive-tinted hips, and before he had completed his discipline, the entire surface was reddened, and Ann's curses and threats had changed to shrieks of pain and frantic pleas for mercy. When he released her, she slipped to the floor and groveled at his feet, weeping stormily and contorting her supple body ludicrously with the smarting of her crimson hips.

"Get up and get out!" he ordered, rising and opening the door. His anger had cooled and he felt a reaction—a feeling of disgust at himself, and distaste for his next task. Joan Kirby was standing near the door, where she had evidently been listening to Ann's howls with mingled emotions—elation at Ann's humiliation, and painful anticipation of the same treatment for herself. Her eyes were dilated, her red lips parted, and she stepped hastily back away from Brent, as he came from the "licking shed."

Brent opened the outer door. "Get your books, Ann, and get going." She obeyed, sobbing and tenderly caressing that part of her anatomy which felt as if it were afire at the moment. At this Joan dimpled with an amused smile, but her fine eyes were shadowed with anxiety on her own account.

"You let her listen to me gittin' licked!" Ann accused bitterly. "But you won't let me stay and listen to her holler!"

"Go on home!" Brent ordered, holding the door open for her. There was some justice in her complaint, but at the moment he hated the sight of her. The experience of exposing and whipping a full-grown girl had shaken him more than he had expected; the reaction was unpleasant, and increased his resentment toward the victim who had forced him into it.

Ann went, weeping furiously, and outside the door she flung back: "Yo're partial to her! Yo're on the side of the Kirbys! I'll tell pap, and then you'll see, you big bully!"

Shaking his head disgustedly, Brent closed the door and turned back to Joan, who stood tall and splendid before him. She had drawn together the torn dress over her bosom, but through the rents still peeped vistas of rounded ivory that fascinated him. His task was growing more distasteful every instant. She was not a spitting, snarling wildcat like Ann Pritchard. There was a certain lissome dignity about her, despite her cheap, torn dress through which her bare legs showed. There was magnificent beauty in the set of her slim white shoulders and the flowing lines of her white neck, the lift of her head, the level gaze of her wide, clear eyes.

"Get into that room," he commanded, harshly to hide his emotion. "Maybe, when you're eating off the mantelpiece for the next few days, you'll learn a little respect for authority."

"You better not lick me," she answered quietly. "Pap ain't like Bill Pritchard. He says teachers has to whup gals. But my brother

Buck won't stand for it. He says nobody's goin' to tetch a Kirby woman but her own kin or wedded husband. He'll kill you shore, if you whup me!"

With an unpleasant start Brent remembered that Buck Kirby *was* this girl's brother. He had heard plenty about Buck, an implacable feudist, with half a dozen notches on his pistol butt already. Even now he was "hiding out" somewhere in the hills, avoiding the law because of a killing done on the streets of a little mountain town. Buck was bad, and he possessed all the fierce clan-loyalty which is such a dominant characteristic of mountain people. Brent turned cold for an instant, then shrugged his shoulders. He was up to his neck now, and he couldn't turn back.

"I whipped Ann," he said briefly. "In fairness to her, I've got to whip you now, whether I want to or not."

He motioned her into the shed room, and she lifted her head proudly.

"I ain't a-goin' to fight agen you like she did. I know yo're too stout for me. But yo'll be sorry for this."

It was more like a prediction than threat, as she walked regally past him into the shed room. There he turned uncertainly and reached for her, but she drew back, curling her lip.

"Don't tetch me with yo' hands! I'll lay on that bench. You don't have to hold me, nor turn up my dress neither!"

And with a scornful gesture, she slipped out of the torn dress and stood before him, fearless and unashamed, nude but for her slippers and stockings, confined with plain elastic garters above her knees. He caught at the door jamb for support, shocked speechless by the abrupt unveiling of all that dazzling beauty. She was no whimpering child of a schoolgirl, not bodily, at least, but a goddess with the full, curving, flowing lines of luscious ripeness. She stood before him, eyes blazing with resentment at his coercion, but without false modesty or self-consciousness. She made no move to shield her tilted breasts or any other of the intimate contours of her glorious body from his startled gaze.

She shrugged her white shoulders and said: "Well, let's git it over with!" and moved toward the bench, on which it was her evident intention to extend herself, hips upward. Brent caught her wrist. In that instant he knew it was impossible that he should ever chastize this gorgeous creature. The very thought was preposterous.

"Wait!" he begged, incoherently, like a man in a drunken daze. The strap fell to the floor. All he could see before him were those white arching breasts, that blinding, maddening naked body. He ceased to be a thinking, reasoning being. Instincts older than Adam took possession of his body, submerging the conscious entity that was Braxton Brent. "Joan!" It was a tortured gasp as he crushed her in his arms, greedily, hungrily, straining her naked, squirming figure against his. One hand slipped eagerly down over the generous contours of her quivering hips. His fingers kneaded a blissful handful of soft, firm flesh. For an instant she struggled, startled, throwing back her head, while fear grew in her fine eyes. Then as he found her parted red lips with his own, and his questing hands grew more insistent, in her eyes lit the expression that is older than Eve. Her arms ceased straining against him, and went convulsively about him. Catching his hand she drew it down between the white mounds of her quivering breasts, pressing it hard and shivering ecstatically. A low moan of delicious torture burst from her crimson lips, half smothered by his flaming kisses.

He was hardly aware when he lifted her, carried her toward the heap of horse blankets in the corner; Time and conscious thought had ceased for both, drowned in an elemental tide that surged again and again and again, until they lay spent and whimpering in each other's arms.

It might have been hours later when Braxton Brent stumbled into the school room and closed the door. He sank down on a seat and dropped his head in his hands, groaning in a chaotic agony of spirit. Joan was gone; a few moments ago she had gone up the road in the gathering dusk toward her home cabin, three miles away. Her eyes had dwelt on him, enigmatically. Only meaningless, inane words had passed between them. Any words, after that emotional storm, would have seemed banal. He had let her go, without a word as to his inner feelings.

But what were his inner feelings? Just then a savage shame and self-accusation. He had committed the unpardonable offense. A young girl, entrusted to him—his office was one of trust and faith, even if he did have to maintain it by brutal force. And he had betrayed that trust. He groaned and beat his fists together in sheer agony. What should he do? He could never remain, to face the silent accusation of Joan's face, day in and day out—and he knew that he could never trust himself with her. Even as he sat there, cursing himself for a scoundrel, he quivered inside with an eager hunger for the softness and regal suppleness of her fair body. She was no wanton, giving herself to any man who asked; she was—had been—a virgin. He had wronged her enough; he would go—leave that very night. Pride objected that people would think he fled in fear of the Pritchards. Well, damn them, let them think what they would—

He started up as the door burst open. In the last light of the dying west that streamed through the windows, he saw the man who stood there—a wiry, booted youth, with a broad-brimmed hat pulled low over smoldering eyes, mouth grimly set, one hand in the pocket of his ragged coat.

"Where's Joan?" he rasped. "Where's my sister, damn you?"

"She's gone home," Brent answered quietly, though his heart skipped a beat.

"You whupped her!" he spat the accusation. "One of the Richardson kids found me and told me you kept Joan and Ann Pritchard in after school for to whup 'em for fightin'."

"Well, suppose I did?" parried Brent, outwardly calm, though he knew his life hung on the crook of a hair-trigger. "I'm their schoolteacher. It's the custom in these parts to whip girls for disobedience—"

The boy spat an oath.

"Custom, hell! It is if you can make it stick. I'm here to see you don't! You think I give a damn what you do to Ann Pritchard? You can skin her rear ever' day if you want to. But you nor no other damn' Yankee's goin' to lick any of my women-folks and git away with it!"

"I'm no Yankee!" snapped Brent. "I was born and raised in Richmond."

"I don't keer," snarled Kirby. "They was a Yankee afore you, and *he* knowed better'n to lick a Kirby gal!"

"No!" growled Brent. "He licked kids belonging to weak families, but he was afraid to whip Pritchards or Kirbys. Finally he was run out for showing partiality. I'm not going to be run out for that!"

"Who said anything about runnin' you out?" ripped out Kirby, his face convulsed with fury. "I'm a-goin' to—"

His hand came out gripping a cocked pistol. But the hammer caught in the lining of the coat pocket for an instant, and in that instant Brent, nerved by the fear of death, snatched up a poker. As the gun came clear he struck with desperate quickness and force. The gun spun from Kirby's numb fingers, but before Brent could strike again, Buck was on him.

The young mountaineer was as quick as a famished panther, and Brent felt his muscles like steel springs in the instant of contact. The poker was ripped from Brent's fingers as the men went down together. Kirby, as the men went down together, twisted his body to land on top, but Brent, employing a half-forgotten wrestling trick of his college days, used this momentum to complete the circle and bring Kirby under him again. He was only half-successful. They struck the floor sidewise, in a dog fall, but Fate was playing her hand for Brent in that deal. Kirby's head smacked hard against the massive foot of the hand-hewn desk, and for an instant he went limp.

Brent tore free, sprang to the fallen pistol and caught it up, just as Kirby came to his feet like a cat, shaking his head, snarling and crouching for another leap. He checked at the menace of the lifted pistol.

"Get out of here!" ordered Brent. "I'm running Whiskey Run School!"

There was no fear in Buck Kirby's eyes, only a black fury.

"All right," he snarled. "You got the drop! I'm a-goin'. But this don't settle it! I'll git you, as shore as yo're standin' there!"

And with an oath the young feudist turned and strode out the door into the twilight. A moment later the drum of hoofs diminished up the road. Brent wiped his brow with a shaking hand, glanced at the pistol as if it had been a snake, and thrust it quickly into his pocket. Suppose Buck, with the recklessness of his warning, had ignored the levelled gun? Brent could not have shot the brother of the girl he had—with a groan he clutched his head, which had begun to throb. What a mess! But this settled it. He *had* to go now, as a matter of self-preservation. Buck had ridden away, doubtless to re-arm himself, but he would be back. And when he came it would be kill or be killed, and Brent knew it was only by sheer luck that he was alive at the moment. Chance had made him victorious in that brief tussle, but he knew that but for some such lucky break, he was no match for the young mountaineer, whose catlike ferocity and strength would make any wrestling or boxing skill useless. But it wouldn't be fist-and-skull next time. It would be a rifle shot from the laurel, or the blast of a pistol at close range. He was no match for Buck Kirby in any event. Besides, he could not fight the boy. He could not seduce the sister and then kill the brother.

Locking the door of the schoolhouse, Brent hurried to the little cabin which, standing in a grove of trees some distance away, served as his home. There was no other house within a mile of it. The dwelling houses along the Run stood wide apart, as they had stood since the first pioneers wandered through the mountains, in pre-Revolutionary days. Lighting a candle he began to throw his things together. He'd walk across the mountains to the railroad, and—he dropped the shirt he was folding and sat weakly down on his bunk. Suddenly he realized that the thought of going away from Joan Kirby was making him sick. Overwhelming almost as the surge of passion that had swept her into his arms, came the realization that he loved the girl, desperately. Well, all right! He'd marry her, take her back to Richmond. There was a job waiting for him there when he got tired of sowing wild oats and came back to settle down—with a jolt he brought himself up short. Why should he take it for granted that she *would* marry him? She had yielded in the intoxication of the moment. That was all. Probably she despised him now. Besides, he could never pay court to her, not with her brother gunning for his life—oh, what a hellish mess! He was caught in a snare he could not break. If he ran away he was doomed to an agonized lifetime of unsatisfied desire. If he stayed Buck Kirby would kill him.

A voice called outside the door: "Mister Brent! Oh, Mister Brent!"

"Who is it?" he asked suspiciously, drawing Buck's pistol.

"Joe Barlow, Mister Brent. My boy's hurt and we want to bring him in there to the light so's we can see how bad."

"Why, sure!" Brent thrust the gun under the blanket that covered the bunk, stepped to the door, opened it and peered out at the cluster of figures, dim in the darkness. "Bring him right in here—"

Even as he realized that there was something funny about this, the cudgel crashed on his head and the candlelight and stars went out in a brief burst of flame.

Braxton Brent groaned, lifted his aching head and stared haggardly about him. His hands were bound behind his back, and he was lying on his rude bunk. He managed to hitch himself to a sitting posture. The first figure he saw was that of Ann Pritchard, who posed insolently before him, a spiteful smile on her lips and her eyes poisonous with obscene purpose. Four rough figures clustered about him. He recognized old Bill Pritchard, bearded, evil eyed, and his three hulking, brutal-faced sons: Jim, Dick and Joe. Something inside him went cold and hard. He had forgotten the Pritchards.

"You whupped Ann here," accused old Pritchard ominously.

"Well, what if I did?" snarled Brent. "She needed it. Isn't it customary for a teacher to whip a disobedient pupil?"

"Yeah!" snarled Joe, the eldest. "But you didn't lick Joan Kirby! Yo're partial to them damn' Kirbys!"

"Who says I didn't whip Joan?" demanded Brent.

"I know you never!" asserted Ann vindictively. "You run me out of the schoolhouse, but I listened outside. If you'd a-whupped her, I'd a-heard the licks, and her hollerin'. I didn't hear nothin'."

Old Man Pritchard's eyes turned red. Hates half a century old smoldered between him and the Kirbys; the feud was a heap of coals that would burst into murderous flame any time either clan had an advantage over the other.

"You damn' furriner!" he said thickly. "You cussed Kirby-lover! You whupped a Pritchard, but you wouldn't whup a Kirby! I'm a-goin' to fix you—not for whuppin' Ann, because I know she needed it, but because yo're a friend of the Kirbys! Because you whupped a Pritchard and let a Kirby listen to her holler, and then didn't whup the Kirby!"

"I—" began Brent, but Joe struck him heavily across the mouth, knocking his head stunningly back against the wall.

"Shet up! Ann, what you want us to do with this skunk? If we cut his throat and throw him in the creek, nobody'll ever know who done it."

Ann shook her head, her eyes gleaming with age-old feminine cruelty, and she made the answer vindictive women have made all down the ages.

"Killin's too good for him. Cut—"

Brent, who had not flinched at the threat of death, paled at the bestial mutilation she named with the gross candor of a mountain woman. Old Pritchard grinned, and Joe guffawed, slapping his sister's hips with fiendish joviality.

"By God, gal, it takes a woman to think of the best things! Jim, gimme yo' knife. Mine's too dern sharp! We don't want to do this too quick and easy!"

Brent sprang to his feet, but Jim and Dick grabbed him, slammed him back down again. Joe tested the knife edge, leering evilly—then all whirled as the door opened. Joan Kirby entered and closed it behind her. She faced her enemies calmly.

"What you all fixin' to do?" she demanded.

"We're goin' to make a steer out of a bull!" shrilled Ann, in vindictive glee. "And now you can stay and watch! We'll teach him to whup a Pritchard and let a Kirby go!"

"What do you mean?" retorted Joan. "He whupped me harder'n he did you!"

"Yo're lyin'!" shrieked Ann. "I listened outside—you didn't holler once! I listened till I got tired and went home. You didn't yell none!"

Joan curled her lip in scorn.

"I reckon not! A Kirby don't yell, like a Pritchard! I'd be ashamed to squall like you did, when he was fannin' yo' bare behind."

"Well, Joan," suggested Joe, an evil leer on his unshaven lips and lurid lights beginning to glow in his eyes, "suppose you jest show us whar he whupped you, and then we'll believe it!"

"Sure I will!" With a scornful toss of her head at him, she turned about and lifted her dress to her waist. Brent caught his breath at the sight of the cruel red welts that crisscrossed her full white hips and her sleek thighs.

"He used a switch on me!" she said. "I bet that hurt worse'n a strap!"

Letting the garment fall, she turned about and said: "Well, are you all satisfied? Will you go on now and let him alone?"

Old Pritchard chewed his beard in scowling uncertainty. Ann cursed sullenly beneath her breath. Joan crossed quickly to the bunk and began to untie the thongs that bound Brent's wrists. Only then, when, with his head close to her bosom, he heard the quick, wild beating of her heart, did he realize her fear and peril.

Suddenly Joe lurched over and pulled her away from the captive.

"Hold on there, gal! We ain't told you to let him go!"

"What you mean?" demanded Old Man Pritchard, while the younger sons gaped stupidly. "If he licked Joan too, we ain't got nothin' agen him—"

"I warn't thinkin' so much about him, now," Joe grinned. "Look what we got!" Gloatingly, as if showing them something they had not seen, he pushed Joan around before him. "It's too good to pass up!"

Vindictive understanding shone on Bill Pritchard's face as he realized that, for the first time in the history of the feud, a woman of his enemies was in the hands of his clan, helpless and unprotected.

Grinning hatefully, he said: "Come on, Ann; we got to get home!" As she followed the old man out of the cabin Ann looked back spitefully at Joan, made an obscene gesture impossible to misinterpret, and laughed poisonously. The door closed behind them, and the three hulking men turned to stare at their fair captive with burning eyes. They ignored Brent, who was frantically working at the thongs on his wrists. Joan had loosened them before Joe grabbed her; he felt them slipping as he wrenched and strained.

"Reckon I'm first!" grinned Joe. The next instant Joan was fighting him like a wild thing. But the Pritchard was like a gorilla. He ripped the dress from her bosom, grunting beastlike as he seized her ripe breasts with his hairy paws. She screamed with pain and outrage. The others snarled about them like wild beasts. And then the remaining thong snapped between Brent's straining wrists. With a groan of fury he was on his feet before they knew he was free. His right fist hurtling from the hip smashed against Joe's bristly jaw, and the Pritchard went down like a pole-axed ox. Brent grabbed Joan's wrist, snatched the hidden pistol from the blanket on the bunk, as the other brothers recovered from their surprize and came at him.

"Back up, blast you! Reach for the ceiling, or I'll drill you both!"

Four grimy paws shot into the air. White lipped, eyes blazing with cold murder, gun menacing, Brent was a fearsome spectacle.

Joan clung to him, sobbing her rage and shame at the humiliation of Pritchard hands on her body. Her bare white breasts heaved stormily.

"Go, quick!" he panted. "While I hold them here!"

"No! I won't leave you! Buck's comin' after you tonight! One of the Richardson boys told me. I came here to warn you, and I seen them hit you and drag you in here There wasn't no time to git my men-folks—I had to do the best I could."

"But why did you run such a risk for me, girl?" It was a question he had to ask, even in that moment of peril.

"Why, I love you!" There was surprize in her wide eyes. "Didn't you know it, mister? Did you think I'd a-done what I done if I hadn't? I didn't know it till you kissed me, but—look out!" The last a shriek as Jim Pritchard's hand stole toward his belt. It jerked up again as Brent snarled: "Reach, blast your filthy soul! Oh, are you coming around?"

Joe was getting groggily to his feet, gaping stupidly.

"Get their guns, Joan," Brent ordered. "Don't get between them and me."

She circled them, reaching around their waists and pulling the heavy revolvers from their belts. She got Dick's and Jim's, but the nearness of her warm body, as she secured Joe's gun, was too much for the half-crazed brute. With a choking cry he grabbed her, swung her around in front of him, the guns flying from her hands and clattering on the floor. And Joe would have died in the first motion of that insane move, for Brent jerked the trigger, aiming for his head. But no report answered. The trigger hung loose in the crook of his finger. And he realized that the poker blow that had knocked the gun from Buck's hand had broken the mainspring. The pistol was useless.

Joe sensed the truth and bellowed, his hands full of the madly fighting girl: "His gun ain't no good! *Git him!*"

Dick and Jim dived for the guns on the floor, yelping. Dick got one first, and Brent hurled his useless pistol just as he fired. Dick staggered under the impact and his bullet tore through the roof. In an instant Brent had grappled with him, forcing his gun hand up, momentarily expecting to be shot in the back by Jim. But Joan and Joe, whirling in a crazy semicircle as she fought with him, lurched between Jim and the other battling pair. Jim cursed and stepped aside, lifting the gun—and then the door crashed open.

A wiry figure was framed against the blackness, there was a crack and a jet of orange flame. Jim grunted and collapsed, and Buck Kirby's wild yell rang to the roof.

"Turn around, you damn Pritchards, and git it in front!"

Dick tore free from Brent, wheeled, fired and missed and went down, hit in the belly, breast and head. The cabin was full of smoke, a murky fog shot by jets of red flame.

Joe, holding Joan in front of him for a shield, ducked and came up with Jim's gun. But Brent knocked up his arm as he shot, and

Buck, firing carefully across his sister's shoulder, killed Joe Pritchard with a slug that missed Joan's soft white neck by a fraction of an inch.

She reeled free as Joe fell and Brent caught her in his arms.

Buck's flinty voice brought him around. The youth's face was grim. "Mister, I got a bullet left in this gun, and I'm a-goin'—"

Dry lipped, Brent braced himself for the tearing shock of the bullet; it was bitter to have his new-found cup of happiness dashed from his lips—to die just as he learned that Joan loved him. The girl sprang before him shrieking: "Don't, Buck, don't! I love him! Don't kill him!"

"Who said I was a-goin' to?" he demanded. "What you think I kept them Pritchards from killin' him if I wanted him daid? He's got to live to do right by you! Nobody can lick a Kirby woman but her kin or her husband. Before I git back in the hills to my hideout, I'm a-takin' you all to the justice of the peace. He's a-goin' to marry you!"

Brent suddenly went weak all over. He wanted to laugh hysterically. Instead he meekly followed Buck out of the cabin and down the road toward the cabin where his dreams were going to come true, with his arm about Joan's supple waist. She nestled against him, and he felt her wince a little as he caressed the superb swell of a velvety hip. Buck was several paces ahead of him. He bent and whispered in her ear.

"Joan, who made those whip marks you showed them?"

"I did!" she answered calmly. "I sneaked up to the winder before you come to, after they hit you, and heard 'em say they was after you because you whupped Ann and not me. So I went back into the bresh and broke a switch and hit myself a few licks. I knowed they'd want to see the proof!"

Miscellanea

"John Gorman found himself..."

(untitled synopsis)

John Gorman found himself in Samarkand, in possession of a letter which proved the guilt of one Abdullah Khan, a Persian, and supposedly a European in disguise, who was located in Kabul as an engineering expert and who was stirring up raids across the Afghan border. The idea being to embroil the Amir in a struggle with the English so as to weaken the empire's hold on India. It was thought that the Amir, if angered by the British, would turn to Russia for support. A radical party in Moscow was working to this purpose, but were not recognized officially.

Gorman had obtained possession of this letter by bribery. But while he sat in a native cafe, a dancing girl showed him a ring worn in the ear of the gypsy who had stolen the letter for him. Knowing she would not have it if the man were alive, he followed her into an inner room and learned that she too was a spy, the spy he had come there to meet and give the letter to. She told him she would lead them on a wild goose chase, while he took the letter to Herat. A man would meet him at a rest house on the road to Herat and take the letter.

Stepping from the house he was attacked by some strangers but fought them off, and without stopping for his luggage, made his way on foot to the depot, where he caught the train which ran to Merv every three days.

When he arrived at Merv he found he had several hours to wait before the train went on to Kushk. He went to a prison-like hotel, and there encountered a girl who seemed out of place in such a joint. She flirted with him, and in the encounter managed to tip over the candle and plunge the place into darkness. In scurrying for the door she upset the chair on the back of which his coat hung. He wondered if she had stolen his wallet which was in his coat pocket, but found it intact.

He went on by train to Kushk, where he hired a horse and rode to the fort at Kara-Tappeh on the Afghan frontier. There he found that his passport had been stolen, and the commandant told him that a wire had come to hold a man of his description for a squad of soldiers who were coming to arrest him. He knew they were not soldiers, but members of the radical organization in disguise. He knocked out his guard and fled in the night.

He rode southward and at Chodchah Molal robat was held up by the girl he had seen in Merv. But he knocked the pistol out of her hand and raped her. Then he rode on to Herat, knowing they had captured the man who was to have met him at the rest house.

He had adventures on the way, and when he came into Herat was captured by a woman who was in love with Abdullah Khan. But the girl of Merv came to his rescue, and rescued him and the man who was to meet him at the rest house. She was in love with Gorman.

The Girl on the Hell Ship

(earliest known draft)

Outside the sea was calm but a typhoon was raging in the cabin of the *Saucy Lass*. Most of the thunder was supplied by Captain Harrigan—vociferous language charged with brimstone and sulphur, and resounding bangs of a hairy fist on the table, across which he was bellowing damnation and destruction at Raquel O'Shane. Together they were making so much noise they could not hear the sudden shouting that burst forth on deck.

"*Shut up!*" roared Captain Harrigan for the fortieth time. "One more word out of you, you Spanish-Irish gutter-snipe, and I'll lay one on your jaw!"

Being a man of his word and also impulsive, he sought to demonstrate what he meant by a fervent swipe of his mallet-like fist across the table, which Raquel dodged with the agility of much practice.

"Pig!" she screamed with other pet names less printable. "You lay a finger on me and I'll knife you!" This was purely rhetorical; the Captain had laid a finger on her more than once; and not only a finger, but a whole fist on occasion, as well as other implements such as belaying pins and rope's ends.

She too banged the table energetically and cursed whole-souledly in English, Spanish and Tahitian.

I've stood all from I'm going to!" she raged. "You've treated me like a dog all the way from Brisbane! Getting tired of me, eh? You, who took me from a good job in San Francisco—"

"*I* took you away from a good job—" the enormity of the accusation choked the Captain. "Why, you waterfront whelp, you climbed aboard that night and begged me on your dash-blank knees to take you to sea and save you from the cops—after you knifed that Wop in the cabaret—"

She did a war dance in her rage.

"You know what he called me!"

"Well, whatever it was, he was probably right," snarled Captain Harrigan, wetting his whistle with a horse-sized snort from a square-faced bottle. "I'm sick and tired of your tantrums. As soon as we raise a civilized port, I'm going to kick you off onto the docks. And you by damn thankful I'm such a goodhearted swab that I don't sell you to the first Kanaka chief I meet, or set you adrift in an open boat, you blasted hellcat!"

This set her off again, like lighting the fuse of a skyrocket. Metaphorically she hit the roof. For a few moments the cabin was so full of female oratory and profanity that it even drowned out Harrigan's impassioned roars.

"And what in the name of the sulphurous inhabitants of hell are we doing lurching around in these God-forsaken seas?" she concluded. "I think you've guzzled so much rum you've got bats in the attic! Where the hell are we going? I want to know! The crew wants to know! Do you know, you square-headed ape? All you do is sit and study that blasted chart—!"

With feminine impulsiveness she hurled the whiskey bottle with one hand and grabbed the chart with the other, which she brandished in his face.

"Gimme that!" he bellowed, grabbing wildly. She jumped back agilely, sensing that it was precious in his estimation.

"I won't! Not till you promise to quit knocking me around! I'll throw it out the porthole if you come any nearer—"

With a frantic roar Harrigan lunged, upsetting the table with a splintering crash. Raquel had raised a greater hurricane than she had expected. She squeaked in alarm and leaped back, the chart wildly waving in her hand.

"Gimme that!" It was the howl of a lost soul. Harrigan's hair stood straight up and his eyes flamed. Raquel yelped with terror, too confused to make her peace by delivering the article requested. She leaped backward, tripped over a chair and fell headlong backward, with a shriek and an involuntary abandon that tossed her ivory-tinted legs revealingly skyward. But Harrigan had no attention to waste even on this entrancing display. For as she fell, her arm, thrown out wildly, propelled the chart through the air; and as the Devil always controls such things, it sailed straight toward the open porthole, and vanished, to the accompaniment of a howl like a stricken Harrigan.

"Ye gods and sacred devils!" screamed the Captain, tearing his hair. "It's gone to hell!" He rushed madly to the porthole, blindly stepping on Raquel in his haste, and glared out. The chart was in Davy Jones's locket.

He wheeled with a howl that paled all his previous efforts, so much so that outside, the bos'n, who had just reached the cabin door, turned and fled precipitately toward the deck. Raquel was just rising and making some necessary adjustments in her garments—which consisted mainly of a thin dress and a pair of slippers.

"You threw that away on purpose!" he roared. "The only chance I ever had to make a fortune—and you threw it away! I'll fix you—!"

He lunged and she skipped back with a squeal, but not quick. His huge paw closed on a shoulder strap. There was a ripping sound, and Raquel fled toward the door minus the dress which remained in Harrigan's hand. She ducked outside and slammed the door, and in her confusion tried to hold it against him until a big fist crashing through the panels convinced her of her folly and, grazing her dainty nose, filled her eyes with stars and tears. She yipped pitifully, abandoned the door and fled out on deck, a startling figure in slippers and pink panties.

After her came Captain Harrigan, a bellowing, red-eyed, hairy-fisted monstrosity whose only desire was to sweep the deck from stern to poop with that slim, ivory-tinted body.

They burst out on deck, aware of a clamor that they had not been able to hear before, and came full onto a scene that halted the Captain momentarily.

Raquel scampered across the deck, unnoticed by the milling crowd in the waist, and sprang into the ratlines before she turned and stared at the spectacle which had prevented the men even from noticing her.

In a ring of yelling, cheering seamen, the first mate, Buck Richardson, was locked in more or less mortal combat with a stranger whose breeches (his only garment) were dripping seawater. That Buck should be battling a stranger was not strange; what was strange was that Buck, an original bucko mate, the terror of a thousand ports, bully and hazer deluxe, was getting the hell beaten out of him. His opponent was as big as he—a broad-shouldered, hard-waisted, heavy-armed man with black hair plastered to his head, blue eyes that blazed with the joy of battle, and lips that grinned savagely even when they were smeared with blood.

He fought with a gusto that Raquel has never seen equaled. He hammered the luckless mate as a blacksmith on an anvil. He kept plunging in, head down, not blindly like a bull, but with his eyes open—except the one the mate had closed—and his maulers lashed like a couple of sledgehammers. Buck was bleeding like a stuck hog, and from time to time he spat a fragment of a tooth on the deck. He was blowing like a porpoise, and in his one good eye there was a desperate gleam.

"Who in the hell's that?" demanded Harrigan aghast. "Where'd he come from?"

"We sighted him while ago," said the bos'n, spitting carefully to leeward. "He was driftin' along in a open boat, balin' and cussin' somethin' fierce. He came right out of a fog bank. His boat sunk under him before he could get to the ship, and he swum the rest of the way. A shark tried to scoff him on the way, but he kicked its brains out or bit it in the neck, or done somethin' atrocious to it. You know who that is? That's Wild Bill Clanton!"

"The hell it is!" grunted the captain, staring with new interest, as Clanton bashed Richardson accurately on the snout, with appalling results. Harrigan swore wholeheartedly. "They're bleedin' all over my clean deck!"

"Well," said the bos'n, "as soon as he clumb over the rail he seen Richardson and went for him. From the remarks they passed before they was too winded to talk, I gathered Richardson gypped Clanton once in a matter of a girl."

Conversation was taking place at present, rather breathlessly.

"Thought you was smart, huh?" quoth Clanton, smiting Mr. Richardson mightily in the midriff, causing the mate to salaam involuntarily. "Smart trick, hey?" He straightened the mate with an uppercut that sounded like the smack of the boom against a sail. "I don't never forget!" Bam! Mr. Clanton's left mauler sank to the wrist in Mr. Richardson's solar plexus evoking an agonized grunt that was heard by the cook in the galley.

Bam! A mallet-like right to the jaw and Mr. Richardson went reeling halfway across the deck to bring up against the rail with a resounding crack that would have fractured the skull of anybody except a bucko mate.

Clanton started after him, tossing aside a sailor who didn't get out of the way quick enough—then his eyes encountered Raquel, poised in the ratlines. He stopped short, and his mouth open as he glared wildly at the ivory tinted vision posed against the sky, clad only in slippers and pink panties which were a mere wisp of filmy silk that tantalized rather than concealed.

"Hell's fire!" quoth Clanton fervently—and at this instant Mr. Richardson, a bloody ruin, lurched away from the rail with a belaying pin in his hand. *Bam!* It crashed on Clanton's head, and the owner of the head measured his length on the deck. Mr. Richardson croaked gratefully and bestowed himself lovingly on the bosom of his victim, naively intent on beating his brains out with the trusty belaying pin. But Clanton anticipated his design by drawing up his legs after the manner of a panther fighting from a prone position, and receiving the hurtling form of the mate on his feet and knees, he catapulted Richardson over his head.

The mate smote the deck headfirst and resoundingly, and this time the impact was too much even for his adamantine skull. Clanton, on the other hand, bounding to his feet, observed some faint signs of life still in his foe, and proceeded to correct this oversight by leaping enthusiastically and with both feet on the mate's torso.

This procedure suited his simple nature so that he repeated it with gusto, and seemed content to keep it up indefinitely, had not the Captain yelled: "Grab him! He's killin' the mate!"

As no spectacle could have pleased the crew better than the violent demise of the aforesaid officer, they obeyed half-heartedly; a lack of enthusiasm not shared by Clanton. The man seemed overflowing with energy and gusto. After a short but violent interlude which much resembled a miniature tornado, the men fell back, decorated freely with black eyes, bloody noses and broken teeth, and told the Captain wrathfully that if he wanted that so-and-so Bengal tiger put in irons, to do it himself and damned to him for a slave-driving lubber.

"Who's captain of this mud scow?" roared Clanton.

"I am!" yelled Harrigan, advancing; the two men glared at each other with mutual interest and dislike.

"You're aboard my ship!" bellowed Harrigan. "And you'll work for your grub, damn you!"

"All right," growled Clanton, spitting blood on the deck. "Who's that?" He pointed to the alluring vision still clinging to the ratlines.

Harrigan remembered and roared like a bull.

"Drag her down!" he yelled. "Bring her here and tie her to the mast! Bring me a rope! I'll take the hide off her!"

"You won't!" shrieked Raquel. "Don't touch me! I'll jump into the sea and drown myself."

She had about as much intention of carrying out her threat as she did of flying to be moon, but she made it sound real. Clanton cleared the space between them with a tigerish bound, caught her wrist and whipped her down on the deck before she knew what was happening.

"Oh!" she gasped, and stared at him with dilated eyes. He was bronzed by the suns of the Seven Seas, and his torso was ridged with clean hard cords of muscles. In his one good eye unconcealed admiration blazed as his gaze devoured her from her trim ankles to the luscious curves of her waist, and then, reluctantly, up to the foamy burnished mass of her hair.

"Good work, Clanton!" roared Harrigan, striding forward, dangling a rope's end. He announced, in a voice like a bull sea lion, that he intended to remove the skin from a certain intimate portion of the slut's anatomy, and he designated the portion candidly and without hesitation. Raquel wailed despairfully, unable to release her wrist from her captor's grasp. But Harrigan, reaching vengefully for her, had his hand knocked violently aside, and he paused and goggled amazedly at Clanton.

"Hands off!" roared Clanton. "What are you up to? Haven't you any idea how a lady ought to be treated?"

"Lady!" yelled Harrigan. "If she's a lady I'm the king of Singapore! Do you know what she just did? Threw away my chart! The only dash-blank chart in the world that told me how to find the island of Aragoa!"

"Never heard of it," said Clanton coldly.

Harrigan did a war dance on the deck.

"Ambergris!" he howled. "A barrel full of it! A black birder went on the beach back in the '90's, and only one man got ashore. They had a barrel of ambergris and it washed ashore. He stood the solitude as long as he could and then took to sea in the ship's boat he'd patched up. He salvaged the chart and marked the island. I picked him up on my last voyage. He was raving. He told me about it; he gimme the chart, and then one night he got to raving deliriously and fell overboard—"

Somebody laughed among the group of sailors and Harrigan glared murderously in that direction.

"That island ain't on no other chart or map. The Kanakas call it Aragoa. And now that daughter of Jezebel has fed the chart to the sharks, and—"

"Why, hell," quoth Clanton. "Is that what all the ruckus is about? Why, I can take you straight to Aragoa and I don't need any chart."

"You can?" yelped Harrigan. "Then for the love of—"

"Wait a minute!" commanded Clanton. "You don't think I'm shipping' on as a forecastle hand, do you? Richardson's not in any shape to do his work. I'll sail you to Aragoa on one condition—I'm first mate!"

"All right!" snarled Harrigan.

"And no kickin' the girl for losin' the chart," warned Clanton.

"All right." This reminded Harrigan of her unclad condition and he roared: "Get into the cabin and get some clothes on, you shameless hussy!"

She scurried for the cabin, squeaking as Harrigan's toe caught her in the seat of her brief panties as an inducement for haste.

Richardson was lifted and borne to his cabin, still senseless, and presently calm of a sort settled on the *Saucy Lass.*

Clanton, having descended on the galley and bullied the morose Chinese cook (who made attempts with a meat cleaver and as a result was kicked into his own stove) into setting him out a feed that would have taxed the capacity of a horse, took the wheel.

The stars of the South Seas above him, the slap of the waves against the ship's keel beneath him, his shoulders bulked against the stars as he held her to her course. He might have posed there for the image of an intrepid adventurer—until a slender figure came gliding to him across the deck.

"Harrigan know you're out here?" he demanded.

"He's asleep," she answered, her dark eyes sad and pensive in the starlight; she was careful to stand so they shone in the starlight. "He sleeps like a pig. He *is* a pig."

"Poor kid," he said compassionately, protectingly passing his arm about her waist—the paternal effect of which was marred somewhat by his stroking of the sloping swell of a ripe hip. She sighed and leaned against him.

"What did the Old Man say the name of that island was?" he demanded presently.

"Aragoa." She jerked her head back suddenly and looked at him startled. "I thought you knew about it!"

"Knew Hell! I never heard of it. I told him that just to save you from a licking."

"Oh!" She stood aghast. "But you can't fool Harrigan long! And then he'll skin us both!"

"It's a jamb that requires deep thought," he agreed. "Sneak down and steal me a few bottles of the Old Man's booze."

She cast him an uncertain glance, but moved away, a lissome shadow in the starlight, and presently returned with an armful of bottles which caused Clanton's eyes to glisten. He lashed the wheel, setting her on the course of a star on the horizon, and sat down, leaning against the rail, and drew her down on his lap. He knocked the neck off a bottle, took a deep drink and passed it to her.

By the time he had tossed an empty overboard, he was saying: "To hell with the Old Man! If he gets fresh with me I'll kick his teeth down his gullet."

A few moments later he said: "I don't believe there ever was an island of Aragoa, anyway!"

"Who cares?" she breathed, leaning supply back and lifting her arms up and back to encircle his brawny neck. He ran an appreciative hand over her swelling breasts and slipped a hand under her skirt . . . .

Grey dawn rising over the sea—and a sudden shock ran through the *Saucy Lass*—a thundering crash of falling utensils and men hurled from bunks! The captain came storming up on deck without stopping for his clothes.

"What the hell?" he roared, and stared aghast.

"We're aground!" he screamed. "What's the meaning of this?"

Clanton rose, yawned, and stared appreciatively at the island that stretched away under the port bow.

"There's your island," he said, with a grand gesture.

"But did you have to run her ashore?" screamed Harrigan.

"That could have happened to anybody," asserted Clanton, and added disapprovingly: "Where's your pants?"

But the captain had seen something else—he howled like a stricken soul at the sight of the broken bottles, and Raquel rising uncertainly from the deck. She blinked and rubbed her eyes with a childish gesture, and made a face, tasting all the square-face she had guzzled the night before.

"You stole my liquor!" bleated Harrigan. "You had my girl with you all night! You've run my ship aground, and by God, I'm goin' to kill you, ambergris or no ambergris!"

He reached for his gun, only to discover that he had neither gun nor belt. Bellowing he snatched a belaying pin from the rail and made at Clanton who replied in kind. Harrigan went sprawling into the scuppers, and Clanton grabbed Raquel by the neck and crotch, tossed her overboard and leaped after her.

Harrigan dived into the cabin and emerged with a triumphant howl and a Winchester, with which latter he employed to throw hot lead after the fugitives, just vanishing among the trees that fringed the narrow beach.

In the shelter of these trees the fugitives paused, dripping and Clanton peered cautiously back at the schooner.

"Harrigan couldn't shoot for beans," he chortled. "He missed us at least a foot every time. The old so-and-so! He's doing a hootch-kootch dance on the poop deck!"

Clanton gave vent to his mirth in guffaws, and Raquel glared at him. No woman could ever see any humor in a situation which found her in a dripping dress that clung to her skin and strands of wet hair plastered over her face. She threw these back and demanded acidly: "Just what the hell is there so funny about this? We're marooned on a desert island and you laugh! I guess if one of those bullets had hit me in the rump as we ran you'd bust yourself laughing!"

"Probably," he agreed. "Well, hell, we're here, ain't we? Look: you sit down here and watch 'em, while I go inland and look around for fruit and fresh water. They're not stuck so bad; they'll get into the boats and pull her off that sand bar."

"All right." She shucked her dress without more ado and hung it up to dry and lay down on her tummy on the soft dry sand while she peered through the bushes at the ship. Clanton strode inland, walking lightly and softly for so big a man.

She watched the men piling into boats, where presently they were engaged in working the schooner loose by main strength and profanity. She watched awhile, then presently got impatient. Clanton had not returned and she was hungry and thirsty—especially thirsty.

She rose, donned her dress, now dry, and started inland. The trees were denser than she had thought, and she soon lost sight of the beach after she had gone a few yards. Presently she had to climb over a fallen log, and, leaping down on the other side, a brambly bush caught her skirt. She swore and twisted about, trying to extricate herself, for the bramble was holding the skirt twisted up high about her ivory thighs, and she could neither reach the limb nor wrench free.

As she wriggled and cursed, a light step sounded behind her, and without looking around she commanded: "Bill, pull me loose!"

Obligingly a firm masculine hand took hold of her skirt and freed it from the branch, this action entailing the lifting of it several inches. But her rescuer did not then lower the garment; indeed Raquel felt him pull it up even higher—much higher!

"Quit clowning, will you," she requested, turning her head to give him a disapproving look—and then she opened her lovely mouth to its widest extent and emitted a yell that startled the birds in the trees. The man who had hold of her dress surveying the prospect with blissful ecstasy was not Bill; he was a big Kanaka, clad tastefully in a breech clout! Raquel made a convulsive effort to go elsewhere, but a brawny brown arm encircled her supple waist and swung her off the ground. Thereafter for a few seconds the peaceful glade was the scene of a brief hurricane of violent action, punctuated by lusty and energetic screams that a big hand clapped over a red-lipped mouth could not altogether stifle.

Clanton heard these shrieks as he glided like a big brown tiger through the trees. He could not mistake their quality and they acted on him like an electric current. In an instant he was in full career through the trees, leaving a blue streak of profanity in his wake. He burst into the glade whence the howls came, and came full onto a scene striking in its primitive simplicity.

Raquel was defending her virtue with as much vigor as nations defend mythical possessions. Her dress had been torn off and her writhing white body and squirming ivory limbs contrasted vividly with the dark brown skin of her captor. He wasn't all brown; he was red in spots, for she had bitten him with fervency and abandon. So much so that an element of irritation entered into his ardour, and, momentarily abandoning his efforts to make her assume a position on her back, he clenched an enormous fist and prepared to retaliate by means of a clout that would assuredly have wafted her into dreamland—and maybe into Kingdom Come.

It was at this moment that Clanton arrived on the scene, and his unshod foot, describing a whistling arc, caught the Kanaka under the haunches and catapulted him in a complete somersault clear over his captive, who scurried to her protector on her all fours.

"Didn't I tell you to stay on the beach?" *Whap!* In his irritation Clanton emphasized his remarks with a resounding, open-handed slap on her pink posterior which her position rendered peculiarly vulnerable. Raquel's shriek was drowned in a roar that told Clanton he had made a mistake in wasting time that way. The Kanaka had regained his feet and was bounding toward him, swinging a knotty-headed war club he had leaned against a tree when he stole up on Raquel. Clanton faced him barehanded; with a yell of triumph the Kanaka lunged, flailing a stroke that would have spattered Clanton's brains all over the glade if it had landed. But it didn't land. It flailed empty air as Clanton left his feet in a headlong dive that carried him under the swipe and crashed his shoulders against the Kanaka's legs. Bam! They hit the earth together and the club flew out of the native's hand, as his back smashed against the earth with an impact that jolted a grunt out of him.

The next instant they were rolling all over the glade in a desperate dogfight. Clanton was too old a hand at rough-and-tumble to try to strangle the bull-necked Kanaka. He let the native grab his own throat in both huge hands, and then, while the Kanaka was trying to drive his thumbs and fingers through the corded muscles that defended the white man's jugular and windpipe, Clanton employed his own hand in every tearing, breaking bending trick he could think of. While with one hand he groped for the Kanaka's eyes, he clenched the other into a fist and hammered away at the brown man's face, while bringing up first one knee and then the other to groin and belly, when he could get a brief purchase in the midst of the frantic revolutions they were performing from one side of the glade to the other. Raquel had secured the club and was dancing about, trying to get a chance to brain the Kanaka, and it was this, knowing the accuracy of women's aim as he did, that drove Clanton into a desperate effort. His eyes were beginning to start out of their sockets as the Kanaka's fingers ground in in spite of the thick neck muscles; but it was the risk of being brained by a well-meant swing of that club which horrified Clanton.

His knee at last found its mark, and the man gasped and doubled convulsively, nose squirting blood and and teeth smashed in already. Clanton broke away, rose and kicked the groaning Kanaka heavily in the belly. The Kanaka made a surprizing come back, with a maddened yell, grabbed the foot and twisted it savagely. Clanton whirled to save himself a broken leg, and fell to his all-fours on the sand. At the same moment Raquel swung with the club that was too heavy for her. She missed as the Kanaka ducked and sprawled on her belly in the sand. Both men gained their feet at the same time, but the Kanaka reached for the club. As he bent over Clanton swung his right overhand like a hammer, and with about the same effect. It smashed behind the Kanaka's ear with an impact like a caulking mallet striking a ship's hull. The Kanaka stretched out in the sand beside Raquel who rolled away in a panic. But he didn't twitch after he hit the ground.

Clanton grabbed the club. Raquel scrambled up and grabbed Clanton, sobbing hysterically. Clanton shook her loose with lurid comments.

"This is no time for a pettin' party! That illegitimate isn't alone. There's a whole village of 'em over towards the other side of the island. I saw it from the trees! I was sneakin' back here to tell you—"

"Look out Bill!" she screamed. He wheeled to meet the rush of three more Kanakas from the trees. They had knives and fan-shaped tomahawks. He met the first with a swing that cracked the native's thick skull like an eggshell; ducked the swipe of a tomahawk and jabbed the end of the club into the man's belly with one hand, while he grabbed a knife arm of the third with the other. The man with the belly grunted and went to his knees, and the man with the knife staggered back with a broken arm. Lifting the bludgeon and drawing a deep breath, Clanton swing for the other man's head like a batter clouting a homerun. It caved in like a pumpkin. The man with broken arm leaped in, stabbing with his left hand, and drawing blood from Clanton's breast muscles. The next moment he was lying on the ground, his neck broken by a left uppercut that white man lifted from his knee.

"Now I know whey they call you Wild Bill!" panted Raquel.

"Come on!" He grabbed her wrist and fled toward the beach with her, panting as he ran: "Thick brush; men cussin' loud onboard the ship. They wouldn't hear the yells."

They burst onto the beach, and saw that the men had worked the *Saucy Lass* loose from the sand bar.

"Ship ahoy!" yelled Clanton from behind a tree. "Harrigan! This is the island, after all! I've found the ambergris!"

Harrigan was lifting a rifle, but now he paused.

"What's that?"

"Sure! I'll show it to you if you'll agree to take us aboard!"

"You fool!" hissed Raquel, kicking his shins. "He'll promise anything and then shoot us!"

"Shut up!" snarled Clanton. Lifting his voice he yelled: "How about it? Come ashore if you don't believe me! Bring Richardson!"

For a bandaged and battered figure was to be seen on deck.

"Alright!" yelled Harrigan. "We're coming!"

They came, in a boat, with half a dozen men.

"Leave them and the girl here," said Clanton. I'll show you where it is."

They marched him ahead of them through the jungle for a short space. Climbing over a log, he slipped and fell.

"Hell! I've sprained my ankle! You'll have to rig up a stretcher and carry me!"

"Carry you, hell!" snarled Harrigan. "Tell us where the loot is and we'll go and find it ourselves."

"Go straight on about three hundred yards," groaned Clanton, heroically suppressing the pain. "Then turn to the left and go till you sight a big mangrove tree. Go straight on past that, and you've find it."

"And if we haven't," said Harrigan, "we're going to shoot you when we get back."

"And we're goin' to shoot you whether we find it or not!" snarled Richardson, with his one good eye resting balefully on his enemy. "How you like *that*, huh?"

Clanton registered despair, and both men chortled brutally as they moved on. They moved out of sight, and Clanton waited a minute, five, ten—he sprang up and sprinted for the beach.

He burst on the men on the beach so suddenly the bos'n nearly shot him.

"Row for the ship, quick!" he yelled. "Cannibals! They've got Harrigan and Richardson surrounded! Listen!"

Back in the jungle rose a sudden clamor of shots and blood-freezing yells. It was enough. In another instant the boat was scudding toward the schooner, and the *Saucy Lass* was making for the open sea before the Kanakas came dancing out of the jungle; one waved a Winchester rifle, another a pistol.

"Jump to it!" ordered Clanton. "I'm cap'n here now! Harrigan and I matched pennies, his ship against my share of the ambergris. I own it! We're headin' for the Solomons to pick up a cargo." He turned to Raquel and pinched her plump hip appreciatively. "As for you," quoth he, "I want to see you down in the captain's cabin, right away!"

Ship in Mutiny

(untitled synopsis)

Setting: a trading schooner, and an island in the South Seas. Characters: Wild Bill Clanton, captain and owner; Raquel O'Shane, his girl; Big Joe Croghan, forecastle hand; King Tanoa, a cynical and European-educated native potentate, whose island, being off the regular path of ships, had kept its independence; native girls. Accomplishment: escape from an English man-o'-war with a hoard of pearls.

Obstacle: mutiny.

Climax: big fight and seizing of the ship again by Raquel and Clanton.

The men, led by Croghan, mutinied off the island of Muweia, none of them being able to navigate. They intended anchoring in the bay and waiting until the British ship-of-war, which they had temporarily shaken off, came off and took them off. They intended to swear they had been pressed into service, and to display Clanton's body as token of their honesty. Mutiny against a blarsted pirate would be accounted honesty and earn them a pardon. They intended to do away with the girl, and keep the pearls for themselves. They would give a few to the English captain to persuade him of their honesty. The English ship was "The Royal Venture" and her captain hated Clanton of old.

But in the brawl Raquel and Clanton escaped ashore, and the wind changed and blew the "Lazy Lass" offshore. A sudden squall drove ashore the boat in which Clanton and Raquel escaped, and they were separated. Raquel was seized by the king, who laughed at her when she tried to pose as a goddess out of the sea. Clanton appeared and broke his neck. Clanton then released a number of political prisoners who had opposed Tanoa's rule. Croghan and his men were lured ashore by dancing girls.

Clanton manned his ship with willing Kanakas.

The men, led by Big Joe Croghan, mutinied and killed the mate; Raquel jumped overboard to escape a Spaniard who tried to seize her for Big Joe. Clanton was hurled overboard and they both got ashore on an island, but some distance apart. Big Joe attacked the Spaniard for letting the girl get away, was fatally stabbed by him, and brained him with a handspike as he fell. Big Joe was the only man who could navigate.

Raquel got ashore and was confronted by the king of the island, to whom she pretended to be a white goddess come out of the ocean. He laughed at her, grabbed her by the ear and the seat of her step-ins, and frog-marched her into his hut. He was Tanoa, a Kanaka who had been educated in Europe, and had recently usurped the rule of Queen Leilu. He was preparing to rape her when Clanton appeared, having heard her shriek and stolen into the village. He gave Tanoa a terrible beating, but was captured by the Kanaka warriors and thrown into a hut to await execution. Raquel escaped.

To Clanton came Leilu, secretly, hating Tanoa, and set him free, telling him the ship had anchored on the other side of the island. Clanton determined to go there, kill Big Joe, and, as the only man able to navigate, force the mutineers to submit to him. They ran until Leilu was out of breath, and while they rested, she allowed Clanton to have intercourse with her. Just as they were through, they heard a rifle shot. Tanoa, while they lingered, had discovered and attacked the ship. They stole forward and met Raquel, who had talked with one of the mutineers and learned that Big Joe had been killed, and they had helplessly worked the ship in to anchorage. They stole forward and hiding on a tree-fringed bluff, looked down on the beach where the Kanakas were attacking. Leilu told Clanton that if he killed Tanoa, she could regain control of the tribe. Raquel showed herself to the chief and lured him up on the bluff alone, and Clanton broke his neck and hurled him down the cliff. The tribe then submitted to Leilu and the mutineers submitted to Clanton who, with Raquel, sailed away in the ship.

Ship in Mutiny

(earliest known draft)

The mutiny the *Lazy Lass* began with a bang—or rather with the thud of a handspike, wielded by Big Joe Croghan, the ringleader, on the mate's unsuspecting head. The mate never knew what hit him; the mutineers, who had crept stealthily out of the forecastle during the fourth watch, were just lifting the limp body over the rail when the head of Raquel O'Shane appeared above the companionway. Instantly her lovely eyes flared and she gave tongue piercingly: "Bill! Bill! They've killed the mate!"

"Blast that loud-mouthed wench!" snorted Big Joe. "Grab her!"

A scar-faced Spaniard was nearest the companionway. His move was a trifle quicker than hers, as she tried to retreat. He grabbed her by her curly blue-black hair and hauled her forth, shrieking and kicking.

"Lock her up in the galley," commanded Big Joe. "I got something to say to her before she goes over the side! Look out! Here comes the cap'n!"

It was a beautiful moonlit night, lovely as only a South Sea night can be. Less than a mile abeam shone the narrow beach of an island, like molten silver. The *Lazy Lass* was a distinct blot in the calm serenity of the scene. A man had just died on its deck; a girl was being dragged galley-ward by her hair, and her language was lurid. While a maddened roar marked the coming of the ship's captain up the companionway. Wild Bill Clanton had heard Raquel's scream; only a dead man could have failed to hear it.

At the fearsome voice the mutineers wavered, and even the man at the wheel showed a disposition to desert and jump overboard, but Big Joe's bellow steadied them. "Stand to it, you swabs! Jack, stand alongside with your belayin' pin and bash him when his head shows! Rest of you standby!"

And then Wild Bill Clanton, the iron-fisted terror of the seas, came gustily up the companionway. Jack made a noble attempt with his belaying pin, but unfortunately Clanton had heard the command, and was ready for just such an action. He ducked the swipe, and Jack, missing, fell full into an uppercut that had behind it the lifting drive of Wild Bill's lunge up the stair. The snap of shattering bone rose plainly above the shrieks of Raquel, and before the horrified mutineers could gather their wits, the ravening captain was among them. Three of them were down with their features permanently altered before they recovered from their surprize, and Big Joe Croghan, having missed a swipe with his trusty handspike, was being beaten to death against the rail before his impassioned howls for aid brought his comrades desperately to the rescue.

Meanwhile the Spaniard was finding his task of escorting Miss O'Shane to the galley no easy one. His captive, assuming a position on her all-fours clutched at every stanchion, hatch-combing and stay within reach, and some of the things she called him, in three different languages, got under even his tough skin. So much so that he took advantage of her position to employ his toe with force and accuracy, and the resultant impact brought a louder scream from her lips. But it was about like kicking a wildcat, for with a desperate wrench she grabbed his leg and began masticating his bare ankle with her beautiful teeth. He howled with agony and tore free, releasing her hair as he did so. She sprang up, looked about her like a wild thing, raking back a strand of her black hair, and staring wildly at the knot of battling figures in the waist.

She looked about for some weapon to go to her sweetheart's aid, but then shrieked and fled toward the stern as the Spaniard, in a killing mood now, came for her with his knife drawn and his bared teeth gleaming in the moonlight. He was close on her heels along the deck, up the ladder to the forecastle head—as despairingly she leaped to the rail, his hand closed on the shoulder of her light dress. The knife went up, but with a wrench that left the empty dress in his hand, she tore clear and left the rail in a long, dive. The Spaniard, glaring over, did not see her come up again.

But in the waist the battle rage, and the combined strength of the crew was none too much to subdue the raging Clanton. With his back against the rail he belabored them right and left, until a blindly thrown belaying pin glanced from his skull, and as pitched backward, slumped over the rail and fell silently to the water beneath.

Croghan spat out some teeth and said, "Well, that's that. Throw some water over them men he knocked out. Where's the girl?"

The Spaniard approached uneasily. "She jumped overboard."

"Oh she did, hey?" quoth Croghan ominously. "I thought I said lock her in the galley?"

And forthwith he took his trusty handspike and bent it over the Spaniard's head.

"Throw him over with the rest," said Croghan. "You, Spike, stay at the wheel. I'm going below and see can I find them pearls. Rest of you stay on deck."

A hearty laugh greeted this suggestion, and he glared.

"All right, come with me then, if you ain't got enough decency to trust a mate. Are you all straight about the story we tells? Well, I'll go over it again. You all know how we been run out of our course by that British warship, which we shook off three days ago. Well, being as we all wants a share of the pearls Clanton has in his cabin or somewhere, we mutinies off this island, where we can run to and anchor, as none of us can't navigate. We waits here till the warship heaves in sight. Which it will, mates, never fear! Then we claims we been pressed by Clanton, the bloody pirate, but has mutinied—and what's a crime for honest sailors is a virtue agen a pirate like Clanton—and we gives him some of the pearls, the little ones, and says we want to go to Sydney and stand trial. I know that ship—she's 'The Royal Venture' and the cap'n's old Richard Harston which hates Clanton like pizen—like pizen, mates! We'll all get a free pardon, and the pearls clear! And now keep a sharp watch for a likely place to anchor."

When Raquel dived, she hit the water with a smack that all but knocked the wind out of her; she sank deep, intending to come up and grasp some rope or chain near the stern as the ship went past.

But when she came up, the ship was out of her reach. The battle was still raging on the deck. She saw the futility of swimming after it, and turning, out for the distant beach. Her scanty brassiere and brief silk panties were no hindrance; she was a good swimmer but it was a long stretch. She knew it would be touch and go if she reached the beach before she became exhausted. Nor would she, had it not been for a reef-like rock jutting up out of the water several hundred yards from the beach. She reached it just as the last ounce of her strength went out of her, dragged her quivering body up on a ledge-like projection, and lay there utterly spent. Helplessly she saw the ship drift on and vanish from sight around a point of land getting close in all the time.

Dawn was a white streak in the east when she felt recuperated enough to try for the shore again. She slid into the water, shivering at the thought of sharks, and presently felt the firm sand beneath her feet. A moment later she emerged, a dripping pink and white image of supple loveliness, onto the beach—and stopped short, confronted by a trio of astounded Kanakas, clad only in loincloths. Apparently they had not seen the ship, and this apparition startled them. She grabbed at a desperate chance. Summoning her sketchy command of the dialect, she struck a lofty pose, and said: "I am a white goddess come out of the sea! Kneel and do me reverence!"

They seemed to understand her. They did not kneel, but they spoke among themselves, too fast and excited for her to understand, and then presently they formed around her, at a respectful distance, and indicated that she should accompany them. She didn't know whether her escort formed a guard of honor, or of captivity, but she believed she was putting it over. Otherwise the command to march would have been emphasized by the prod of a spear in the soft flesh of her hips, molded by the wet fabric of her panties.

So she marched, trying to carry herself with a regal hauteur, and succeeding fairly well, until they, after following a winding path from the beach, burst into a clearing where stood a rather large village. The Kanakas must have been feasting the night before, with the usual drunkenness and sexual sports. Few were stirring, and those were heavy eyed and sluggish. But the sight of a white woman roused them, and they came pouring from their huts.

Out of a big hut near the edge of the clearing came a splendid specimen of Polynesian manhood, a brown-skinned giant, with a keenly intelligent, though rather subtly cruel face.

"Tanoa," quoth one of the warriors. "King Tanoa, him!"

Raquel favored him with a haughty stare, and began to intone: "I am the daughter of the goddess, returned from far to my own land to receive the homage of my people—*ow!*"

It was an outraged shriek of surprize and pain. Tanoa had slapped her resoundingly across the tight-fitting seat of her wet panties!

"The homage due you, oh daughter of the gods!" said he cynically, and in perfect English. "A good act, sister, and it might have worked if I had not been educated in Europe! Come in, goddess!"

And forthwith he seized her by one pink ear and the seat of her step-ins and frog-marched her into his hut. Her ears burned with shame at the jeers of the crowd, and that wasn't the only place she burned. That spank had been administered with a hearty goodwill.

In the hut she cringed and begged for mercy; before his cruel cynicism her audacious pretense had been stripped away. He laughed at her, jeered at her, and flicked her brassiere from her. With a beastly light in his eyes he advanced and she shrieked, recognizing his next move. She tried to duck beneath his arm, but he was too quick. He grabbed her—a salacious laugh, a despairing scream, the wild, futile thrashing of white legs—and he held up her pink panties in gloating triumph, while Raquel fled sobbing to the far corner of the hut, striving in vain to conceal her nudity in the instinctive feminine manner. Tanoa laughed at her.

"You'd have to have three hands for that, sweetheart. But enough of frivolities. Now for the real sport!"

The mockery on his brown face gave way to a fiercer, more intent expression as he advanced. She had no strength to run or fight. Her legs gave way and she sank to her knees, whimpering: "No, no!"

With studied cruelty he caught her chin and forced her to look up into his implacable face, gloating over the terror in her tear-wet eyes. He caught her in his arms, and she screamed at his touch, as his hands ruthlessly sought out every intimate detail of her writhing figure, crushing her attempts at defense. He lifted her, carried her toward a bed on the opposite side. Then a step behind caused him to whirl.

Clanton stood in the backdoorway.

"Bill!" sobbed Raquel. Tanoa, recognizing his deadly danger, released her and she ran to Clanton, weeping hysterically.

"I thought they'd killed you!"

He disengaged her clinging arms from his neck and spoke quickly: "I swam ashore. Didn't know you'd made it till I heard the screams comin' from this hut. Out the door, quick!"

She snatched some sort of a garment from the wall—a man's shirt it was—and scurried. And Clanton went at Tanoa like a panther.

The Kanaka was bigger than Clanton, taller and heavier. And he knew the Kanaka way of fighting, which is ruthless and primitive; also he had learned something about boxing in Oxford. But he found his arts helpless before the fury of the white man. To the Anglo-Saxon alone is given the gift of battling mightily with his bare hands, and this Tanoa quickly learned. He was battered and beaten from side to side, from wall to wall. But for his insane fury Clanton might have knocked him down and escaped, but the white man was in the grip of one of those berserk rages which only white men have.

Intent on smashing his enemy to a bloody pulp, he was scarcely aware when the hut was flooded with warriors, until a war club, glancing from his head, told him he was trapped. He turned on his enemies like a cornered tiger, and the floor was littered knee-deep with writhing figures before a hard-swinging club beat him to his knees, where they cast a rope about his arms and bound him fast.

"Throw him in a hut!" panted Tanoa, who was ghastly to behold. "We will find the girl and make her watch while I skin him alive! I will make of his hide a garment and force her to wear it always about her loins to remind her how her lover died!"

They scattered through the jungle. Presently, to the hut in which Clanton lay bloody and bruised, a woman stole, a native woman, with a golden skin and dark eyes and luscious breasts and hips and thighs.

"I am Leilu," she whispered. "I was queen until Tanoa returned and usurped my power. Listen, white man, I will aid you if you will aid me! I will set you free and you can go get the other white men to aid you!"

"What other white men?"

"Those in the ship anchored on the other side of the island!"

"What? They anchored? By Judas, if I can get to them and bump Croghan off, they'll have to take me on. They can't navigate."

She cut his bonds and they ran for the opposite side of the island. They were nearly across when she panted and sank down, exhausted. He caught her in his arms as she fell and eased her to the grass. They lay there a moment, her head on his shoulder, her firm young body melting against his. As if by chance one hand cupped a velvety breast, the other caressed a dimpled knee, slid up the warm, smooth length of thigh, under the scanty skirt, until to came to rest. . . . She sighed gustily, wriggled and flung back her head against his shoulder to look up at him with liquid dark eyes.

The crack of a shot off to the north roused them.

"They have found the ship!" cried Leilu, starting up. "They are attacking!"

Clanton swore as he leaped up and ran for the north side of the island. That was one time when a idle dalliance might cost him his life. Leilu followed, contrite but not regretful. Even as she ran she relived in blissful memory the more excruciatingly sweet moments of the past half hour.

An instant later they met Raquel, whose lovely eyes dilated with anger at the sight of Leilu, and the dreamy reminiscence in

Leilu's eyes; the queen understood and smiled cryptically, a smile Raquel understood perfectly. "They're attacking the ship, Bill," she said hurriedly. "I sighted it, when you were captured, and met one of the men who was hunting fresh water ashore. He said Croghan was dead and they had to anchor here because none of them could navigate. He hurried back to the ship to get some men to rescue you, but I didn't trust them and hid on the shore. And then the Kanakas came and started fighting."

They crept forward and on the edge of a tree-fringed bluff, looked down on the beach below. The ship was anchored a short distance out in the little natural bay, and the Kanakas were swarming in the water and on the beach, firing with old-fashioned muskets and hurling spears. Already a few lay littered at the edge of the water, as the crew fired with their rifles.

"There's Tanoa," said Leilu. "If you could kill him, I could regain control of my tribe."

They saw him, standing well back out of range, near the foot of the cliff, directing the attack. Raquel turned up her small nose scornfully at Leilu, and picking up a pebble, threw it so it rattled down close to Tanoa. He turned and saw her standing there, apparently in an attitude of panic because of her discovery. She yelped and ducked behind the bushes, and he promptly abandoned the fray and came swarming up the cliffs. He plunged into the bushes—and stopped short at the sight of Clanton. They came together like plunging bulls, grappled and went over the cliff, and when they ceased that rolling tumble, Tanoa lay still beneath Clanton with a broken neck.

The Kanakas wheeled and started toward the victor, who rose dazedly, but up on the cliff Leilu raised an imperious hand.

"Stop! Tanoa, the usurper, is slain! I am your queen!"

Without a leader there was nothing to do but submit.

Clanton yelled at the mutineers: "You fools, will you let me come aboard, or am I goin' to have to lead these devils over the rail? They won't leave one of you alive!"

They submitted and Clanton and Raquel went aboard the ship.

Desert Blood

(earliest known draft)

The lazy hum of ancient Tebessa's streets was only a faint echo in the little room, with its gilded ornaments and woolen rugs, where Wild Bill Clanton scowled in disgruntled puzzlement at the girl who stretched with feline luxuriousness on the couch opposite. Clanton was a broad-shouldered, hard-fisted, lean-waisted man whose face was browned by the suns of the Seven Seas. It was not the first time he had come to Tebessa on business not to be shouted from the housetops.

"What the hell?" he demanded of the world at large, and particularly of the girl who smiled with mocking malice at him. "What's the matter with you, Zouza?"

She rolled over on her supple stomach and propped herself on her elbows. There was no veil to hide her roguish features, her full, pouting red lips and *kohl*-darkened eyelids, which now drooped alluringly over dark eyes that sparkled with hidden meaning. Her *gandourah*, the robe worn by Algerian women, was so light it scarcely veiled the warm ivory flesh which shone beneath. Her broad girdle, drawn close about her supple waist, emphasized the swelling ripeness of her hips. One leg was thrust out in a straight line, the other kicked up her small heel in the feminine joy of tantalizing a male. The little crimson slipper barely clung to one saucy toe.

"Women love valiant men!" she announced.

"Nobody ever called me a coward," he growled. He could not understand her attitude. He had been a week in Tebessa; he had fallen in with her the first day of his stay. She had bestowed on him the full flavor of her exuberant charms with a zest that custom had not had time to stale. But today she was tantalizing, repulsed him. And it was not whim of coquetry, rising from a desire to be deliciously mastered. If it had been he would not have hesitated.

"You fight men!" she mocked. "Have you fought beasts—the king of beasts?"

"What do you mean?" He was fascinated by the swell of her ripe young breasts under the filmy robe. His fingers itched to cup them as he had so often before. Impatience was playing hell with his temper.

"The man I love must be a slayer of lions!" she announced. "If you would hold me, bring me the pelt of a lion!"

"And where the hell would I get a lion's pelt?" he demanded. "Nowhere around here, sure! An Englishman told me—"

"Allah blight your Englishman!" she interrupted rudely. "There are lions in the forest of Alloufa, one day's ride from this spot. If you were a *brave* man—"

"Shut up!" he snapped, stung by her taunt. He was no hunter, but his mallet-like fists had impacted on human jaws on every sea that ships sailed, and in every port from Frisco to Singapore; he had all the pride and vanity of a fighting man. Mingling with his fierce desire to crush this tantalizing armful of warm, scented flesh in his arms, there was a wish to answer this challenge to his manhood. He had business in Tebessa; he was no hunter; but he was not the first man to wander off at a tangent in response to the flirt of a petticoat—or in this case, the careless toss of a *gandourah*.

"Well, I'd have to get a guide, and some kind of a license or permit or somethin', wouldn't I?" A man of the sea, his ideas of such things were extremely hazy. Zouza bent her head to hide a triumphant smile; this iron-jawed, hard-fisted bucko was wax in her small hands.

"Don't bother with getting a permit from the French! They would cheat you. I have a cousin, himself a famous lion hunter, who will guide you. He is Ahmed ibn Suleyman. Have you been south of the city?"

He nodded.

"Then you know where is the Well of Mansourah? Good! Go there tonight, before moonrise. My cousin will be waiting for you, with horses and a rifle."

"You take a lot for granted," he grunted. "How do you know I'm goin' to chase off to Alloufa to shoot a lion for you? You're not the only woman in Tebessa!"

"But I am Zouza!" she assured him, with the naive vanity that always amused and stimulated him. "You will prove yourself a man for me!"

She turned lithely and sat up, heedless of the disarrangement of her *gandourah* which displayed an expanse of softly gleaming thigh. She slipped out of Clanton's grabbing hands, with a peal of silvery laughter, snatched her robe away from him and took refuge on the other side of the couch.

"No, not yet! Not until you have heard the lion call! '*Ana wa el-bin el-mera!*' Not until you bring me his skin!"

A few moments later Clanton, swearing under his breath, strode out into the streets, and almost bumped into another woman, the very antithesis of Zouza. Instinctively he lifted his cap. He knew her, as white people in Oriental cities quickly learn each other's identity. Miss Augusta Evans, a New England schoolteacher, on vacation and prying into strange and exotic places as people of her sort have a way of doing, of both sexes.

She returned him a frigid stare. Evidently she knew enough about Tebessa to have an idea about the place he had just come out of. She was not at all unhandsome, in a cold, aloof way. There were plenty of curves displayed by the riding habit she wore, and there was a wealth of light hair under the English sun helmet New Englanders feel obliged to wear anywhere south of the twenty-fifth parallel. Her features were classical, regular, not hard to look at, in spite of the tight-lipped expression she usually wore, denoting her disapproval of anything that differed from the ways and habits of Boston.

Clanton was impelled to address her merely by a desire of being helpful to a fellow countryman.

"Good afternoon, Miss Evans. I understand you're interested in archaeology. There are some Roman ruins a few miles south that I'd be glad to show you—"

Her voice dripped icicles as she answered.

"Yes, Mr. Clanton, I am quite aware of that fact. I am also, I assure you, in no need whatever of your assistance. I am quite capable of hiring a mount and guide and exploring those ruins myself, thank you.

"Okay, sister!" Clanton left her instantly, smarting.

"Damn', prudified, stuck-up snip! Serve her right if some Bedouin would kidnap her."

In a state of extreme irritation in regard to women in general, Clanton sought his quarters where he made such inroads on his own personal stock of alcoholics, that, when he sallied forth after dark, he was scarcely in condition to steer a course, much less lay one.

However, he presently found himself astride of a donkey and forging steadily southward, the city behind him, and a wind out of the desert in his face. It sobered him, but not soon enough. He realized that he had passed the Well of Mansourah in the darkness and that while not exactly lost—in that he still knew in which direction the Mediterranean Ocean and the Sahara Desert lay—he had wandered into a stretch of country unfamiliar to him.

Presently he saw a light glinting in the darkness to the northwest, and headed in that direction. He saw a tent ahead of him, and the light came from within. As he dismounted the tent flap was pulled aside and a slender figure was silhouetted against the glow. A soft voice called: "Ahmed! Ahmed ibn Suleiman! Is it you?"

"No, it's his friend!" announced Clanton, striding out of the darkness.

The girl cried out and drew back, but Clanton caught her wrist. He was just drunk enough to be indifferent to consequences, and the sight of her supple figure outlined against the light had set hammers going in his temples, and the blood sizzling in his veins.

"Don't be afraid," he soothed, following her into the tent as she backed away from him, trying to disengage her wrist. "I won't hurt you. I'm the man Ahmed was to meet at the Well of Mansourah, but I missed him in the dark. He your boyfriend?"

There was no one but themselves in the tent. She was prettier than Zouza, a little taller, and possessing suppleness that belongs only to Bedouin girls. Below the waist she was clad in voluminous pantaloons, girdled at the waist and caught in at the ankles. Above the waist her only garment was a sleeveless, low-necked vest of embroidered silk, caught together with a single gold brooch, which left bare her rounded throat and the upper swells of her ivory breasts. Her lips were full and red, her eyes dark and expressive. That was about her naked arms and shoulders at once a suppleness and frailness that most excites a man.

She nodded mutely in reply to his last question.

"And he leaves you here alone? Looks like he'd be more careful."

"No man would dare touch a woman claimed by Ahmed ibn Suleiman," she declared. "He is a trusted man of Shaykh Ali ibn Zahir!"

"The hell he is!" Clanton seated himself on a couch and drew her down on his knee. She struggled only a little. Clanton was forgetting lions, Ahmed, and everything else in the fascination of this lovely being in his arms. Presently she melted into his arms with a sigh, and thereafter Zouza might have been on the moon so far as he was concerned.

"It is a trap," she said presently. "I know all about it. But now—I love you, *sidi*, and I cannot see you go to your doom. Ahmed is not Zouza's cousin—the treacherous hussy, may she sit upon hot coals! He went to her and gave her money to trap you. There are no lions in Alloufa. She lied about many things. Ahmed waits at the Well of Mansourah to take you, with half a dozen men. You are to be brought to Shaykh Ali ibn Zahir—but for why, I do not know. There are strange things in the *douar* of ibn Zahir these days. Men say his favorite wife Zulakha, who was a princess and rules him even as he rules his tribe, has turned from him and has set him a task to perform before she will grant him her favor. She is the sister of Muhammad Pasha, the Turk."

He began to wonder at the significance. Muhammad Pasha was an adventurer, scheming in Tripoli. Clanton was waiting for an agent of a certain Berber chief with whom he intended making arrangements for delivering a cargo of rifles. There was more than money involved; Clanton saw these tribesmen as free men battling for life against a tyrannical European power.

"The moon has risen!" said the girl, Ayisha, lifting her curly dark head from his shoulder. "Let us go, quickly! If Ahmed returns and finds you here—"

Even as they stepped outside the tent door six men swept over a rise and were upon them, leaping from their horses. No time to run. Oaths, shouts, the impact of blows rang to the sky. Ahmed, his face convulsed, forgot his command to take the *Roumi* alive, and lunged in, dagger lifted. Clanton met him with the swing of a heavy branch picked up from a heap of firewood. Ahmed dropped with his skull shattered. The rest leaped on the white man and bore him down. A gun butt smashed on his own head; vaguely he heard Ayisha scream, saw her sprang clear and dart toward the horse tied behind the tent. Then he knew no more.

He came to himself bound in a saddle, with his captors around him. They were taking him, they told him, to the tents of Shaykh Ali, who had moved in from the desert for that very reason. The sun was well up when they reached the tents. Shaykh Ali, a tall, self-possessed man with a pointed black beard, met Clanton and said, quietly: "Your enemy, my wife, awaits you within her tent. It was at her command that you were brought here."

"I'm no enemy of hers," grunted Clanton.

"She says you are. Because of you her young brother was cast into prison."

Clanton was led to a large tent.

Shaykh Ali said grimly: "Never in the history of Islam before has a *shaykh* led an unbeliever in to his wife, and retired! But the eunuch is my servant, and your hands will be tied!"

Clanton strode into the tent. A dark-haired, dark-eyed beauty, unveiled, lounged on a couch. Near the door stood a huge impassive Soudanese, with a scimitar in his hand, like an image cut out of black basalt.

"I had you brought here," she said abruptly. "I am Zulakha. I want you to write a letter to your employers telling them to deliver the rifles to a certain island in the Gulf of Gabes. The island I will designate."

"And they'll eventually find their way into your brother's hands," he said.

"Yes."

"I won't do it."

"There are ways to make a man do what he is told."

"Not me," growled Clanton. "I'm a gone goose anyhow. Go ahead and tell your boyfriend to bump me off. Those guns are goin' to men who are fightin' for freedom, like my ancestors fought—not to a big fat-bellied Turk who's plannin' nothin' but his own advancement."

Zulaykha eyed him calculatingly, recognizing a man who might be led—by a woman—any length, but who was not to be driven. She rose suddenly, came to him and released his hands.

"Let us talk and be friends," she said caressingly. "Never mind the black man. He is my servant—not Ali's."

He understood her game, but he was a man who plucked fruit as he found it. Nothing loath, he sat down beside her and slipping an arm about her supple waist, began to explore the perfumed recesses of her *gandourah* and the silk vest beneath. She was a young woman, healthy and passionate as are all Turkish women. Presently the game merged into something more than a game.

A voice shouted outside: *"Sidi!* A white woman! Not more than a mile from camp!"

Instantly all was in confusion. The lawless Shaykh could not resist such a tempting game as this. He had a penchant for white women. Thinking Clanton bound and a prisoner of the eunuch's, he leaped into the saddle with his men and galloped away. But inside the tent Clanton came to life.

"Hell! I can't let him get away with this!"

"What do you care?" Zulaykha had no jealousy for a chance-caught captive. "Stay—let the fool take her. I begin to like you."

"To hell with that!" He knocked the black sprawling, snatched the pistol from his girdle, ran out into the camp, sprang on a horse and rode. From the crest of the ridge he saw a figure on a horse, riding hard. The horse looked familiar; it was the one he had seen tied behind Ayisha's tent. And the figure in the saddle was familiar—riding breeches and sun helmet! Miss Augusta Evans! She was riding as he had never expected to see Miss Evans ride. The Arabs were scattering, closing in on her. Her horse fell, throwing its rider over its head. Shaykh Ali swept in with a triumphant yell.

Clanton charged down the slope, yelling, just in time to see Ali dash his captive to the ground in a paroxysm of anger Clanton could not understand. At his yell the Shaykh turned. They fired simultaneously, and the Bedouin fell with a bullet through his head. The others broke, scattering in all directions. Only the presence of the Shaykh had emboldened them into aiding in the capture of a white woman. Now they fled in terror, not realizing what it was that Ali had caught.

Clanton recognized this, as he went to pick up the girl.

"Ayisha!"

She clung to him.

"Oh, *sidi*! It was blind chance. I knew Ali could not resist the chance to catch a white woman. So I rode within sight of the camp, hoping to draw him away. I hoped to outrun him and double back to aid you, but the horse stumbled."

"But where'd you get these clothes?" he asked.

"I sprang on the horse and fled toward Tebessa, meaning to ask aid of the French, though I feared they would arrive too late. But within four miles I met a white woman on a donkey, with a boy I knew, Yussef, son of Hassan, guiding her.

"So I told Yussef my plight, and we took the white woman's garments—"

"What?"

"Aye. Yussef helped me strip her when I gave him money—she made many lamentable cries and seemed much ashame. Then when I had her garments, I made Yussef put her back on her donkey, and the beast ran away toward the city, and—"

The thought of Miss Augusta Evans approaching the crowded streets of Tebessa on a runaway jackass, clad only in horn-rimmed spectacles, was too much for Clanton; he burst into a roar of mirth, while Ayisha watched, pleased that he should find pleasure in what she had done, but naively seeing nothing hilarious in what he found so amusing.

Desert Blood

(list of characters)

Characters:

Wild Bill Clanton, American sailor, in Tunis seeking to dispose of a cargo of rifles.
Zouza, a prostitute, desired by Clanton.
Shaykh Ali ibn Zahir, chief of a Bedouin tribe.
Miss Augusta Evans, a New England schoolteacher on vacation; handsome in tight-lipped way; schooled to disapproval of everything that differed from the ways of Boston; spectacled, with classical features.
Ayisha, a Bedouin girl, mistress of Ahmed ibn Suleiman.
Ahmed ibn Suleiman, spy for Shaykh Ali. Zuleykha, favorite wife of Shaykh Ali.
Yussef, guide of Miss Evans.

The Purple Heart of Erlik

(untitled synopsis)

Arline Ellis was told by the adventurer, Duke Tremayne, that she must steal the purple ruby of Woon Yuen, Chinese antique merchant, or that he, Duke, would turn her over to the police for the killing of a wealthy Japanese official. It had been self-defense, but she knew she would be convicted. Only Duke knew her connection with it and she was completely in his power. He was tall, suave, ruthless. As he talked to her in the little curtained nook of the cabaret, his fingers investigated the velvety warmth of her thigh, under her dress. She loathed his caress, but dared not resist him. He told her she must go to Woon Yuen's antique shop and steal the ruby, which was hidden in a wall safe in an inner chamber where only the wealthiest collectors were ever admitted. To gain entrance to that chamber, she was to pose as Lady Elizabeth Willoughby, a beautiful and eccentric young heiress who had a passion for jade. Arline faintly resembled her, and was dressed as she dressed, and could imitate her English accent. She was to enter the inner chamber, where Woon Yuen always served tea to his fair guests, and then sent away the servants, for frequently women made strange bargains with the wealthy Chinaman, who did always sell his rarest antiques for money. But he would not part with the purple ruby, of which he made a god. He believed that any woman who touched it must make a sacrifice to it of her virtue. Tremayne told her to get the ruby and bring it to him in a certain chamber in the native quarter.

As she left the cabaret, which was on the edge of the native quarter, she was accosted by Wild Bill Clanton, American sailor, who had long admired her. She repulsed him and went on, to Woon Yuen's shop. There she was admitted to Woon Yuen, showed him the card given her by Duke, who had stolen it, and was bowed into the inner chamber. To gain access she was forced to walk along a corridor floored with mirror, by which Woon Yuen obtained an idea of the intimate charms of his fair customers.

Woon Yuen, a powerful North Chinaman in a velvet robe, excused himself for a moment, but quickly returned, and tea was served them by a pretty Chinese girl clad only in a brief silk jacket that only partially concealed her charms. Arline knew that Woon Yuen believed that the sight of feminine nudity put a woman in the proper state of mind to accept his advances. But he made none toward her. As they sipped their tea, she pointed out an article on an ivory shelf and when he went to fetch it, she dropped a k.o. pellet in his tea. He showed her the object, an obscene statuette, and drank his tea, almost instantly falling senseless. Arline found the wall safe, curiously concealed by ornaments, and opened it easily. She had the great purple gem in her hands when a cynical voice brought her about to face Woon Yuen! He told her that the drugged man was his shadow, made up to look like him. They had changed places when Woon Yuen excused himself. He told her he knew she was not Lady Elizabeth Willoughby when she walked across the mirror, for the British woman always wore jade-green step-ins. Arline's were peach colored. He then raped Arline and kicked her out by a back alley. Then he told a hatchet man and a boy to follow her and see where she went. He believed a man was back of the scheme, and it was an obsession of his to feed the ruby blood with his own hand.

Arline, fearing Tremayne would make good his threat, started to cast herself in the bay when Clanton stopped her and persuaded her to tell him her troubles. She did so, and he accompanied her to the place where she was to meet Tremayne. The Chinese boy ran back and told Woon Yuen that they had tracked her to the man who plotted the theft.

Clanton knocked Tremayne senseless, and Woon Yuen entered with a pistol to shoot Clanton, thinking him the thief. Arline created a diversion and Clanton shot the Chinaman. Knowing there would be a hatchet man near, he put the gun in the hand of Tremayne, just coming to, and he and Arline hid. The hatchet man, hearing the shot and entering, thought Tremayne had shot Woon Yuen, and split his head. Clanton and Arline slipped out the back way.

The Dragon of Kao Tsu

(earliest known draft)

Wild Bill Clanton was sipping a whiskey-and-soda in a back room of the Anglo-American Bar and considering the merits of a pearl-poaching venture into the Solomons as opposed to a gunrunning job up the China coast, when his meditations were startlingly interrupted. The girl that stormed into the room without knocking looked as much out of place in the Anglo-American as a Fifth Avenue debutante in Bowery honkytonk chorus. If class means wealth and blue blood, she advertised class from her insolently tilted beret to her high French heels. And if class means looks, she had plenty of it. She was tall and slender, but all her lines were supple and rounded, with melting curves that a sweetly athletic suggestion kept from being too delicate. But she was no shrinking violet; her purplish eyes warned of a nature full of fire and ginger, and just now they flashed wrathfully. Under light silk her pertly tilted breasts swelled stormily, and her first words crackled blue lightnings.

"You," she addressed Wild Bill without preamble, "are a thief, a liar and a double-crossing rat!"

"So what?" retorted he, unimpressed, as he reached for a selzer-water bottle.

"Why, you low-lifed—!" Her refinement skidded a trifle in her resentment of his tranquility. She began tracing his genealogy with language she never learned in the Junior League, but he interrupted her peremptorily as some of her remarks got under even his rhino-like epidermis.

"Now you hold on! Some things nobody can call me, not even a lady! Sit down and cool off, before somethin' unpleasant happens to you—unpleasant and embarrassin'!" He added with meaning and relish.

She wilted at the threat. He was, she knew, not a man to waste words idly. She drooped into a chair opposite him and took the drink he shoved across the table.

"This," she said bitterly, "is what I get for associating with a gorilla like you. Why I do it I don't know."

"I know," he retorted. "Because you're afraid to trust anybody else with your dirty work. Because, in this case, you wanted Gop Kang's ivory elephant and I was the only man who could get it for you."

"Yes, you were!" There was rancor in her tone and she fixed him with a basilisk glare that made him a trifle uneasy. You never could tell about these society pets! If she yanked a knife out of her garter he'd smack her down first and ask questions later.

But she had no knife in her garter, as he could tell when she crossed her silk-clad legs with the regal indifference of a true aristocrat. She twitched down her skirt an inch or so in grudging respect to conventions, but not before he had a glimpse of gleaming white flesh that made the blood boil to his head. Her indifference to his emotions was maddening and irritating. Probably it had never occurred to old man Allison's daughter that a man on such a different social plane from herself would even think of making a pass at her, but he had to clench his hands to keep them off of her.

"What's eatin' you?" he demanded.

For answer she produced something from her handbag and smacked it down accusingly before him. It was a small ivory elephant, exquisitely carved and yellowed with age.

"It's a fake!" she declared.

"It's the one Diego de Strozza stole from Gop Kang and gave me," he asserted.

"It's a fake," she contended moodily. "Either you've gypped me, or Diego has, or Gop Kang's fooled us all. This isn't the genuine Mogul elephant. Never mind asking why. I know!"

"Well, what of it?" he asked. "All you want it for is to show to your society friends back in the States and brag about gettin' hold of a rare antique. They won't know the difference."

"Some of them will," she answered, lighting a cigaret with an injured air. "We idle rich must have our hobbies, and recently, among my set, it's been the collection of Oriental antiques. It's been the fad to 'see' the East and bring back some rare relic—the rarer the better. I don't care anything about antiques, but I'm not going to be outdone. Betty Elston's been crowing over all of us since she got hold of a Ming vase in Canton. She said a mandarin gave it to her—I wonder what she gave him for it! She's strutted about with it till I wanted to kick her little—well, anyway, that's one reason I came to Singapore. In San Francisco I heard about the Mogul elephant. It's so rare very few people know anything about. It's Persian work, made for Akbar. That's what makes it so rare. The Muhammadans are forbidden to paint or carve the shapes of beasts or men, you know. But Akbar was broad-minded and when a Hindu rajah presented it to him, he kept it. It dates beyond Akbar. It is supposed to have been carved by a Persian in the army of Alexander the Great, when he invaded India. It's absolutely unique! Other relics are more costly, but there's not anything else like this. That's why I must have it!"

Clanton picked up the yellow figure and turned it about. He knew no more about Greek art than he knew about Mars.

"I dunno," quoth he. "Diego got into Gop Kang's house and swiped this thing. He's the slickest thief on the Peninsula, but he might not work it again. He's in a blue funk as it is. Gop Kang's bad business."

"But it's not the right one!" Marianne's small fist drummed with nervous irritation on the table. "He's got to get the right one! I've paid him plenty! He's not going to take money under false pretences, is he?"

Clanton grinned at her righteous indignation.

"That's like you rich folks. You bribe a man to be a thief, and then think it's awful if you turns around and gyps you! Well, now keep your pants on! I'm a man of my word, and I promised you I'd get you that elephant. Diego's so scared after stealin' that thing that he's fixed him up a bed in an old abandoned warehouse down on the waterfront and is hidin' down there. That's where I went last night to get that elephant and pay him his money. Now maybe he just got the wrong elephant. Or he may be holdin' out on us. You leave that thing with me, and tonight I'll go down there again and have it out with him. If he's honest, maybe he'll try again. If he's tryin' to put somethin' over on us—well, we'll see."

"I'm going with you," she decided. "I don't trust you any too far."

"It's a bad place for a white woman to go," he warned her.

She tilted a scornful nose.

"I can take care of myself, *Mister* Clanton—otherwise I'd never have had any dealings with you! I'll pick you up on Pahang Street just about dark. And you be there! I don't want to have to go snooping into some dive to find you and drag you out from under some table, or off some native wench."

"I'll be there," he asserted. "But have some more whiskey before you go."

"No thanks!" she declined. "I prefer to keep our relationship on a strictly business basis—and whiskey has too much of an elevating effect on a man's mind—and a woman's dress. I'll see you, at dusk."

And she swung out of the room with a long-legged, hip-swaying gait that made Clanton moan with despair and grabbed the whiskey bottle desperately. She had him buffaloed. If she'd been somebody else he would have grabbed her and headed for the nearest bedroom, regardless. But there was a limit even to his audacity and he didn't dare try any rough stuff on old man Allison's daughter, millionaire and woolly wolf of ruthless finance that the old devil was.

He turned the ivory elephant about in his hands and frowned.

"Antique collectin', eh? Balogna!"

Rising he bellowed to a half-caste waiter, plunked a coin on the wine-stained table, and barged out of a side door. A few moments later he was seated in a little candlelit shop kept by one Yakub a bearded old Jew who had a finger in many businesses besides the one the sign over his silk shop advertised, and who was wise in the ways of the East. Clanton set the ivory elephant before him and demanded: "What's that?"

Yakub donned square, steel-rimmed spectacles, and regarded it.

"That's the Mogul elephant," he said. "But I wouldn't handle it for you. You must have stolen it from Gop Kang. I love life too much to handle anything stolen from that devil."

"You're wrong," asserted Clanton. "It's a fake."

"If it's a fake I'm a Gentile," answered old Yakub, lovingly fondling its smooth surface. "I saw it once, years ago. Tchk, tchk! Such a pity! I'd buy it from you myself if it wasn't for Gop Kang. You better give it back. Then maybe they won't find you with your throat slit some morning."

"You're willing to swear this is the genuine?" Clanton demanded.

"My head on it!" asserted the old man placidly.

"Hmmm!" Clanton's scowl deepened. "I wonder what that supercilious hussy is tryin' to put over on me?"

Then he put a question direct to Yakub.

If Marianne Allison had heard the answer Yakub gave Clanton, she might have worn a less-assured poise when she purred up to the curb in her big coupe just as the streetlights were coming on. He climbed in beside her and she turned off down a side street according to his directions.

"We'll leave the car on a lighted street not far from the waterfront," he said. "The only way to reach that warehouse where Diego's hidin' is down a crooked alley. Did you bring any money, in case he wants more?"

"I should say not," she retorted, narrowly missing a coolie who was shuffling across the street. "That idiot! If I'd run over him, they'd have blamed me! Men are such fools! No, I didn't bring any money. I've already paid him more than enough. He owes me any future service it takes to get that elephant."

"You're an arrogant wench," he observed, his eyes fixed in fascination on a rounded knee. Through design or accident her dress had worked up again, baring an inch of white flesh above the stocking top.

"When you get through studying my legs," she suggested, "you might tell me which way to turn at this next intersection."

She smiled wickedly as he reluctantly turned his attention to the street. Feeling perfectly safe from him, she took an essentially feminine delight in tantalizing him. False modesty not being one of her traits, she was perfectly aware of her effect on him, and she enjoyed seeing the veins of his forehead swell in impotent desire. So now with a twitch she thought he didn't observe, she bared some more white flesh to his harassed gaze. But he was more observant than she thought, and if she could have read his mind at that moment she would probably have jumped out of the car with a shriek.

"Pull up here," he directed and when she observed that it was a shabby neighborhood to leave a nice new car unguarded in, he answered: "It's a damn' sight more respectable than where we're goin'! But I'll 'tend to that." He called a loitering Malay, spoke to him in his own tongue, and then took the girl's arm and started up the winding street.

"He'll watch the car till we get back. Otherwise they'd have the wheels off of it. Here—we turn in to this alley."

It was dark there, faintly lighted by a distant streetlamp. They groped their way along and presently the alley opened into a sort of court, lined on one side by a row of crumbling and deserted wharves.

"That's the warehouse," muttered Clanton, indicating a building that loomed darkly before them, almost overhanging the wharf. "Come on. He's got a room fixed up with a camp cot downstairs."

He led the way to the door, knocked and called: "Diego!" softly. There was no answer. He tried the door and found it unlocked. He pushed open and they entered. She jumped and grabbed his arm as they stood in the darkness.

"The door! Somebody pushed it to behind us!"

"Just the wind blew it to," he grunted. "But where the hell is Diego?"

"Listen!" She was still clutching him, and he could feel the tense quivering of her body against his. Somewhere in the darkness sounded a steady drip-drip as if somebody had left a faucet partly open. But Clanton's hair began to rise, because he knew there wasn't any faucet in that room. In a sort of panic he struck a match and held it up. Marianne clapped a hand over her mouth to stifle a shriek. Clanton swore. In the wavering light of the match they saw a table, and Diego de Strozza sat bolt-upright at that table, bound in a chair. But his head lolled on his breast and his eyes were glassy. And from a slashed throat blood still oozed sluggishly to fall drop by drop in a widening puddle on the floor. "Godlemighty!" hissed Clanton. "We've got to get out of here—*hell!*"

Something that glinted swished at him out of the darkness. Marianne had a brief glimpse of an arc of gleaming steel and a dark, contorted face behind it. And then the match went out, clipped from Clanton's hand by that slashing blade, and the dark was full of sounds of combat. Marianne, following her instinct, deposited herself at full length on the floor, and began scurrying on all-fours in the direction she hoped the door was, but the darkness confused her. She had lost touch with Clanton, but he couldn't be dead, because no corpse could put up the fight he seemed to be putting up, judging from the sounds. Once, when a strong voice panted Anglo-Saxon oaths, she knew he was still in the land of the living, and she felt almost an instant of pity for his adversaries as she heard what sounded like beeves being knocked in the head with a maul, but which she knew to be the impact of his massive fists on human skulls. Howls of pain and rage filled the room, there was the crash of a table being overturned, and then somebody fell over her in the dark.

It wasn't Clanton, but a Malay. She could tell by the smell, even in the dark. She heard the fellow floundering on the floor as she slipped away, and her blood was frozen by the vicious soft *wheep-wheep* of a keen blade being whirled at random in the darkness. It was close behind her and the flesh of her hips crawled as she scuttled away on all-fours. Her hands touched something—a door that led into a flight of steps. But any avenue of escape from that blind blade flailing the blackness was welcome.

She went up as fast as she could and eventually emerged into an equally dark space that felt big and empty, and smelt musty. There she crouched, trembling, while the noise of battle went on below, and presently culminated in an amazing crash that sounded as though somebody had been knocked bodily through a closed door. Then the sounds died away and silence reigned. She lay there too scared to move, and time passed. Hours it seemed. What had happened down there? Surely those were Gop Kang's men who had been hiding in the dark, after killing Diego. But had they killed Clanton as well? At last she could stand the suspense no longer. She groped for the stair, found it and stole down. And as she went she heard somebody enter—somebody that wore the boots of a white man, surely, for though he was trying to go softly, still he made more noise than a barefooted or sandaled native would have done. Then she heard a smothered oath that sounded English.

Had Clanton defeated or eluded his attackers and returned? Light stole through the crack under the door as a match was struck, and she ventured to open the door a little. Through the track she saw a brawny figure in a seaman's cap and garb bending over the corpse bound to the chair. His back was toward her, but she had no doubt who it was.

She opened the door, sprang into the room and exclaimed: "Clanton!" and then stood frozen as a perfect stranger whirled toward her with an oath. The appearance of that stranger was not such as to inspire confidence, either. He was as big as Clanton and much uglier. His eyes were small and piglike, he was bearded, and altogether he looked a great deal like a timber wolf with an ingrown disposition.

He held, moreover, a snub-nosed revolver in his hand and this was levelled at her quivering tummy.

"Don't shoot!" she gasped. "I—I won't hurt you!"

The stranger's reply was unprintable. Evidently her sudden appearance had given him a bad shock. She heard some language that startled even her, sophisticated as she was.

"Who in the blasted, blightin', blinkin' hell are you and what're you doin' here?" he concluded. "Well, talk, before I start sweepin' the floor with you!" He brandished a fist the size of a breakfast ham under her shrinking nose.

She shuddered and spoke hastily, though scarcely convincingly: "I—I was lost and just wandered in here by mistake, and—"

"Stow it!" bellowed the irate intruder. "You can't pull the wool over *'Hurricane'* Davies' eyes like that!" The aforesaid eyes narrowed suddenly. "Oh, I get it!" he muttered. "Of course! Why didn't I think of it before! I know you! You're old man Allison's daughter! Naturally you would be after the elephant. So you killed Diego here to get it! All right, hand it over!"

"I haven't got it," she answered. "And I didn't kill Diego."

"Then who the hell did?"

"It must have been Gop Kang's men. They must have traced him here, killed him, and then heard me coming, and blown out the light and hid in the dark. There was a man with me—I don't know what happened to him, or where they went."

"Likely yarn," grumbled Mr. Davies, absently spinning the pistol on his forefinger. "Diego knew I was after the elephant. He sent me word to come here tonight and make him an offer. I got here just now—and find him dead and the elephant gone. It ain't on him—it must be on you!" He pointed a hairy and accusing finger at Marianne.

"No!" she exclaimed, paling, with a characteristic feminine gesture. "I tell you I haven't got it! Listen! Help me get it! I'll pay you—"

"Jum Noy's already paid me," he growled. "He's paid me as much as you would, and furthermore if I don't deliver the goods, he'll have my throat cut. You've got that elephant on you somewhere! You dames are mighty smart about hidin' things on you! Off with those clothes!"

"No!" she started to back away, but he grabbed her wrist, twisted it until she fell to her knees with a yelp of pain.

"Are you goin' to strip, or have I got to tear 'em off of you? If I have to it'll be the worse for you, blast you!"

"Let go of me," she begged. "I know when I'm licked. I'll do it."

And under his burning, piglike eyes she shed garment after garment until she stood before him clad only in a scanty brassiere, and ridiculously brief pink panties. As she had discarded each garment he had snatched it up and ransacked it, snarling his anger at finding his quest fruitless. Now he glared at her, silent and wrathful, and she squirmed and made protecting motions with her hands. A red glow that was more than rage was beginning to glimmer murkily in his bloodshot eyes.

"Isn't this enough?" she begged. "You could see if I had anything on me the size of that ivory elephant."

"Well, maybe," he admitted grudgingly, laying a heavy hand on her naked shoulder and turning her about to inspect her from every angle.

"Baby, you've got what it takes!" he muttered thickly, slapping a hot, sweaty hand down on each curving hip. "No, you haven't got that ivory elephant hid in your pants—nor in your bust band!" He grinned wickedly as he slipped a finger inside the bandeau. The contact of his hand on her naked breasts was too much. She shrieked and slapped him, and instantly regretted her indiscretion. He grabbed her in a bearlike embrace, and the glassy stare of the dead man grinning at the table didn't seem to lessen the Cap'n's ardor.

He was carrying her toward the camp cot in the corner when he stiffened, turned toward the door. Outside sounded a faint babble of voices. With a stride he turned through another door, still carrying Marianne. When she tried to scream he clapped a big paw over her mouth and hissed: "Shut up, you little fool! Do you want your throat cut? That's Gop Kang's men!"

He seemed to know his way about the warehouse, even in the dark. He stooped, fumbled at the floor, raised a trapdoor, hissed: "If I hear one peep out of you I'll come down there and twist your head off! I'll get you out when they leave—if you're a good girl!" and dropped her.

She was too scared to yell if she'd had breath for it. She didn't fall far and she hit on her feet on a slimy floor. She stood there in the darkness, scarcely daring to breathe, and then she was paralyzed with fear at the sound of scurrying and the sight of small red eyes winking fiercely at her from the gloom. Rats! She had all a woman's natural terror of rodents, and she had heard horrifying stories of the great ghoulish grey wharf rats. But they made no move to attack her and she began to explore her prison, shivering in her nudity at the dampness. The floor seemed to be stone, standing in a few inches of water, and the walls were of stone and wood. She found no opening. She had been dumped into a cellar below the warehouse and the only way out was up through that trapdoor above her head.

She squealed as a rat ran across her foot, and scurried back against the wall, bruising her tender hip and tearing the seat of her panties on the jutting end of a broken board. She felt very sorry for herself at the moment, and intensely humiliated. Imprisoned in a rat-haunted cellar below a deserted warehouse, practically naked—

"This is what I get for associating with people like Bill Clanton," she told herself bitterly. And then the rats started fighting in a corner. Their hideous racket snapped her taut nerves. She screamed. In fact she yelled. She was a supple, healthy, athletic girl, and she had a robust voice. She was too panicky to care for Davies' threat. At the moment she would have welcomed the sight of his bearded face. Having her head twisted off seemed preferable to being devoured by rats in that black well. She lifted her voice in lamentation and appeal. She didn't care who heard her. All she wanted at the moment was for somebody to get her out of that damnable cellar, and she didn't much care what they did to her afterward.

And almost instantly her cries were answered by sounds from overhead. The trap was lifted and she blinked in the glare of a lantern. But it was not Davies' bearded countenance which was framed in the opening, but a dark, saturnine, handsome Oriental face—the face of Shareef Ali! At the sight of her white, terrified, upturned face he smiled with quiet satisfaction.

"Well, our little guest did not escape in the darkness after all!" he remarked, and then spoke in quick staccato to someone near him. This person evidently caught hold of Ali's girdle, for the Arab reached his arms down in the trapdoor, caught her lifted wrists and lifted her lightly up. The trapdoor fell again and she found herself standing in the center of a dozen or so Malay's, whose eyes, like those of Ali, dwelt burningly on her naked limbs and her firm breasts, only partly concealed by the brassiere.

"A curious interlude must account for your presence in that cellar, and your present state of undress," he smiled cynically. "You enter fully clothed, with that dog Clanton. You apparently escape in the melee. Then, less than an hour later, we find you imprisoned in the cellar, lightly clad—and even such garments as you still wear rather impaired. For instance your panties are torn!" And he lightly slapped the expanse of white hip exposed by the accident. She winced but did not reply or resent the indignity. She was scared as only a woman can be in the power of men whom she knows are absolutely cynical in their attitude toward men, merciless and see only a cruel humor in the manhandling of a woman.

When Ali ordered her into the other room she went with a meekness that would have astonished any of her masculine friends.

There she faced him, her mind working rapidly.

"Yes, I had the ivory elephant. I found it where Diego hid it. But Hurricane Davies came and—"

"Davies?" It was a snarl from Ali. "Has that dog been here?"

"He *is* here—hiding somewhere in the warehouse. And he has the elephant."

"Search the place," snapped Ali, and his men scattered from the room, soft-footed as weasels, with naked blades glimmering in their hands.

"What became of Clanton?" she asked.

"He fought his way out the door and got away. We removed the body of Diego and threw it in the river. But what should interest you more is what is going to happen to you!" He was about to rape her when his men brought in Hurricane Davies, a prisoner. They began torturing him to make him tell where he hid the elephant when Clanton returned with a gun he'd got out of Marianne's car and held them up.

They backed against the wall, hands high, and Clanton told Marianne to untie Davies, who glared at her, his hairy breast heaving. Then Clanton told Davies to tie them, which he did. He ran Davies out of the place; weak with torture he was glad to go. Clanton ran swift hands over them all, including the Chinaman, and then stepped back, while they glared at him.

"I knocked out the fellow you had trailin' me. I've got him tied up. I'll untie him and send him back to let you scuts loose. The elephant's gone. Nobody knows where. Better forget it. Ali, you know what the British will do to you for cuttin' Diego's throat. Better let bygones be bygones. We'll keep quiet. You better do the same."

"Come on, Marianne." In the room where the cot was, Clanton drew something from his pocket—an ivory elephant! She snatched at it, but he drew it back from her.

"You wait a minute. I've learned some things since I hired Diego to steal the Mogul elephant for you. You don't care anything about art collections. Your old man sent you to Singapore to get hold of an elephant because you were smarter than any of his employees.

"Years ago Gop Kang and your old man made a contract, that gave the old man valuable concessions in China. They wrote up the contract according to Gop Kang's wishes, on a bit of parchment placed in the belly of an ivory elephant which was a copy of the Mogul elephant—a whim on Gop Kang's part. It was placed in the possession of Shareef Ali's uncle, and was safe as long as he lived. But he died and Shareef Ali got hold of it. And then your old man decided to develop his holdings, but Gop Kang repented of his bargain and wanted to get the contract and destroy it so he could back down on his bargain without losing face.

"But Shareef Ali had anticipated that, and he began bargaining with your old man and with Gop Kang. Your old man's been hit hard in the stock market and he was afraid he couldn't outbid Gop Kang, so he sent you to steal the contract.

"Well, Diego got both elephants. He gave you the genuine article, but he knew what was in the other, so he got in touch with Davies, one of Gop Kang's agents. The rest is easy. Ali's Chinese servant had the elephant you wanted all the time. He was the one that killed Diego, and he found it on him before the others got there. I found it on him when I searched him. But he won't dare tell Ali, because that would be to betray his own treachery. Now then, you can have this elephant, but you've got to pay for it. I told you I'd get you the Mogul elephant for a thousand dollars. And I did. That was the original. This is extra."

"How much money do you want?" she demanded.

"Money ain't everything. You know what I want. You been askin' for it ever since I've known you. You'd better come across, young lady. You're in this up to your hips, you know. It won't hurt me any, but you and your folks can't afford a scandal—murder, torture, and such stuff. Great headline story!"

"Give me the elephant," she acquiesced.

He handed it to her, trustfully and she snatched it and banged him over the head with the chair leg she still held. The next instant she was streaking for the door. But she underestimated the strength of his skull. To her dismay he did not fall; he merely staggered with a gasping curse, and then righted himself and leaped after her. He caught her as she grasped the knob and swung her back into the room, picking her up and carrying her to the camp cot.

"You little cheapskate!" he snarled. "You've never kept your part of a bargain yet! Well, you're goin' to keep this one, whether you like it or not. And you can't squeal, because you don't dare to!"

"You won't!" she gasped. "You can't—"

Even as she spoke she realized the fallacy of her conviction. He could, and would—and did. After an amazingly lengthy interlude he rose and grinned down at her humorously.

"Well," he said philosophically, "that's what you get for associatin' with people like me!"

Marianne's reply was not printable.

Murderer's Grog

(earliest known draft)

When Wild Bill Clanton climbed the stair that led up from the mud-walled courtyard to the rooms of Olga Valisky, he was already fighting mad. Who wouldn't be, when faced with the prospect of losing all his investments and future profits, and a possible jail sentence as well? The incessant clamorings and babblings that were the noises of the streets of Peshawur whetted the edge of his irascibility. Here, in the greatest trading city south of Bokhara, there were fortunes to be made, both legal and illegal; one of those golden troves had been almost within his fingers, but eluded his eager grasp. His brow was dark as he climbed the stair, but his expression lightened somewhat and the angry resentment in his eyes gave place to another, more pleasurable expression as he heard a silvery feminine laugh gurgle above him. That was Olga, and his blood pressure rose a trifle, just to hear her.

Hastily he mounted the stair and rapped on an ornately carved door. It opened a crack and a pretty, dark-eyed Punjabi girl looked out at him. Her eyes widened a bit, as if she had expected to see someone else, and was not too pleased to see Clanton. She made no move to open the door wider, but Clanton attended to that himself. Over the girl's shoulder he had glimpsed Olga, reclining in voluptuous ease on a silken divan, and the maid had as much chance of keeping him out of the room as she would have had of barring a wild Indian from a bottle of whiskey. Clanton pushed open the door and brushed the maid aside, ignoring and indeed scarcely hearing her indignant protests, and strode across the threshold, his eyes glowing.

Olga glanced idly over her ivory shoulder, then came to life and sat up with a suddenness which, had Clanton been in any mood to analyze, was scarcely flattering. Nor was there much encouragement in the way she drew her light *harim* robe together over her luscious thighs, scarcely veiled by the gauzy ankle-length trousers that adorned them.

Olga was one of the mysteries of that city of mysteries. She was the one white woman who habitually lived in the native city, and as such was scarcely welcome in that other world on the other side of the railroad, where the white residents of Peshawur made a little Western world of their own amidst their bungalows and rose gardens. But Olga was indifferent to what the people in the British cantonment thought of her. If she could not go to them, they could come to her—and the loiterers in the bazaars whispered strange tales of sahibs, both in khaki and mufti, who climbed her stair by night. Yet no man could boast truthfully that he had had his way with her, whatever he may have had in the way of information and secret tales that drift up and down the long caravan trails between Samarkand and Karachi. The winds blew these tales through Olga's house and her slim, white fingers sifted out what she desired. So many men sought her, some with the lust of gain—and others like Clanton, with just plain lust. She claimed to be a wealthy young woman, who, tired of society and the conventional ways of the rich, had come to the East to study Oriental psychology at first hand. At which claims the British population snickered in its sleeve.

She made a ravishing figure as she lounged on the couch, even after she had pulled her light silk robe about her lower parts. She was blond, with a wealth of light gold hair, and her flesh was as purely white as unstained Northern snow. Her eyes were deep, grey and enigmatic, with that touch of mysticism and allure characteristic of the Slav, and Clanton knew they could burn and smolder with passion. On the one former occasion when he had seen her he had glimpsed a lighting of spark, and he had come back hoping to fan it to a full-grown flame.

But there was no gleam of fire there now. They were frigid as the surface of ice, though still enigmatic.

"Oh, it's you!" The greeting was not ardent. But Clanton was used to the ways of women and their moods, real and assumed, and he was not at all abashed.

"Sure! Didn't I tell you I'd come? Tell the girl to beat it."

The maid salaamed and exited at an impatient wave of her mistress's hand, and Clanton sat down on the couch, devouring his reticent hostess with eager eyes. Her manner had changed distinctly since he had met her in the bazaar the day before and received her invitation to call on her, but he gave no heed. A woman like Olga had to be always on the defensive—at first. He believed he could break down that barrier of reserve which so many men had failed to do. After all, he came at her own invitation. His gaze dwelt hotly on her bare, superb neck, the arrogant swell of her breasts only half confined by a low-necked, armless velvet vest fastened with a single clasp. She had not bothered to draw her open robe across her bosom, and he glimpsed generous contours of white flesh which seemed to be about to burst their confines. From beneath the robe peeped slender red slippers, sewn with pearls, and the trimmest ankles he had seen north of Lahore.

"Do you want wine?" she asked, but he shook his head and put an arm about her waist. He was a man of impulse and action. The extreme uncertainty of life—as he led it—had taught him to take what he wanted when it was offered—and frequently when it wasn't. She did not exactly resist him, but she did not yield to him. The contact of her smooth flesh went to his head quicker than any wine she could have offered him. His other hand defeated her efforts to keep the robe pulled together over her knees. The feel of her delicious contours, even beneath her filmy trousers, was intoxicating.

"Don't!" She squirmed, crossed her legs and pushed his hand away by main force. It instantly ascended and began fumbling at the brooch which held her vest together, and which, for the moment, defied his ingenuity. A glint of amusement showed maliciously in her marvelous eyes.

"I hear you had a run-in with the British commandant," she said. "You'd better be careful. Your reputation isn't any too good with them, as it is. And after all, they run India."

"That's what he told me," grunted Clanton, scowling again at the memory of his troubles. "In fact, he gave me just twenty-four hours to get out of Peshawur."

"You'd better go," she advised.

"Where? Into Afghanistan? I came down through that way, and believe me, I outstayed my welcome. I was lucky to get across the border with a whole skin. Hell, I couldn't get a pass back there for all the gold in India."

"You'll have to go south," she suggested. "Or into the Independent Territory."

He shot her a quick glance. There was a hint of mocking malice in that last remark. Could it be that she knew it was the Territory into which he desired to go—must go, if he was not to be beggared?

"If I go south without any money, the British will find some excuse to pick me up and heave me into the brig," he muttered. "Listen, I'll tell you a little—I'm here in Peshawur on business. I need to go into the Territory—oh, hell, I know the British wouldn't give anybody permission to go in there, not even me, though they'd like to see some bandit shoot my head off. But to Hell with them. I don't need their permission. I can slip over the border and be out of their reach any time I want to—but—"

"But what?" Was she interested, or merely encouraging conversation to divert his attention from her charms? His hands were still when he talked.

"You know what," he growled. "If I stepped over the border without the protection of some chief, they'd hang my hide on a rock before I could turn around. Those Afridis, Mahsudis and Waziris don't recognize either British or Afghan authority. But if I went into their country under the protection of some big chief—like Baber Ali Khan of the Adam Khel Afridis, I'd be safe from his tribe, and the men of the other clans would hesitate offendin' him. If they shot me, it'd be an insult to his tribe, and he'd feel obliged to declare blood feud. Well, I been waiting for word from him to come ahead, but it hasn't come. I don't understand it. I sent him word of what I wanted before I came down the Khyber Pass. It's to his advantage as well as mine, confound him!"

"You intend putting over a deal in the Territory, and splitting the profits with him, for protection?" she asserted, rather than asked.

"Yeah. And I've tied up plenty of money in the deal. If I don't hear from him within twenty-four hours, I'll have to pull out, flat broke. And the British will get me in jail and deport me as an objectionable character, as sure as hell."

"I could lend you money enough to get to Bombay," she suggested, not enthusiastically.

He shook his head, with stubborn pride.

"Hell no. I ain't borrowin' money from any woman, much less you! Damn it, I didn't come up here to talk business! Not that kind! I came up here to forget my troubles, and—"

His expression was elegant as his arm tightened about her waist, drawing her to him unwillingly. In spite of her reluctance, the silk robe slid off, leaving her arms and shoulders bare. Her baggy pantaloons, of sheer silk, concealed little of her contours from his eager eyes. The brooch gave way to his efforts and his gaze was dazzled by the magnificent arrogance of her ripe breasts. He was endeavoring to unfasten the drawstring of her trousers when her resistance became determined. She jerked free and sprang up, a vibrant figure, resentful and resistant.

"What's the matter?" He too rose, sensing at last that her resistance was not feigned.

"Don't you know when you're not wanted?" she lashed at him, her eyes growing tawny in her anger. There was something feline about her now, something elemental and ready to rend and tear.

He grew angry in his turn.

"Well, what the hell? What's changed you? You gave me plenty of encouragement in the bazaar yesterday. You said plenty with your eyes when you asked me to call on you. Blast it, you did everything but pull up your dress right there!"

"I can't afford to have anything to do with a man who's out of favor with the British," she answered coldly, turning away with a gesture as if dismissing an underling. But Bill Clanton wasn't so easily dismissed.

With a curse he grabbed her shoulder and jerked her about.

"That's a lie! You never showed the door to a man before because of the British! It's your boast that you don't give a damn what they think! There's something else—another man—"

"Yes, another man!" she lashed out, trying to strike his hands aside. "When I saw you yesterday, I was attracted to you—because of your size, strength and animal vitality. I did contemplate an affair with you—I admired you as I might admire a stallion or a tiger. But within a few hours I'd met a real man! The first man I've ever wanted to possess me! The sight of him swept you out of my mind! And now get out of here, before I have you thrown out!"

"Why, you little—!" Smoldering anger at the world in general, stung vanity, thwarted desire, combined to make Bill Clanton a raging demon. He grabbed her, ignoring her biting teeth and clawing nails, swept her off her feet and carried her to the couch where he deposited her, shrieking and kicking. She fought his hands away from the waist of her pantaloons for an instant, and then the triumphant gleam of her eyes, as she looked over his shoulder, gave him unintended warning. He wheeled sidewise, and the bludgeon swung by a huge Shinwari man-servant crashed numbingly on his shoulder instead of braining him. A groan burst involuntarily from his lips and his knees buckled, but with a supreme effort he drove a right hook deep in the servant's belly as the man was lifting the club again.

The Shinwari gasped and collapsed, and Clanton was stooping for the club when another servant landed squarely on his back, bearing him to the floor. Other servants rushed through the doors and fell on the American with a hearty good will. Clanton fought, as only he could fight, but his right arm was useless and the odds were too heavy. Three or four were gasping on the floor, green faced from kicks in the belly or groin, or left-handed clouts delivered in spite of the close grapple, but the others heaved the white man up, rushed him tumultuously across the room, urged on by Olga's cruel laughter, and tumbled him down the stair into the courtyard, where he lay half-stunned.

Indeed he looked so much *hors-de-combat* that the spiteful Punjabi maid ventured down, carrying his cap, to indulge in the age-old feminine sport of taunting the fallen. But she underestimated his recuperative power. She carelessly came within his reach, to toss his cap down at him, with cutting and obscene remarks, and was caught off-guard when he sat up suddenly and grabbed her. There was a brief struggle, feminine shrieks, and then the maid fled up the stair minus her trousers, and Clanton rose and cast the tattered remnants of the garment after her. The sight of bare feminine hips twinkling up the stair in humiliated haste gave him an angry satisfaction which, however, was but a drop in the raging maelstrom which was his present state of mind.

He rose, glared balefully at the door at the head of the stair, now closed and doubtless bolted on the other side, and then he turned and strode out into the street.

He didn't know which made him madder—the treatment he had received at Olga's hands, or the delay in hearing from Baber Ali Khan. Why was the old devil holding up on him? Clanton had brought a batch of rifles down from Russia—the fine, breech-bolt guns the Soviets manufacture especially for the tribes subject to their rivals. These guns were far superior to the native-made weapons, and cheaper than the guns smuggled up from Karachi on the Persian Gulf. But the Soviets didn't give them away. Any man who handled their guns had to pay in advance, though they would aid him in getting them past certain borders. Clanton had sunk his whole wad in this camel load, sure of about three hundred percent profit if he could get them into the Independent Territory. He couldn't work the Afghan tribes proper, because Russian agents were there ahead of him, and jealous of their privilege. He winced as he thought of the work he'd had in getting the guns down through Afghanistan, bribing officials at every turn. There was no bribing of British officials, but there were ways of getting even smuggled guns across the border. The soldiers couldn't watch every mile of it. The rifles were hidden snuggly near the border of the Independent Territory, and only Clanton and his trusted men, three loyal, taciturn Turkomen, knew where. But he didn't dare try to sell them on this side of the line, and he didn't dare cross the border without Baber Ali Khan's protection.

"Sahib!"

He whirled to see just the man he had been wanting to see—Ahmed Shah, a Persian who said he was a prince and acted as Baber Ali Khan's agent. He was a tall, slender man, no darker than Clanton, with aristocratic Caucasian features. Undeniably of high blood, black sheep of a fine Persian family.

Clanton grabbed him, shaking off amazed inquiries as to his appearance.

"Never mind that! Have you the word from Baber Ali Khan?"

Ahmed Shah spread his hands helplessly.

"I have a word, but not what you wished. Baber Ali Khan will have nothing to do with it. He says the British will not like it if he buys Russian guns, or protects their sale, and the money he would get is not worth risking their friendship."

"The British!" raged Clanton, clenching his huge fists convulsively. "Always the damned British—well, all right."

Turning, he strode away down the street, with the lurching roll of a seaman, and natives scrambled out of his way. Even the tall hillmen, truculent and with knives in their shawl girdles, stepped aside after a glance at his dark, convulsed face. Ahmed Shah watched him go, smiled enigmatically, then turned and entered a certain courtyard. He climbed the stair down which Clanton had tumbled shortly before, and was admitted through a certain door by a Punjabi maid who wore a brand new pair of baggy trousers.

Olga rose and came toward him, arms outstretched, tawny eyes glowing. The Oriental look in them was emphasized now. Lithely she slipped into his arms and lifted her lips for his kiss. He caressed her with the nonchalant air of a conqueror.

"You have done what we planned?"

He nodded, smiling.

"He will not dare stay here now. He'll leave Peshawur before midnight."

But Clanton wasn't leaving just yet. He was surging into a certain dive and demanding something with a kick. Frustration turns some men to drink; and Clanton had had his bellyful of frustration that day. He was seething and the capering and wriggling of the dancing girls only brought a scowl to his brows.

"Opium?" queried the dive-keeper hopefully. "Brandy? Charas?"

"Anything," growled Clanton. "Just so it's got power."

The man who trailed him followed the dive-keeper into a back room.

"Give the ferengi *bhang*," quoth he. "It will drive him mad; he will remember his enemies and go forth and smite the deputy commissioner. Then the British will imprison and deport him and he cannot compete with us. My brothers and I make good lever-action rifles in our hand factory. We make a gun in ten days for which we ask eighty rupees. The Russians smuggle guns in which are better than ours, bolt action, with a heathenish range, but until recently they demanded four hundred rupees, and only rich men could buy them. But this man means to sell his guns for a hundred and seventy rupees, and all men will buy them."

The other nodded as he mixed *charas*, made from crushed hemp-plant leaves, with water, mare's milk and sugar. Clanton drank it, made a wry face—possibly because of the unfamiliar taste of the water—and called for more. A few drinks and his brain began to do cartwheels. Men sitting near him, seeing his eyes turn red as coals of fire, moved hastily away from him. A saucy dancing wench, swaying seductively before him, was rewarded with a resounding smack of his open hand that sent her squealing in flight, tenderly caressed her smarting hip. Dashing the cup on the floor, Clanton rose, flung a few coins on the floor and rolled out the door.

"He has gone to cut the throat of the deputy commissioner," said the gunmaker piously. "Wonderful are the ways of Allah!"

"Allaho akbar!" agreed the dive-keeper, dexterously thieving the money pouch of a drunken Tajik.

But again they were wrong. Clanton was heading for Olga's house under full sail. He did not reel or stagger in his gait. No man could have told that he was drunk, unless one looked at his eyes, which blazed in the light of the streetlamps like those of a mad dog. He was utterly reckless of consequences—a natural result of *bhang*.

But he was crafty, too. He did not invade Olga's house from the front, but came up a narrow alley, and rapped subtly on a door. It was opened and the Shinwari thrust out a turbaned head.

"What —" Bang! He crumpled at the impact of Clanton's right mauler on his jaw. Clanton fought his way upstairs and found Ahmed with Olga, he knocked out Ahmed and found the pass on him, then raped Olga and skipped the town.

Guns of Khartum

(earliest known draft)

Emmett Corcoran shook the perspiration out of his eyes and cursed the heat that racked him, the glare that beat up from the dusty, deserted street. A pulse in his temple throbbed sickeningly, but above that he heard the deep rumble of the cannon, as he had heard them for longer than he could remember, in his present daze of fatigue. He knew they spelled the doom of Khartum. For ten months the wild hordes of the Mahdi's fanatics had ringed the city; for ten months they had beaten in vain at its crumbling walls. But the defenders could not hold out for ever.

The street along which Corcoran walked wearily was deserted. Whites and blacks kept indoors these days as much as possible. The whites in despairing fear, the blacks in sinister anticipation. There were traitors in the city, Corcoran knew. He wiped his brow with a shaky hand. His face was blackened with gunpowder smoke, and the bosom of his shirt gaped, revealing his hairy, muscular breast. A Dervish saber had slit that shirt, narrowly missing the flesh beneath—and the Dervish had died, quickly—grimly Corcoran touched the bone hilt of the saber at his side. He had learned to use a sword since he came Eastward.

A sudden shriek, startlingly loud in the tensely silent street, brought him about. He was passing a flat-roofed house with barred windows, and the sound came from within. A woman had screamed, and she had not screamed as a black wench howls under the lash—a fairly common sound in Khartum. Corcoran reached the door with a single stride, preparing to burst it inward. But it opened at his touch, and he stepped inside, blinking in the comparative darkness. Sounds of a struggle came from beyond a curtained doorway, and he sprang across the room, tore the curtains aside.

He was looking into a room which opened onto an enclosed courtyard. It was lighter there, for the last radiance of the setting sun came through an open doorway. Two women were struggling before him, and one was white—a slender, supple girl whose black hair caught the dying sun in glints of burnished bronze. It was she who had screamed, and now she cried out again, in pitiful terror, as her assailant, a pantherish Somali half-caste, forced her down across a couch. The brown girl's handsome face was convulsed with rage and as she pressed the white girl down on her back, she lifted an Egyptian dagger. Her victim's dress had been torn open at the bosom, exposing her quivering white breasts. Between those lovely ivory mounds the Somali obviously meant to plunge her lean blade.

Corcoran had never struck a woman, white or brown. But his blood was still heated from the fury of fighting and killing; months of bitter strife had roused all the color feeling in his soul, making him hate the sight of any skin not white. Now at the spectacle before him he saw red. With a stride he reached the struggling pair. Before the knife could fall he gripped the brown girl's arm and wrenched her about to face him with a violence that brought a scream of pain from her lips. It was cut short as he smashed his fist against her jaw. She stretched her length on the floor and lay still, blood trickling from the corner of her mouth. Still trembling, he stooped, grasped her by her hair and dragged her through the front room, thrusting her out into the street. She tumbled into the dust and lay whimpering.

He slammed the door and turned back into the inner room. The white girl had risen and was clutching at a hanging for support. The other hand fumbled her torn dress together. He halted before her and stood unspeaking, devouring her with his eyes. White women were scarce enough in Khartum; women of her blond beauty were scarce anywhere. Even the distant hammering of the guns was forgotten as he stood there, silent. Desire, numbed in his soul by the constant stress of fighting, was waking. Her white flesh, against a remembered background of black and brown and yellow skin, was like a cool Northern dawn.

"Who—who are you?" she gasped, frightened by his silence, by his haggard and formidable appearance.

He shook himself out of his trance.

"Corcoran," he said. "Emmett Corcoran. I was passing your house when I heard you scream. I should have killed that slut."

She shook her head, then shuddered.

"She is—was my servant—Zelda. She's been growing more and more insolent since the siege. A little while ago she became so insulting I told her I would give her a whipping. It's the custom to chastise servants here, you know. At that she flew into a fury and attacked me, saying she'd kill me. We were alone in the house. I'd don't doubt that she would, if you hadn't come—you are wounded!"

He shook his head, involuntarily rubbed his hand on his pants' leg.

"It's not my blood. We made a sortie, outside the walls—"

"Oh, please forgive my stupidity!" she exclaimed contritely. "Sit down and let me get a basin of water for you—and food—there's still a little in the house."

He sank down on the couch, grateful for its softness and suddenly realizing his exhaustion.

"You are not a soldier?" she asked, as he plunged his hands and face into the bowl she brought.

"No. I'm an American. Was hunting ivory in the lower Sudan when the Mahdi rebellion broke. I was lucky to get into Khartum ahead of them. I've been helping defend the town as well as I could."

"I have heard of you," she said, her fine eyes lighting with interest. He watched them in fascination, so different from the hot brown eyes he had been used to for so long. "They say you are a crack shot, and use a sword like a master."

He grinned wryly.

"I learned to shoot on the Texas ranch where I was born. Never touched a sword until I came to Africa. But cold steel's handy when powder gets scarce—like it is now."

"Was the sortie successful?" she asked.

He shrugged his shoulders.

"They ran before us; we lopped a few heads and chased them for a few hundred yards—then rode back with a thousand Dervish devils yapping at our heels. These sorties are mainly to keep them occupied—to keep them from rushing the walls in full force. There are breaches in the walls we can't mend—if they ever find them—"

"We can't hold out much longer unless Kitchener gets here with reinforcements," murmured the girl, seating herself on the couch beside him. Her fine eyes were shadowed with haunting fear. "My name is Ruth Brenton. I came here to visit my uncle, a merchant. He was killed in the first part of the siege. I couldn't get away, of course. I'm afraid—terribly afraid. This whole country and its people terrify me. It's so different—so utterly different from England. And there's a man in the Mahdi's army—a French renegade—Gerard Latour. I met him at Cairo, and he followed me here—annoyed me until my uncle ordered him from the house. Later we learned he was even then a spy and agent for the Mahdi. He's out there, with them—" Her white hand swept vaguely in the direction of the Nile, and her face paled. "He's sent me a message that he'll have me, if he had to tear the city to pieces."

Suddenly she turned and threw her arms about Corcoran's corded neck, as if seeking security in the contact of a strong man.

"Oh, I'm afraid! I'm afraid!"

Corcoran gathered her in his arms, held her close. Their faces were close together, his fierce blue eyes blazing into hers. The feel of that supple white body in his arms, the first white woman he had touched for three years, drove a pulse of fire through his veins. He forgot the encircling menace drawing closer and closer about the walls of doomed Khartum—forgot the fatigue and the longing for sleep that, after thirty-six sleepless hours had driven him from the wall. As she read the flame in his eyes she tried at first to draw away from him. But his arm was about her supple waist, pinning her to him. His other hand fumbled her torn dress apart, and a deep sigh escaped his lips as his fingers cupped a firm warm globe of white and pink flesh. He felt her resistance melting; the supple arms straining against him glided once more about his neck. With a gasp he thrust his fingers deep into her flaxen curls, pressing her face forward, until her red lips were crushed against his. The tip of her tongue was sweet as burning honey against his lips, and as she took fire from his flaming kisses, her embrace became convulsive, a low whimper of ecstasy escaped from her lips. His hand glided lower, drew her dress upward.

The sun had set; the swift African dusk was deepening into night. Outside the street was silent. Over the flat roofs of the houses came the mutter of the guns of Khartum.

On the couch in the room that opened on the courtyard where palm trees hung their fronds in the windless air, Emmett Corcoran awoke suddenly and sat up, a sense of impending peril clutching at his throat. There was no moon, but enough starlight filtered in through door and barred window to let his make out the figure of the girl who slept beside him. Her white limbs were a soft glimmer in the shadows. He rose swiftly, reaching for his pistol belt and saber, which hung on a chair near the couch. The guns were ominously silent. A tense, shuddering stillness hung over Khartum.

Ruth awakened and sleepily reached her arms for him.

"Is it dawn?"

He kissed her, gently caressed her firm young breasts.

"No. But get up and put your dress on. Something's brewing. I don't like this stillness. It may presage a night attack—*God!*"

Ruth screamed as she sprang frantically from the couch and clutched him, but her cry was drowned in the devil's clamor that had burst outside. All hell had broken loose in Khartum. The silent town came to frenzied life in a cataclysm of hideous screams, yells, curses and shots. A red glare of burning houses rose over the flat roofs.

"The Mahdists!" gasped Corcoran, electrified. "They're inside the wall!"

And they were. Fifty thousand of them. In the darkness they had crept through a breach in the wall cut by the river. They were in the city and at their work of butchery before the defenders knew their peril. After that it was massacre.

In Ruth's house Corcoran snatched on his boots and spoke quickly to the terrified girl.

"We've got to find some place to hide until we can get a chance to steal a boat and slip down the Nile. This house isn't so far from the wall, but—"

A rush of feet in the street, a bestial, exultant howling drowned his words. The Dervishes were upon them. The outer door began to splinter under the assault of hammering musket-butts, and above the savage yells a fierce European voice was yelling commands.

"Latour!" cried Ruth, paling.

"Out into the courtyard!" snapped Corcoran. "No time for you to dress now. Maybe we can get out that way—"

They ran into the courtyard, just as a small door in the wall opened to admit a flood of wild black faces and tossing torches. Sabers gleamed, eyes rolled whitely in the lurid light. At the sight of the girl, clad only in slippers and a thin low-necked chemise, a wild beast roar went up. The soft gleam of white limbs and naked breasts maddened these brutes from the southern grasslands. Beyond them Corcoran glimpsed the triumphant face of Zelda, the Somali girl. She had led the ravishers upon them.

Corcoran backed into an angle of the wall, thrusting Ruth behind him. Sword in one hand, pistol in the other he faced the oncoming warriors. One threw up an ancient musket and when it flashed and bellowed the ball whistled close by Corcoran's ear. Corcoran shot the Dervish through the head, and his bullets raked the court, spilling writhing figures on the flowerbeds, sending the charge reeling back in red ruin. But they came on again, fired to frenzy by the sight of the woman cowering behind him, and his Colt was empty. The first black to come within reach dropped with a split skull as Corcoran's saber cut the torchlight like a flicker of blue lightning. Again and again and again he struck, and a man dropped at each stroke. His muscles were like cords of steel. He loomed like a grim figure of death among the tall Dervishes, and the fury of his strokes beat down their blades, the swiftness of his onslaught blinded and paralyzed them. For an instant the impossible happened, and one man held a whole horde at bay.

Then another band came pouring into the court from the house—the group which had shattered the street door. A tall figure in Arab garb lifted a pistol and fired over the heads of the milling mob. Corcoran swayed and his sword clanged on the flags. He fell as a tree falls and lay still, blood oozing from his head. A dozen spears went up, but before they could fall Ruth had flung herself, screaming, on his body, sheltering his flesh with her own. The spears paused, hovered. Then the crowd was split by the rush of the man in Arab dress and his band. The leader bent, grasped Ruth's arm and hauled her to her feet. In the light of the torches a lean, mocking, saturnine face smiled at her from beneath the flowing Arab headdress.

"Latour!" she sobbed.

"Your faithful admirer, mademoiselle," he answered ironically. "Come to claim you—as I swore I would!"

"You beast!" she moaned. "You've killed him!"

"I seldom miss," he agreed calmly. "Enough! I have what I came for! Why struggle, you little fool? Would you not rather be my slave than the slave of one of these black brutes? Khartum has fallen; the Mahdi is master of the Sudan—and I am high in his favor! Come! In my tent we shall celebrate the victory of this night!"

Laughing at the revealing whirl of white limbs as she struggled vainly, the renegade lifted her in his arms, crushing her resistance, and strode toward the open gate. Though she fought him like a wild thing, she hardly felt his lustful hands on her naked thighs, her bare breasts. She was not aware of the brutal laughter of the warriors, mocking her nudity. Staring over her captor's shoulder, her dillated, tear-filled and horror-misted eyes were fixed in frenzied despair on the figure that lay limply in the angle of the wall, amidst a litter of mangled black figures.

The gate closed behind the renegade and his straggling horde. A slim, brown-skinned figure, vague in the glow of a fallen torch, stole from the shadows and bent over the senseless American. He was heavy, but her slender arms were strong and supple. Still it was all she could do to drag him across the court and into a room. There she drew the blinds carefully before she lighted a candle.

Perhaps it was the gleam in his eyes that roused Corcoran. He blinked stupidly about and sat up, fumbling at his belt. He stared in amazement at Zelda, standing over him, her hands on her hips.

"Where is Ruth?" he demanded. Now that his head was clearing he could hear the sounds that accompanied the sack of Khartum—distant screams, howls of triumph, and shots. He reeled to his feet, stood unsteadily. Blood was dried on his scalp. A sudden weakness caused him to sink down on the couch.

"Latour took her," answered Zelda. "He shot you, but the ball only cut your skin and grazed your skull. They all thought you were dead."

Corcoran cursed deep throatedly, and again reeled to his feet.

"I'll kill him! He shan't have her!"

"He *has* her!" Zelda moved before him, swaying her insolent hips, molded by the short skirt she wore, slit on each side from waist to hem. Her sleek brown flanks gleamed in the dim candlelight, and her scintillant eyes were less an invitation than a demand. "Don't be a fool! He has taken her to the Mahdi's camp in a plain on the river shore. Thousands of warriors guard the camp. How can you hope to reach her, much less rescue her?"

Despair settled over him like a cloud.

"What's your game?" he muttered. She came close to him with a swaying, provocative gait that revealed to him the full length of a sleek thigh and the contour of a full ripe hip through the gaping skirt. She pressed her hands below her already tilted breasts and forced them even more prominently upward.

"Am I not beautiful?" she demanded. "As beautiful as the white woman? I love strong men. You are strong. You struck me senseless with a blow. I did not hate you for that, as a weak white woman would hate you! I could love you, white man! When you slew the warriors in the garden I was hot with desire for you!"

He scowled at her, knowing women of her sort admired strength and brutality. With the feel of Ruth's white body still tingling his nerves, Zelda was almost repugnant to him, as much so as a handsome woman can be to a normal man. Zelda was beautiful, in a wild, bold, sensual way. She was no negress.

"I hold you in my power," she said scornfully. "Khartum has fallen; Gordon is dead. I have seen his head, stuck on the point of a spear. The Mahdi is the master of all the Sudan. I saved your life because I love a strong man, but I can cry out and men will come and take your head. Choose!"

His mind was working swiftly. Dead, he could never hope to follow and take Ruth from Latour as he determined to do; living, there was still hope for rescuing the girl. He choked down the urge to seize the sneering brown girl and break her neck.

"Choice?" he growled. "This is my answer!"

Catching her roughly in his arms he tore the skirt from her body and threw her on the couch. And as his hands explored her breasts and all the intimate mysteries of her bold, brown body, he did not have to feign the fire that kindled in his veins.

Ruth Brenton looked wearily through the gilded bars of the small window which formed almost her only contact with the outer world. The sun was setting over the straggling mud houses grass-thatched *tokuls* of Omdurman, the barbaric capital of the Mahdi. Five months had passed since the fall of Khartum—five months of shame and fear and terror to Ruth Brenton. From beyond the curtained doorway of the room in which she stood sounded the voices of other women—Turkish, Arab, Egyptian women who shared her slavery. She was Latour's favorite—not his only woman. The Frenchman had sunk as low as any wild tousle-headed Sudanese who followed the banner of the Mahdi. The Dervishes were growing rich with plunder; they were building them houses of stone and mud, instead of the grass-thatched huts they were born in, and the slave markets were thronged with captive women, the markets with stolen merchandise. Ruth was dressed like any seraglio slave, in little red sandals and a light silk *gandourah*, which was belted at the waist by a broad velvet girdle into which pearls were sewn thickly; the garment displayed the contours, while barely veiling the intimate details of her dainty figure.

She sighed as she looked out on the barbaric scene. The alley quickly gave way into a market square in which she could see black men and women moving about, jesting, laughing, quarreling, making love. One solitary figure was idling in the alley near the window—a tall man, dressed in the headdress and robes of an Arab. Something about his bearing sent a strange, nameless throb of familiarity through her, though she knew she had never seen him before. He moved idly toward the window and she was about to withdraw, out of sight when he lifted his headdress and looked full at her. The last rays of the sun fell on his lifted face and she almost cried out. She caught the bars of the window to keep from falling as a deadly weakness surged over her. It was the face of a man she had mourned for five months as dead—the face of Emmett Corcoran!

In an instant he had drawn together the fold of his *kafieh* and paused below the window, leaning on a staff. Idly he scribbled in the sand with the tip, as Arabs often do. But there was method in the scribbling. Plainly traced in the sand, she read: "Be ready; I'm coming for you as soon as it is dark."

Then he drew his sandal across the sand, erasing what he had written, and moved away up the alley, to mingle with the crowd in the market. Ruth moved away from the window, feeling stifled by the drum of her heart. Hope for her own rescue for the moment was submerged by a wild joy that he was alive, a sick terror that he would fall into the hands of their enemies. He knew the awful risk he ran, moving among them in disguise, when a false word or gesture might unmask him, and doom him to a hideous death. She had seen men burned alive in the market, had seen women flayed on a scaffold, for merely disobeying the commands of the fiend who called himself the Prophet.

Then followed a fear that she would betray her excitement. She must hide it, especially from Zelda. The girl had come into camp and joined Latour's household shortly after the sack of Khartum. She had been sullen and savage, as if harboring a bitter disappointment or frustration. And she had not failed to vent her spite on Ruth whenever she dared. She feared Latour's anger too much to venture far, but in many small, spiteful ways she had had her revenge on her former mistress. Ruth hated and feared her. Of late there had been a new and vicious meaning in Zelda's leering smile, promising some cruelty of which only she was aware.

Ruth sprang up as Latour entered. The Frenchman had degenerated. Continual debauches had weakened him, made his features coarser and flabbier. Physically and mentally he was crumbling, just as men whispered the Mahdi too was crumbling. Latour had no love for his master; he lived in fear that Muhammad would learn of Ruth and take the white girl away from him. For that reason he kept her more closely confined that he would have otherwise; there was no chance for her to escape the city alone. Ruth, too, lived in horror of such an event. She loathed and hated Latour, but her fear of the Mahdi was a nightmare. She had seen him, riding through the market, huge, black, bearded and hideous, and he haunted her dreams with fear.

But she feared Latour only a little less. Of late the Frenchman had treated her cruelly, even for him. He had taught her many things, including the sting of a rhino-hide *kurbash* on her naked, writhing body. Now he kissed her roughly, began playing with her breasts and pulled her down on his knee. She submitted perforce, but with greater reluctance than ever. The sight of Corcoran, the knowledge that he was alive, made her slavery seem more abominable than ever. Latour sensed her reluctance, and it angered him.

"So you cringe at my caresses!" he snarled. "Must I teach you obedience again? You need a taste of the whip!"

"No!" she begged, forcing herself to clasp her arms about his neck. The threat terrified her. "Please don't whip me! I always obey you!"

"Yes," he snarled, "but with reluctance. With evident loathing. You hate me, damn your British soul—don't try to deny it! I—"

A sudden tramp of feet sounded in an outer corridor. There was a squealing of women scattering in the adjoining room, and then the curtains of the door were jerked aside and a band of warriors stood before them, led by an ostrich-plumed chief in full barbaric regalia, a sword in his hand.

Latour sprang up, angrily.

"What do you mean by entering my house in this manner?"

"I need give no explanation for obeying the command of our lord, the Mahdi!" replied the *emir* arrogantly. Latour paled. "I have come at his order to convey that English girl there to his palace."

Latour trembled and for an instant it seemed that he would draw his sword and leap at the speaker, who waited, smiling grimly. There was no love between the renegade and the native chiefs. But fear mastered the Frenchman's anger. A grey pallor overspread his swarthy cheeks and he said sullenly: "Take her, then. I obey the Mahdi's command."

"Well for you, white man," said the *emir* haughtily. "You know the law—all captives must be brought to the Beit-el-Maal, the treasure house of our master, there to be apportioned or appropriated by himself as he deems fit. This law you disobeyed when you took the white woman for yourself. The Mahdi generously spares your life, because of your past services. But beware!"

Seizing Ruth roughly by her shoulder he thrust her into the hands of a grinning warrior.

"Latour!" she cried frantically, writhing in her captor's brutal hands. "Don't—for God's sake don't let them take me to that beast!"

Sullenly the Frenchman lowered his eyes, refusing to meet her frantic gaze. Her captor slapped her contemptuously across her soft hips and pushed her ahead of him. Helplessly she was marched out of the room and down the corridor. Presently the outer door banged with a brazen clangor.

Latour staggered toward a wine jug on a table, cursing vilely. As he lifted the jug he caught a movement of the tapestry on the wall. Dashing down the jug he sprang, jerked the hanging aside and dragged Zelda, the Somali girl, from her hiding place.

"Why were you hiding there?" he demanded.

"I was in the other room when the soldiers come," she answered. "I was afraid and ran in here and hid."

"When did you ever run from men?" he snarled. "You lie! You—" Suddenly, at the sight of the malicious smile lurking on her lips, light came to him in a grand burst. Cursing he grasped her slim shoulders and shook her savagely: "Damn you, you are the cause of this! You told the Mahdi I had a white girl in my *harim!* You hated her—knew she feared him even more than she did me!"

She screamed as he ripped out his saber—her scream died to a gurgle as his blind thrust ripped through her breast. She caught at the blade with her bare hands and sank down writhing. As he tore the steel free she went limp. Cursing like a madman, Latour kicked her limp body and again staggered toward the wine jug. Again he halted. The curtains billowed and a tall figure stood there before him. A man in Arab garb, whose eyes burned under the shadow of his *kafieh*. A big pistol in the man's hand menaced the amazed Frenchman. In English the intruder spoke: "Where is she, Latour?"

"Who?" gasped the renegade.

"Ruth Brenton!"

"The Mahdi took her! I swear it!" Latour's eyes narrowed. "By God, you are Corcoran! I thought you were dead!"

"So did others. That wench on the floor there saved me for her own purposes. I finally got away from her and slipped down the river one dark night. I couldn't speak Arabic well enough to get into the Mahdi's camp. I had to go away where I could get a disguise. I was grabbed by slave traders who started to the Abyssinia border with me. It's taken me this long to get away and get back here. And now you lie to me!"

"I swear I do not!" The Frenchman was lashing himself into a frenzy of jealous hate. "You shall not have her, though! I had rather the Mahdi had her than you! You were the one she loved! That's why she hated me! I will send him your head to give to her1! Oh, you dare not shoot! A shot will bring a hundred men about your ears! I'll take your head!"

And whipping out his saber he rushed at Corcoran, laughing wildly.

He was right in believing that Corcoran feared to fire. The American stepped aside, thrusting the big Colt back into his girdle, drawing his saber. Latour laughed like a wolf. Confident of his skill with the naked steel he came on. He had learned swordsmanship in the fencing schools of Paris; but Corcoran had learned his in warfare or in naked deserts, where no one had the chance to repeat a mistake.

Latour feinted and lunged; Corcoran swayed his body at the waist, took the point in the loose *abba*, under his armpit. Too late Latour saw his mistake. The scream that rose in his throat was severed as the downward-lashing saber in Corcoran's hand split his skull to the teeth. He fell across Zelda's body and lay still, his shattered head in a ghastly puddle of blood and brains. Corcoran spat at the corpse and turned hurriedly away. There had been no clang of steel to rouse the household, and the thick carpets had muffled the stamp of sandaled feet. None saw or heard the vague figure that glided out of a side door and melted into the darkness of the alley.

Corcoran hurried toward a certain point of the town, near the market. There he was to meet a Copt who had fled from his master and yearned for Egypt. The Copt knew where a boat could be stolen. In it they would attempt the perilous journey down the river. Corcoran had expected to meet the man at the appointed rendezvous, with the girl. Now he must tell him that they must postpone their flight until he, Corcoran, could attempt the desperate venture of stealing her out of the Mahdi's palace. Already his quick brain was working out a plan. He had not spent several days in Omdurman without having obtained a good idea of the plan of Muhammad's palace, though he had not expected to have to invade it.

Fires blazed in the market and men reeled and shouted drunkenly. A few steps more and he would reach the alley where the Copt would be waiting to tell him where he had hidden the boat. Corcoran absently glanced at the severed heads adorning the rows of posts. In that hell-town fresh heads adorned the points almost every day. And he froze, with an icy hand clutching his heart. In the firelight he recognized one of those heads, grinning vacantly, glassy eyed. It was the Copt who had intended escaping with him. He must have been recognized, on his way to the rendezvous, by some one who knew he was a runaway slave. Punishment had been instant.

Corcoran stood paralyzed, while the world crashed about his ears. Then everything floated red before him—red figures reeling against a hellfire background. In blind fury he turned toward the Mahdi's palace. Fate had dealt the hand against him, but at least the author of their misfortune, his and hers, should not survive it. He would kill the Mahdi, kill the girl, mercifully, and then wreak havoc on the black hordes until a merciful sword thrust quieted his tempestuous soul.

Like a shadow he glided along a meandering side street and melted into an alley that ran along the side of Muhammad's palace. It was dark there, but not too dark for him to see a man squatted on his haunches, a naked scimitar by his side, his chin resting on his knees. He was asleep. Ostrich plumes nodded over his head. Corcoran knew the man was a high official in the palace, and in temporary disfavor with the Mahdi. This menial task had been set as punishment. The Mahdi posted guards only as a sort of formality. Not a man in his army but believed he was the rightful successor of the Prophet, a sort of god on earth; the pagans in his horde worshipped him as a god. No enemy could reach him, in the midst of his city, the Mahdi believed. After all, he was a Negro, with all a Negro's carelessness.

Like a shadow of doom, Corcoran loomed over the sleeping *emir*, saber lifted. The alley was a blind one; this was the only entrance. He could not enter without stepping over the man, and that would surely awaken him. Three times he lifted the blade, and three times he lowered his arm, cursing his squeamishness. But he could not bring himself to kill a sleeping man, not even one of Muhammad's devils. Lifting the saber again, he brought the hilt down with a force that stretched the *emir* senseless.

Corcoran glided down the alley until he reached a certain door. He tried it gently. It was barred, but a thin knife blade slipped between door and jamb lifted the bar. The next instant he was inside, finding himself in a short hall, lit with brass lamps. Within a few feet it ended at a curtained doorway. And beyond that doorway came sounds that brought the red mist floating before his eyes again—gasping, hysterical sobbing of a woman, and the brutal, low laugh of a man.

He tore aside the curtains. A huge black man whirled to meet him. In the sight of his followers the Mahdi affected a tattered *djibbeh* and garments. They would scarcely have recognized the resplendent figure in silk and gold that faced the maddened American. Beyond him Ruth dropped the golden vase she had been using to fight off the slavering brute and sank to the floor, crying out with relief.

The Mahdi had been a notable fighting man in his youth. He was still quick enough to elude Corcoran's first, vengeful thrust. It slit the skin of his fat neck and brought a stream of blood. Before Corcoran could strike again, the Mahdi had closed with him, and for an instant Corcoran felt the play of giant muscles. But he had gripped the fat throat, strangling the Mahdi's yell, and suddenly the struggling figure in his grip crumpled. Evil living had made a shell of a once mighty frame. The Mahdi's eyes distended, he caught at a dagger, and Corcoran smashed his hilt against his jaw, too close to use the blade. The Mahdi fell and lay sprawling, blood from the scratch on his neck mingling with blood from his mangled jaw. Corcoran lifted the sword to strike off his head, then a sound brought him around.

The *emir* he had struck down in the alley stood in the curtained door, eyes wide with horror.

"The Mahdi!" he gasped. "You've killed him! His throat is cut—"

"Yes, I killed him!" snapped Corcoran. "And you helped us!"

The man recoiled, his dusky skin going ashen.

"You—you are mad!" he stuttered.

"Yes? Who'll believe you say you didn't? You were in disfavor, or you wouldn't have been doing guard duty out in that blind alley. That's a slave's job. How could I get in without your assistance?"

"You can't prove this!" panted the *emir*. "The people will tear you to pieces!"

"Sure! But they'll tear you, too! I won't have to prove anything. I'll just tell them you were our ally. They'll be eager for victims. You won't have a chance."

"Mercy, in the name of Allah!" begged the wretch. "Let me go! Let us slip away! I will keep silent, and you do the same."

"That's not enough," said Corcoran inexorably. "You've got to help us get away, and come with us! You've got authority—use it in getting us out of the city! We'll go to your house, and get camels and pull out. People know the Mahdi had a new woman, and won't interrupt. They won't find him until morning. We'll have a good start then. Come with us and surrender to the British. I'll promise you they'll give you your life."

A moment later they were stealing down the alley, Ruth muffled in a robe snatched from a couch. Corcoran kept close to the *emir*, pistol ready. They appropriated three racing camels in a court near the palace, the *emir's* word being enough authority.

Only when they were racing across the desert, with distance rapidly widening between them and danger, the girl whispered to Corcoran: "Was the Mahdi really dead?"

He placed his lips to her ear: "No. The *emir* only thought he was, and I didn't finish him; that would have put him wise. But he won't live many days; I heard his rotten heart pumping like a war-drum."

He spoke with confidence, and as it later proved, prophetically. But just now he was more interested in the girl in his arms than anything else. With a deep sigh of satisfaction he drew her close to him. Behind was terror and peril. Ahead was safety and happiness; he fondled a soft breast and was aware of a great content.

Daughters of Feud

(untitled synopsis)

Braxton Brent, schoolmaster in a little mountain-country school, was confronted with the task of disciplining Joan Kirby and Susannah Pritchard, nineteen-year-old girls, for fighting each other. They were defiant and insolent, and he knew he must whip them, as he had been warned he must do in order to make them respect him, by Judge Harrison, the only educated man in the community, and head of the board of trustees. Harrison had warned him that he must punish his pupils in the fashion of a century ago, and perhaps fight their parents if he did. Angered at being driven into such a position, Brent took the girls off into a shed off the main school building, used for such purposes, after dismissing school, where after a struggle, he whipped Susannah soundly with a well-worn strap that hung there for the purpose—his predecessor had been run out of the country by the pupils for his failure to use it. Then he sent Susannah, sobbing and promising vengeance, out of the room, and started to whip Joan, who made no resistance. He lost his nerve when he started to whip her, and had sexual intercourse with her instead.

Returning to his cabin, some distance from the school, he was confronted by Buck Kirby, Joan's brother, who covered him with a pistol and began cursing him for whipping his sister. Buck was a wild young feudist, wanted by the law. He had met a youngster going from school who told him Brent had taken Joan into the licking shed to whip her. Brent knocked the gun from his hand with a poker, and in the ensuing struggle, Buck was stunned by a fall, and Brent got the pistol and drove him away, swearing vengeance. Brent knew it was only by chance that he had got the best of the young outlaw, and did not see how he could escape Buck's wrath. But his newfound love for Joan would not let him run away.

Called to his door, he was set upon by a gang of men and carried captive to a cabin in the mountains. His abductors were the Pritchards, who were intent on mutilating him, not because he had whipped Susannah, but because she had not whipped Joan. Susannah said she had listened and had not heard the sound of blows, or Joan crying. They were about to emasculate him when Joan appeared, alone, and swore that he did whip her, displaying red welts on her body to prove it. But they refused to let him go, and seized her, to glut an old lust and an old spite on her. In desperation Brent broke away and began fighting, and in the midst of it, Buck appeared and shot down three or four of the Pritchards. Brent then tensed himself for the bullet he expected, only to be told that he had to marry Joan—the very thing he most desired.

Daughters of Feud

(earliest known draft)

Braxton Brent, new schoolmaster in the little mountain school of Whiskey Run, sprang from behind his hand-hewn desk as smoldering hatred burst into a flame of feminine rage between Joan Kirby and Ann Pritchard, daughters of feuding families. They came together in the aisle between the rude, handmade desks, in a whirl of skirts and thrashing white limbs. Garments disarranged by their violence displayed generous expanses of smooth pink flesh. Mountain girls fought like wildcats. The other pupils, used to such scenes, sprang up and moved back, giving them room. They did not shout and jeer, like city-bred children; they maintained a tense silence, but blazing eyes and pale, hard-set lips told of fierce emotions within. Whiskey Run School, where old hates smoldered, was a powder keg that might explode any instant with devastating violence.

Ann screamed like a wild thing, clawing, tearing, trying to gouge the other girl's eyes out, but Joan fought in silence, striking and kneeing like a man. Before they could damage each other much, Brent had reached them and grabbing each by a straining, slim shoulder, tore them apart by main strength. The new schoolmaster was young, well built and athletic; it was his first experience as a schoolteacher, and he was getting plenty.

Ann writhed in his grip, trying to get at her enemy, but Joan stood passively, her lip curled in scorn as she looked at the other girl. Her splendid bosom, heaving, told of her controlled passion. Her dress had been ripped open, and the sight of those full, white globes as they rose and fell stormily quickened Brent's pulse. The sight of a sleek white thigh peeping through a rent in her skirt that ran from hip to hem did not tend to make him any more calm. Ann was not so disheveled as to clothes; Joan had fought to damage her enemy, not her garments. A trickle of blood seeped from the corner of Ann's sullen mouth.

"Let go me, damn you!" raged the Pritchard girl. "Let me git my hands onto her! I'll tear off every stitch she's got on!"

"Why didn't you do it when you had the chance?" retorted Joan disdainfully. "If he hadn't pulled me off, I'd a-beat yo' haid into mush. You better let go of us, mister; we'll have it out in spite of you!"

"Shut up, both of you!" he snapped, interposing his trim, strong frame between them. "Didn't I say there was to be no fighting in school?"

Behind him some boy laughed jeeringly. Ann spat at him, and Joan laughed in his face, amusedly. She was a magnificent figure as she stood there, scornful and angry, yet smiling defiantly, heedless of the display of her splendid bosom. She was fair, Ann was dark; both were handsome as only mountain girls can be. And both were wild, untamed young barbarians, eager to make life hell for the "foreign" schoolmaster. Brent realized he faced a crisis and in spite of himself he turned cold inside. There was insolence and mockery in all the faces all about him, the pupils realizing he faced a test of mastership, and doubting his ability to conquer it. The mockery in the faces of the girls he held apart was unendurable. Ann sneered openly, wiping the blood from her lips, tossing back her black hair insolently; the quiet, dimpling smile on Joan's lips was just as arrogant. A slow anger began to stir in Brent's bosom.

He had been warned of some such situation by Judge Harrison, the one cultured, educated man in the community and the head of the board of trustees, who had hired Brent. Harrison was wise, with the hard, cynical wisdom of a man who knows the people of the backwoods as well as their softer cousins of the cities. Concisely he had told Brent what he might expect, and how he must meet his problems. Brent stood aghast.

"Why, good God, man, that's barbarous! Outrageous! A custom that went out of fashion a hundred years ago, even in Europe! It's medieval!"

"Whiskey Run's medieval," answered the Judge. "These mountain people are all living in the seventeenth century, actually. You've got to meet barbarity with barbarity—or rather, anachronism with anachronism."

"And you mean to tell me that I'm expected to punish nineteen-year-old girls in this barbarous and indecent manner?"

"That or let them kick you all over the place. You've got to make your pupils respect you, and the only way you can do that is with a strap. If you let them get the idea that you're afraid to handle them roughly, they'll make life hell for you, and eventually run you off, just as they did the fellow—a Yankee he was—who tried to teach school before you."

"But won't their parents object?"

"Perhaps. But in that case you'll just have to fight the parents! You look capable—but remember, mountain men don't fight according to the civilized rules!"

"A nice position!" quoth Brent bitterly. But when a man is flat broke, he can't be choice. He had taken the job; and now he was face to face with a crisis which would determine his status in Whiskey Run. If he let these girls get away with this, his pupils would run him off the place. If he did whip these nineteen-year-old culprits in the customary mountain manner, he'd probably have their relatives gunning for him. He was in for it, whichever way he turned. And resentment at the position into which he was forced, rebounded on the culprits. At the insolent smiles on their faces, he saw red. All right! They'd put him on the spot, and they'd take the consequences. Whatever happened to him afterwards, he'd take it out of their skins now.

"School's dismissed," he said crisply. "All pass out except Ann and Joan. As for you young ladies, we have a date in the woodshed!"

Ann snarled, and the smile was wiped off Joan's face. In the faces of the other pupils grew a grudging respect. The new teacher was not a scary softy, after all. Silently they gathered their dog-eared books and trudged out, boys and girls, from tiny tots in long-tailed shirts to gawky boys and strapping girls almost grown. Without a word they filed out, and Brent locked the door after them. The windows had heavy wooden bars, and the only other door in the one-room building led into the woodshed. Pocketing the key, he turned grimly to the culprits who faced him still scornful, but with apprehension beginning to mingle itself with their disdain.

"You don't dast lick me!" Ann spat at him. "My folks'd skin you alive!"

He thought it quite probable. Might made right in the mountains; because a method of procedure was a custom didn't necessarily mean that folks would put up with it. Customs, like laws, were obeyed only when somebody had the power to enforce them. But he was too mad to answer Ann's taunt. He grabbed her by her shoulder and propelled her through the door, into the small lean-to shed where the wood was piled. There was a bench there, too, and on a nail near the door hung a leather strap, worn smooth by frequent use. It was because of reluctance or inability to use that strap that Brent's Northern predecessor had been run out of the school and the county, and beaten to a pulp by the young barbarians for good measure. The most successful teacher the school had ever known had been a giant raised in the country who licked boys and girls impartially and mercilessly into submission, battled enraged parents with knives and shotguns, and retired honored and beloved after years of triumphant pedagogy. Since then one teacher after another had been routed in ignominious defeat.

"Damn, you let go a-me!" gritted Ann, kicking viciously and fighting like a wildcat, as Brent took the strap from its peg. "You don't dast lick me—you bastard! You don't dast—"

She was quickly disillusioned. She was strong and supple as only a mountain girl can be, and she fought like a wildcat, but Brent was an athletic young man, and he was fighting mad. There was a brief whirl of struggle, and then his superior strength made itself evident. Crushing her resistance, he sat down on the bench and imprisoned her, cursing and kicking, across his knee, and pulled up her skirt. He had already learned that the girls of Whiskey Run wore no underwear.

"Now, you little devil," he said grimly, "I'm going to show you who's boss here!"

And firmly grasping his raging, writhing captive, he employed the strap on her bare, squirming, upturned hips with a vigor inspired by a determination to assert himself once for all. He didn't want to have to repeat this experience. At each reverberating smack a broad crimson weal appeared on her olive-tinted hips, and before he had completed his discipline, the whole surface was reddened and Ann's curses and screaming threats were changed to lusty howls of pain and pleas for mercy. When he released her, she slipped to the floor, bawling loudly, and groveled at his feet, contorting her supple body ludicrously with the smart of her crimson hips.

"Get up and get out!" he ordered, rising and opening the door. His anger had cooled and he felt a reaction—a feeling of disgust at himself and distaste for his next task. Joan Kirby was standing near the door, where she had evidently been listening to Ann's howls, with mingled feelings—elation at Ann's pain and painful anticipation of the same treatment for herself. Her eyes were dilated, her red lips parted, and she stepped hastily back, away from Brent as he came from the "licking shed."

Brent opened the outer door. "Get your books, Ann, and get going." She did so, sobbing and tenderly caressing that part of her anatomy which felt as if it were on fire at the moment. At this Joan dimpled with an smile of mocking amusement, but her fine eyes were shadowed with anxiety on her own account.

"You let her stay and listen to me gittin' licked!" Ann accused bitterly. "But you won't let me stay and listen to her holler!"

"Go on home!" Brent ordered, holding the door open for her. There was some justice in her complaint, but at the moment he hated the sight of her. The experience of exposing and whipping a full-grown girl had shaken him more than he had expected; the reaction was distinctly unpleasant and increased his resentment for the victim, who had forced him into it.

Ann went, weeping, more with anger than pain now, and safe beyond his reach outside she flung back: "Yo're partial to her! Yo're on the side of the Kirbys! I'll tell pap, you watch and see, you big bully!"

Shaking his head in disgust, he closed the door and turned back to Joan, who stood tall and splendid before him. She had drawn together the torn dress over her bosom, but through the rents still peeped vistas of rounded ivory that enflamed him. He was still angry with her, but his task was growing more distasteful every instant. She was not a spitting, snarling wildcat like Ann Pritchard. She was calm, sensible, with a certain lissome dignity about her, despite her cheap, torn dress through which her bare legs showed. There was magnificence in the set of her white shoulders and the flowing lines of her white neck, the lift of her head, the level gaze of her wide eyes.

"Well, what are you waiting for?" he asked harshly, speaking roughly and coarsely to hide his emotion. "Get on in that room. Maybe, when you're eating off the mantelpiece for the next few days, you'll learn a little respect for authority."

"You better not lick me," she answered quietly. "Pap ain't like Bill Pritchard. He won't care. He says a teacher has to warm a gal's behind now and then. But my brother Buck won't stand for it. He says nobody's goin' to tetch a Kirby woman but her own kin or wedded husband. He'll kill you shore, if you whup me!"

With an unpleasant start Brent remembered that Buck Kirby *was* this girl's brother. He had heard plenty about Buck—a wild young mountaineer, a fierce fighter and an implacable feudist, with half a dozen notches on his pistol butt. Even now young Kirby was "hiding out" somewhere in the hills, avoiding the law because of a killing done on the streets of a little mountain-town. Buck was bad, and he possessed the full flavor of the fierce clan-loyalty which is such a dominant characteristic of mountain people. Brent turned cold for an instant, then shrugged his shoulders. He was up to his neck now, and he couldn't turn back.

"I whipped Ann," he said briefly. "In fairness to her, I've got to whip you now, whether I want to or not."

He motioned her into the shed room, and she lifted her head proudly.

"I ain't a-goin' to fight agen you like she did," Joan said. I know yo're too stout for me. But yo'll be sorry for this."

It was more like a prediction than threat, as she walked regally past him into the shed room. There he turned uncertainly, and reached for her, but she drew back, curling her lip.

"Don't tetch me with yo' hands! I'll lay on that bench. You don't have to hold me, nor turn up my dress neither!"

And without a word, scornfully, she slipped out of the torn dress and stood before him, fearless and unashamed, nude but for her slippers and stockings, confined with plain elastic garters above her knees. He caught at the door jamb for support, almost overwhelmed by the abrupt unveiling of all that dazzling beauty. She was no whimpering schoolgirl, not bodily, at least, but a goddess with the full, curving, flowing lines of ripeness. She stood before him, eyes blazing with anger and resentment at the action to which he was to deliver her, but without false modesty or self-consciousness. She made no move to shield her luscious, tilted breasts or any of the other intimate contours of her glorious body.

She shrugged her white shoulders and said: "Well, let's git it over with!" and moved toward the bench, on which it was her evident intention to extend herself, hips upward. Brent caught her wrist. In that instant he knew it was impossible that he should ever lay a strap on this gorgeous creature. The very thought was preposterous.

"Wait!" he begged, dazedly, incoherently, like a man in a drunken daze. The strap fell to the floor. All he could see before him was those white arching breasts, that blinding, maddening naked body. He ceased to be a thinking, reasoning being. Instincts older than Adam took possession of his body, submerging the conscious entity that was Braxton Brent. "Joan!" It was a tortured gasp as he crushed her in his arms, greedily, hungrily, straining her naked, squirming figure against his. One arm encircled her white shoulders, the other imprisoned her generous hips. His fingers kneaded a blissful handful of firm, resilient flesh. For an instant she struggled, startled, throwing back her head, while fear grew in her fine eyes. Then as he found her parted red lips with his own, in her eyes grew the expression that is older than Eve. Convulsively her arms went about him. Catching one of his hands she drew it down between the white mounds of her quivering breasts, pressing it hard, and shivering ecstatically. A low moan of delicious torture burst from her lips, half-smothered by his passionate kisses.

He was hardly aware when he lifted her, carried her toward the heap of horse blankets in the corner; Time and conscious thought had ceased for both, drowned in a tide of elemental passion that surged again and again and again until they lay spent and whimpering in each others' arms.

It might have been hours later when Braxton Brent stumbled back into the schoolroom, and closed the door. He sank down on a seat and dropped his head in his hands, groaning in a chaotic agony of spirit. Joan was gone; a few moments ago she had gone up the road toward her home cabin, three miles away, in the gathering dusk. Her eyes had dwelt on him, enigmatically. Only meaningless, inane words had passed between them. Any words, after that storm of passionate experience, would have seemed banal. He had let her go, without a word as to his inner feelings.

But what was his inner feeling? Just then a savage shame and self-accusation. He had committed the unpardonable offense. A young girl, entrusted to him—his office was one of trust and faith, even if he did have to maintain it by force and brutality. And he had betrayed that trust. He groaned and beat his fists together in sheer agony. What should he do? He could never remain, to face Joan's questioning face day in and day out—and he knew that, despite his present self-hate for what he had done, he could not keep from repeating his sin, if sin it was. She was no wanton mountain filly; she—had been—a virgin. Even as he sat there, cursing himself for a scoundrel, he quivered inside with a hungry eagerness for the girl—for the supple melting of her delicately molded waist, the free, proud swing of her long limbs, the regal tilt of her arching breasts. Now—he must go. He would leave that night. Pride told him that if he went people would attribute his fleeing to fear of the Pritchards. Well, damn them, let them think what they would—

He started to his feet as the door burst open. In the last light of the dying west that streamed through the windows, he saw the man who stood there—a wiry, booted youth, with a broad-brimmed hat pulled low over smoldering eyes, mouth grimly set, one hand in the pocket of his ragged coat. There was menace in every line of his catlike figure.

"Where's Joan?" he rasped. "Where's my sister, damn you?"

"She's gone home," said Brent quietly, though his heart skipped a beat.

"You licked her!" he spat the accusation, his shoulder hunching slightly.

"I was heading for my home cabin for supper, when I met one of the Richardson kids. She told me you kept Joan and Ann Pritchard in after school for to whup 'em for fightin'."

"Well, suppose I did?" parried Brent, outwardly calm, though he knew his life hung on the crook of a hair-trigger. "I'm their schoolteacher. It's the custom to whip girls here if they disobey—"

The boy spat an oath.

"Custom, hell! It is if you can make it stick. I'm here to see you don't! You think I give a damn what you do to Ann Pritchard? You can skin her rear ever' day if you want to. But you nor no other damn' Yankee's goin' to whip any of my women-folks."

"I'm not a Yankee, confound you!" snapped Brent. "I was born and raised in Richmond."

"I don't keer," snarled Kirby. "They was a Yankee before you, and *he* knowed better'n to lick a Kirby gal!"

"That's right," growled Brent. "He licked girls who didn't belong to the feuding families, though, and finally people ran him out for showing partiality. Well, you can't run me out that way!"

"Who said anything about runnin' you out?" ripped out Kirby, lurching toward him, his face convulsed with fury. "You laid hands on my sister, and—"

His hand came out of his coat pocket, gripping a cocked pistol. But the hammer caught in the lining of the pocket for an instant, and as it came free Brent struck with the poker he had snatched up, struck with desperate quickness and force. The gun spun from Kirby's numb fingers, and Brent lifted the poker again. But before he could strike, Buck was on him with the blinding speed of a maddened panther.

In the instant of contact Brent felt the young mountaineer's muscles like steel springs under his hands. The poker was ripped from his fingers as the men went down together. Kirby, even as they fell, wrenched himself around to land on top, but Brent, employing a half-forgotten wrestling trick of his college days, used this momentum to complete the circle and bring Kirby under him again. He was only half-successful. They struck the floor sidewise, in a dogfall, but Fate was playing her hand for Brent in that deal. Kirby's head smacked hard against the massive foot of a hand-hewn desk, and for an instant he went limp.

Brent tore free, sprang to the fallen pistol and caught it up, just as Kirby came to his feet like a spring shooting erect, shaking his head, snarling and crouching for another leap. He checked at the menace of the cocked pistol.

"Get out of here!" ordered Brent. "I'm running this school to suit myself! Get going!"

There was no fear in Buck Kirby's eyes, but a black fury.

"All right," he snarled. "I'm goin'—*this* time! But don't think this settles it! I'm git you, as shore yo're a-standin' there!"

And with an oath, the young feudist turned and strode out the door into the darkness. A moment later the drum of hoofs diminished up the road. Brent sighed gustily and wiped his brow with a shaking hand, staring at the pistol as if it had been a snake. Suppose Buck, with the recklessness of his breed, had ignored the warning? He could not have shot the brother of the girl he had—with a groan Brent thrust the gun into his belt and held his head, which was beginning to throb. What a mess! But this settled it. He *had* to go now, as a matter of self-preservation. He couldn't kill Buck—not after what he had done to the boy's sister, and he knew Buck intended to kill him. Buck had ridden away, doubtless to get another gun, but he would be back. And when he came, it would be kill or be killed, and Brent knew he was alive at that moment only because of sheer luck and chance. If it came to hand-to-hand fighting, he knew all his boxing and wrestling tricks would be useless against the catlike ferocity and strength of the young mountaineer. But it wouldn't be fist-and-skull; it would be a rifle shot from the laurel, or the blast of a pistol at close range. He was no match for Buck Kirby in any event; besides he could not fight the boy. Buck was right in what he was doing, now. He could not seduce the sister and then kill the brother.

Locking the door of the school, Brent hurried to the little cabin which, standing in a grove of trees nearly a mile from the school building, served as his home. There was no other house within a mile of it. The dwellings along Whiskey Run were isolated, even from each other, as they had been since the first pioneers wandered through the mountains, in pre-Revolutionary days. Lighting a candle, he began to throw his things together. He'd walk across the mountains to the nearest town, and—he dropped the shirt he had picked up and sat down on the nearest chair, weakly. Suddenly he realized that the thought of going away from Joan Kirby was making him sick. Overwhelming almost as that surge of passion that had swept her into his arms, came the realization that he loved the girl. Well, all right! He'd marry her, take her back to Richmond. There was a job waiting for him there when he got tired of sowing wild oats, and came back to settle down—with a jolt he brought himself up short. He had no way of knowing her feelings regarding him. Why should he suppose she cared anything about him? She had yielded in the intoxication of the moment. Probably she despised him now. Besides, he could never pay court to her, not with her brother gunning for his life—oh, what a hellish mess! He was caught in a snare he could not break. If he ran away, he would spend the rest of his life in an agony of unsatisfied desire. If he stayed, Buck Kirby would kill him.

A voice called outside the door called respectfully: "Mister Brent! Oh, Mister Brent!"

"Who is it?" he asked suspiciously. He did not recognize the voice.

"Joe Barlow, Mister Brent! My boy's broke his leg and we want to bring him in there so's we can set it."

"Why, sure!" Brent stepped to the door, opened it, and peered out at the cluster of figures, indistinct in the darkness. "Bring him right in here—"

Even as he realized that there was something funny about this, the cudgel crashed on his head and the candlelight and stars went out in a brief burst of flame.

Braxton Brent groaned, lifted his aching head and stared haggardly about him. His hands were bound behind his back, apparently with rawhide thongs. He was lying on his rude bunk, and he managed to hitch himself to a sitting posture. The first figure he saw was that of Ann Pritchard, who posed insolently before him, with a leering smile on her lips and her eyes poisonous with spite and obscene meaning. Four rough figures clustered about him; he recognized old Bill Pritchard, bearded, evil eyed, and his three hulking, brutal-faced sons, Jim, Dick and Joe. Something inside him went cold and hard. He had forgotten the Pritchards.

"You whupped Ann here," accused Old Man Pritchard ominously.

"Well, what if I did?" snarled Brent. "She needed it. Isn't it the custom in these parts?"

"That's all right," snarled the eldest, and most vicious looking of the sons, Joe. "But you didn't lick Joan Kirby! Yo're partial to them damn' Kirbys!"

"Who says I didn't whip Joan?" demanded Brent.

"I know you never!" asserted Ann vindictively. "You chased me out of the schoolhouse, but I listened outside. If you'd a-whupped her, I could a-heard the licks, and heard her hollerin'. I didn't hear nothin'."

Old Man Pritchard's eyes turned a murky red; old hates, half a century old, smoldered between him and the Kirbys; even now the feud was a heap of coals that might burst into flame anytime either had the advantage of the other.

"You damn' furriner!" he said thickly. "You Kirby-lover! You whupped a Pritchard, but you didn't whup a Kirby! I'm a-goin' to fix you—not for whuppin' Ann—I 'low she needed it— but because yo're a friend of the damn' Kirbys!"

"I—" began Brent, but Joe struck him heavily across the mouth with his open hand, knocking his head stunningly back against the wall.

"Shet up! Ann, what you want done with this skunk? Le's cut his throat and throw him in the creek. Nobody'll ever know who done it."

Ann shook her head, her eyes gleaming with the age-old feminine cruelty, and her answer was old as the pleasure vindictive women have always derived from certain forms of torture.

"No, I don't want him killed! I want him to live and suffer. Take down his pants, and—"

Brent, who had not flinched at the threat of death, paled at the mutilation she mentioned, with the gross candor of a mountain woman. Old Man Pritchard grinned, and Joe guffawed, slapping his sister's hips with fiendish joviality.

"By God, gal, you can think up the best jokes I ever heard! We'll do it! Jim, gimme yo' knife! Mine's too dern sharp! We don't want to do this too quick and easy!"

Brent sprang to his feet, but Jim and Dick grabbed him, slammed him back down again. Joe tested the knife grinning evilly—then all whirled as the door opened. Joan Kirby entered and closed it behind her. She faced her enemies calmly, imperturbably.

"What you all fixin' to do?" she demanded.

"We're goin' to make a steer out of a bull!" shrilled Ann, almost hugging herself in vindictive glee. "And now you can stay here and watch! We'll teach him to whup a Pritchard and let a Kirby go!"

"What do you mean?" retorted Joan. "He whupped me harder'n he did you."

"He didn't neither!" shrieked Ann. "You're lyin'! I listened outside the schoolhouse—you didn't holler once!"

Joan curled her lip in scorn.

"I reckon not! A Kirby don't yell, like a Pritchard! I never hard nobody squall like you did, when he was fannin' yo' behind. I'd be ashamed to holler like that."

"Well, Joan," suggested Joe, an evil leer on his unshaven lips and lurid lights beginning to glow in his eyes, "suppose you jest show us whar he whupped you, and then we'll believe it."

"Sure I will!" With a scornful lift of her head at him, she turned about and lifted her dress to her waist. Brent caught his breath at the sight of the ugly red welts that crisscrossed her full white hips and her thighs.

"He used a switch on me!" she said. "I bet that hurt worse'n the strap!"

Letting the garment fall, she turned about and said: "Well, are you-all satisfied? Will you go on now and let him alone?"

Old Pritchard chewed his beard and scowled uncertainly. Ann cursed sullenly beneath her breath. Joan crossed quickly to the bunk and began to untie Brent's thongs. Only then, when, with his head close to her bosom, he heard the quick, wild beating of her heart, did he realize her fear and peril.

As if coming to life suddenly, Joe lurched across the room and pulled Joan roughly away from the captive.

"Hold on there, gal! We ain't decided to let him go!"

"What you mean?" demanded Old Man Pritchard puzzedly, while the younger sons looked on stupidly. "If he licked Joan too, we ain't got nothin' agen him—"

"I warn't thinkin' so much about him, now," Joe grinned. "Look what we got!" Gloatingly, as if showing them something they had not seen, he pushed Joan around before him. "I've wanted this girl for years. Now I ain't goin' to let her run home so easy!"

Vindictive understanding shone on Bill Pritchard's face. Here was an opportunity to wreck havoc on the hated Kirbys. He merely said: "Come on, Ann; we got to be goin'!" As they left the cabin

Ann looked back at Joan, made an obscene gesture impossible to misinterpret, and laughed jeeringly, poisonously. The door closed behind them and the three hulking boys turned to stare at their fair captive with burning eyes. They ignored Brent; frantically he was working at the cords on his wrists. Joan had loosened them before Joe grabbed her; he felt them slipping.

"I'm first!" asserted Joe. She sprang for the door, but he was before her. He seized her, ripped the dress from her bosom, grunting beastlike as he seized her ripe breasts with his hairy paw. The others snarled about them like wild beasts. And then Brent snapped the remaining thong. With a groan of mad fury he was on his feet before they could turn. His right fist lunging from the hip, smashed against Joe's bristly jaw and the Pritchard went down like a pole-axed ox.

Brent was on him like a cat, snatching the pistol on his belt before the others could move, stunned as they were by the fierce quickness of his attack. He faced them, white lipped and blazing with cold rage.

"Get back! Back, damn you, or I'll drill you! Come here, Joan!"

She ran to him, panting sobbingly and clung to him, unnerved by the experience of brutal Pritchard hands on her supple body. Her bare white breasts heaved stormily.

"Take their guns away from 'em and run 'em off!" she begged. "Hurry! You got to get away! Buck's comin' after you! I came here to warn you, and looked in the winder and seen them and heard them say there was goin' to fix you for not lickin' me when you licked Ann."

Even in his rage and haste he paused and stared at her.

"You came to warn me? Why, girl?"

"I love you!" She met his eyes squarely, without flinching. "Didn't you know it? Did you think I'd a-done what I done if I hadn't a-loved you? Look out!" The last a shriek as Jim Pritchard stealthily started a hand toward his belt. He paled and his hands jerked up again as Brent snarled: "Reach, blast you! So, you're coming around, eh?"

Joe was getting groggily to his feet; he began to curse vilely as he recognized the situation, then ceased as Brent snarled at him.

"Get the guns the others have, Joan," Brent ordered. "Don't get between them and me—"

She moved to obey. As she reached for Jim's pistol, Joe grunted and grabbed her. Brent instantly jerked the trigger, aiming for Joe's heart, but only a click answered him. Joe bellowed and swung the struggling girl in front of him.

"I dropped the gun in the creek on my way over!" he bellowed with furious triumph. "*The powder's wet!* Git him, boys, while I 'tend to the girl!"

Yelling, they drew their pistols, while Joan screamed madly and fought like a wildcat. Brent hurled the useless pistol at Dick just as the Pritchard fired. It saved Brent's life for Dick staggered from the impact, and his shot went wild. Joan and Joe, whirling in a crazy semicircle, lurched between Jim and Brent, causing him to hold his fire, cursing savagely. For an instant there was chaos in the cabin, as Brent grappled with Dick, forcing his gun hand toward the roof. Jim was springing about, trying to get a shot at Brent without hitting one of his brothers—and then the door smashed open.

A wiry figure was framed against the blackness and there was a crack and a jet of orange flame. Jim cried out and collapsed, and Buck Kirby's wild yell rang to the roof.

"Turn around, you damn Pritchards, and git it in front!"

At that yell Dick Pritchard started convulsively, tore free from Brent and wheeled, firing point-blank. A lock of hair jumped from Buck's head, and Dick staggered and went down, hit in the belly, breast and head. The cabin was full of smoke, a murky fog through which the gun-flame spurted like jets of lightning.

Joe, holding Joan in front of him for a shield, ducked and came up with Jim's gun. Yellow teeth bared, crouching behind the terrified girl, he fired just as Buck changed his position. Lead smacked the wall behind the place Buck's head had been an instant before and Buck, aiming carefully and firing across his sister's shoulder, killed Joe Pritchard with a slug that missed Joan's soft white neck by a fraction of an inch.

She reeled free as Joe fell and Brent sprang caught her in his arms, eased her to the bunk. Buck's flinty voice brought him around, to face the gun in the boy's hand.

"Mister, I got a bullet left in this gun; I'm a-goin'—"

Brent braced himself for the tearing shock of the slug; it was hard to have his cup of happiness dashed from his lips. Joan sprang in front of Brent, shrieking: "Buck, don't! I love him! Don't kill him! Please don't?"

"Who said I was goin' to?" he demanded. "What you think I kept them Pritchards from killin' him if I wanted him daid? He's got to live to do right by you! Nobody can lick a Kirby woman but her kin or her husband! Before I git back into the hills to hideout again, I'm takin' you to the justice of the peace. He's a-goin' to marry you!"

As they went Brent bent his lips to Joan's ear and whispered: "Joan, who whipped you? Who made those marks you showed them?"

"I did!" she answered. "I sneaked up and heard 'em talkin', so I went back in the bresh and broke a switch and slashed myself several times. I knowed they'd want proof!"

ROBERT ERVIN HOWARD (1906-1936) grew up in the boomtowns of early twentieth-century Texas, eventually settling in Cross Plains where he lived for the remainder of his short life. Deciding early on a literary career, he spent the bulk of his time crafting stories and poems for the burgeoning pulp fiction markets: *Weird Tales*, *Action Stories*, *Fight Stories*, *Argosy*, etc. Howard's literary reputation was assured with the publication of "The Shadow Kingdom" in 1929, which featured a unique blend of Fantasy and Adventure which has since been termed Heroic Fantasy. The creation of Conan the Cimmerian in the pages of *Weird Tales* has earned him lasting recognition.

DR. PATRICE LOUINET, from Limoges, France, is a renowned scholar in Robert E. Howard studies. His passion for Howard's work was ignited in 1983 upon discovering the Conan stories. He completed his Ph.D. at La Sorbonne, Paris, focusing on Howard in 2020. Patrice has edited the definitive three-volume Conan series for Del Rey Books and authored Le Guide Howard, published in France. His editorial and scholarly contributions extend across numerous publications in Europe related to Howard. Honored with the Lifetime Achievement Award from the Robert E. Howard Foundation in 2014 and the Special Award at the Imaginales in France (2012), Patrice's work continues to significantly influence the understanding and appreciation of Howard's legacy.

ROB ROEHM has edited more than a dozen Howard-related books for the REH Foundation Press as well as a couple with his own Roehm's Room Press. He has won multiple awards for his research and writings in a variety of Howard-themed publications. He has traveled to every location in the United States that Howard mentions visiting—from New Orleans to Santa Fe, and dozens of Texas towns in between—verifying and expanding our knowledge of Howard's biography. His research has also uncovered lost Howard stories, letters, and poems. He writes about these discoveries, infrequently, at howardhistory.com.

PAUL HERMAN, long-time engineer and intellectual property attorney, began publishing REH in 1999 via his own Hermanthis Press and later, Wildside Press; he has edited well over one million words. His etexts have been the starting material for a significant number of REH books published in the last 25 years. His REH bibliography, *The Neverending Hunt* became the new standard when it was first published in 2006 and is the basis for the HowardWorks website. His wife of 40 years, Denna, continues to tolerate his hobbies. Paul currently resides in Weatherford, Texas, a few miles from Robert E. Howard's birthplace.

MARK WHEATLEY holds the Eisner, Inkpot, Golden Lion, Mucker, Gem and Speakeasy Awards and nominations for the Harvey Award and the Ignatz Award. He is also an inductee to the Overstreet Hall of Fame. His work has often been included in the annual Spectrum selection of fantastic art and has appeared in private gallery shows, the Norman Rockwell Museum, Toledo Museum of Art, Huntington Art Museum, Fitchburg Art Museum, James A. Michener Art Museum and the Library of Congress, where several of his originals are in the LoC permanent collection.

STÅLE GISMERVIK has been passionate about Robert E. Howard since discovering his work in 1990. In the mid-1990s he created one of the earliest and largest websites devoted to Conan and Howard's fiction, and today manages the comprehensive Howard resource *The World of Robert E. Howard* at https://reh.world. He also administers the Robert E. Howard Foundation and REH Foundation Press websites, overseeing the design, editing, and digital production of the Foundation's eBooks. Since the summer of 2024, he has led the preparation of the Robert E. Howard Foundation Ultimate Editions, contributing to the preservation and promotion of Howard's literary legacy.

www.ingramcontent.com/pod-product-compliance
Lightning Source LLC
Chambersburg PA
CBHW060708190726
48289CB00002B/590